IN THE HISS OF SUMMER

Another Case of Detective Lyle Odell

Paul John Hausleben

God Bless the Keg Publishing LLC

Copyright © 2022 Paul John Hausleben

All rights reserved

The characters and events portrayed in this book are fictitious. Any similarity to real persons, living or dead, is coincidental and not intended by the author.

No part of this book may be reproduced, or stored in a retrieval system, or transmitted in any form or by any means, electronic, mechanical, photocopying, recording, or otherwise, without express written permission of the publisher.

The eBook cover design is by https://selfpubbookcovers.com/VonnaArt
Final editing services by Cyclops of the Paper Editing Services
The photographs of the author are by Ms. Cali Rose
The Detective Lyle Odell Logo is by Paul John Hausleben
Copyright © 2022 by Paul John Hausleben
Published by God Bless the Keg Publishing LLC
Henrico, Virginia, U.S.A.
All rights reserved

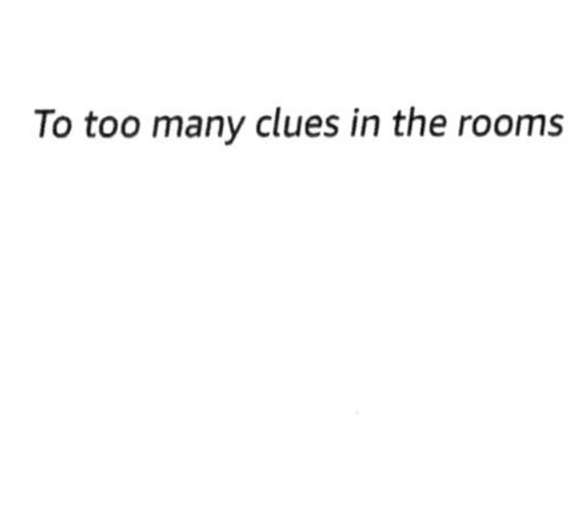

To too many clues in the rooms

"Mark my words that this guy is sick and evil. Very evil. It is okay. I will drown the clues and the facts in Irish whiskey tonight and find some answers. Tomorrow, I will set foot to get 'em. I need him to make seven mistakes and I will nail 'em. Seven mistakes and he will be dead and be history or in handcuffs."

THE CHARACTER OF HOMICIDE DETECTIVE LYLE ODELL

PAUL JOHN HAUSLEBEN

MARCH 2022

CONTENTS

PROLOGUE

The lake was like a perfectly round mirror. No imperfections. You could not see or detect a single ripple anywhere upon the surface of the lake. It was that kind of day. No telltale signs of any disturbances. Not detectable—at least.

Beside the lake, inside a rustic cabin built for hunting and fishing, and for enjoying the lake, a man ran a knife along a sharpening stone. Despite the bucolic atmosphere of the lake inside the cabin, evil surrounded the man.

As he worked the knife blade along the stone, the man mumbled, "It is really not my fault. They made their choices. They killed first and when they did so, they killed all that was right and wonderful in this world. Not me. Now, they need to understand what that means. What the repercussions of killing are. They need to know what it is like. To kill. To end life in such a horrific manner. So suddenly. So violently."

He finished sharpening the knife. He held it up to the light to check the edge. His generous muscles bulged in waves of ripples as he held the knife up into the light to check it. The edge was perfect. Sharp. It harbored no mercy.

With a smile upon his face that wandered from sadistic to uncaring to downright evil, the words came out of the man's mouth and the ominous tone of the words hung in the air as if they were a fog.

He held the knife up in the air and scrutinized the blade while he held it up to the light to check the sharpness of it.

"Just a little more. I love knife blades when they are razor sharp and slit throats and carve up bodies like I am carving a Thanksgiving turkey. It is such an enjoyable and rewarding experience. I have been waiting. Finally, an endless heatwave is here. I love heatwaves. It is perfect for my plans. Everyone is miserable, and it makes for excellent killing weather. After all, where this all began was miserably hot for months on end. Miserable."

The setting sun over the lake shone through the window of the cabin, and the rays of the sunset cast an ominous beam of light across the man's face. The shadows of his body as he worked the knife blade along the stone danced across the floor in waves of evil.

"They all said that they cured me."

The next words came out of his mouth as if they were a whisper.

"Unfortunately, they were wrong."

CHAPTER ONE

It was about to be an interesting first meeting between Captain Connor Moore and Homicide Detective Lyle Odell.

"Ah . . . this horrific homicide and the gory details of the crime scene are very disturbing to me. Perhaps I might be a little antsy about horrific violence in Mohawk City so soon after taking over this position, Detective Odell . . . we did not have such violence in Hagerstown. Maybe I just need to get used to it. I read the initial report, but have yet to see yours cross my desk," Captain Connor Moore said with a hint of sadness in his voice. He paused for a few seconds, then continued, "I am not sure of my expectations, but this is not what I wanted during my first week on the job in this new position. Far from it." The newly minted police captain stopped speaking. Now, since he had not yet seen or heard any response from the police detective sitting opposite him in the guest chair in front of his desk, Captain Moore leaned back into his desk chair, crossed his arms in front of his chest and studied the man sitting there in front of him.

Captain Connor Moore's own appearance was in stark contrast to the man sitting in front of his desk. The captain kept a squared up, perfect appearance. He was in his mid-forties, his dark skin and perfect complexion as a stalwart and handsome black man did him proud. He was tall, standing well over six feet, and his build revealed his dedication to physical fitness. He had dark eyes, and a close-cropped perfect haircut, that kept his preferred hairstyle from his years in the United States Army Reserve, where he served for over twenty years as a military police officer, and his hairstyle gave him away as being a military man. Captain Connor Moore was a picture-perfect police officer.

He was nothing like the police detective sitting opposite him at his desk.

That man was the much decorated and valued, yet very unorthodox, and very messy Mohawk City Homicide Detective Lyle Odell, who sat in front of his new boss. Odell's head was down, his eyes glued on a cellphone that he held in his hands, while he pressed and pushed all the buttons on the keyboard of the device. It appeared as if Detective Odell was so engrossed in his electronic device that he did not hear a word that Captain Moore had said, nor had he paid even the slightest bit of attention to his new boss.

Captain Moore uncrossed his arms from his chest and he leaned forward in a careful study of Detective Lyle Odell. Moore sniffed the air a little, trying hard to detect a hint of Irish whiskey that he had heard that the good detective dabbled in, but he could smell nothing. Yet, it sure appeared as if it had been a long and difficult night and perhaps a morning for Odell. Odell's former commanding officer, the now retired, Captain Tucker prepared him for dealing with Detective Odell, but experiencing firsthand the eccentric but undeniably brilliant Homicide Detective Lyle Odell was a unique experience.

Odell's hair stuck out from his head in many directions. Tousled and unruly hair that was too long to comply with police regulations for grooming requirements made it look as if Lyle Odell just crawled out of bed. Tousled and unruly hair was a description that fell short of describing the hair upon his head. It was more as if it was an uproar of hair. As if his hairstyle was a victim of the tail winds of a hurricane. His suit jacket was full of layers of wrinkles, and it looked as if Odell had slept in his clothes. What little that Captain Moore knew about Odell and from the information he received from his predecessor, Captain Tucker, Odell sleeping in his clothes was a distinct possibility. Around Odell's neck hung a wrinkled necktie with the necktie cloth behind his neck hanging stuck over the collar of his shirt; the necktie knot was not actually a knot; it was more as if it was a crisscross of the cloth and his necktie hung askew. It was either too short or too long; since the detective sat in the guest chair, it was difficult to tell. He wore no police badge that was visible. Perhaps it was on his belt somewhere, but Captain Moore could not see or detect it.

Odell was a mess.

"Ah, Detective Odell . . . have you heard a word that I have said?" Captain Moore finally asked.

Odell looked up, nodded, and then immediately went back to punching the buttons on the phone.

"Captain Tucker warned me about you, Odell," Moore huffed and added, "he told me that you could not, or would not . . . understand how to . . . use cellphones."

Odell looked up again, and he blinked twice and said, "I am so sorry, Cap, this blasted thing seems to have a mind of its own," Odell said. He waved his hand in the air and then, in surrender, handed the phone to his boss. "It won't; turn on. However, this is not Hagerstown. It is Sin City. Mohawk City, New York. Home to all things rotten."

Odell then looked at Captain Moore, he tapped his suit jacket pockets, first the left side, then the right side, and then finally with a nod of his head in a hint of recollection, Odell reached into his shirt pocket and mumbled, "Shirt pocket." Odell pulled out a neatly folded piece of paper and Captain Moore sat there in silence, while remaining mesmerized by Odell's peculiar actions. Odell unfolded the paper and began to read from the words on the paper, "Connor William Moore, Born six November nineteen-sixty-five in Mohawk City Baptist Hospital. Your dad served as a first sergeant in the United States Army and then worked as a postal worker after his service in Korea. A great man. An honorable man. A patriot. He was highly decorated for combat actions." Odell looked up and smiled at Captain Moore, and then he directed his attention back to the paper and continued to read, "Your very dear mom was primarily a homemaker, but she worked part time in a pharmacy to help make ends meet. You are an only child. Graduated Mohawk City

High School as an above-average student. At eighteen years of age, you joined the United States Army Reserve. You worked your way up to master sergeant in the military and served in combat in Afghanistan and other sensitive locations. You, as your father is, are highly decorated for valor and bravery in combat. You went to college part time for many years on the G.I. Bill and earned a degree in criminal justice. While you served in the military in the reserves and attended college, you took a full-time job at the Hagerstown Police Department. First, as a patrolman, then you worked your way quickly up the ranks, because of earning your college degree and because you are an excellent police officer, who works very hard. You excelled at your career, all while marrying your beloved high school sweetheart," Odell again looked up and he smiled. This time, he winked and then tried in vain to fix his tousled hair and then added, "Louise. With all due respect, because as a detective, my job is to observe every detail. Your wife is an exquisite woman. Gorgeous. You are a very lucky man."

Captain Moore sat dumbfounded and all he could manage to do was to mumble, "Thank you."

Odell then continued, "Two amazing children, Spencer and Claire, twenty-three and twenty years of age, respectively, who both take after their mom in appearance." Odell winked again and continued, "That is not so bad. You retired from the Army Reserve two years ago, this past October. When Captain Tucker retired three months ago, Mohawk City Police Chief Neil O'Donnell lured you back home to Mohawk City with this captain position and perhaps a shot at the chief's job when O'Donnell retires in two years. You are a churchgoing man and family. Second Baptist Church here in the city. You were an elder back in your old church in Hagerstown. Maybe you will be one at the new church, too. Time will tell." Odell finished speaking, then he folded the paper back up and mumbled, "Suit jacket, right side," and he stuffed the paper into his pocket. Odell looked up, and said, "by the way, I hate to tell you this, but this is a serial killer at work in the city. Welcome aboard. Captain Tucker spoke highly of you. It is my pleasure to serve with you, Captain Moore." Odell stood up, gave a less-than-perfect salute and then sat down in the chair and he pointed at the cellphone in the stunned Captain Moore's hands. "Can you get that stupid thing to work, or is it me?"

Captain Moore looked down at the phone. He pushed the on-off button, and the phone jumped to life.

With a shake of his head, he reached over the desk, and he handed Detective Lyle Odell the phone, and said, "It is you, Odell. By the way, that was some remarkable research on my career, my life and me. Do you ever rest?"

Odell grabbed the phone, studied it, and said in a low whisper, "Thanks, Cap. I think. Damn thing is a curse. I swear that I pushed every button. I will rest when the bad guys decide to rest. That means when I retire or I die. Whichever one comes first."

"You are welcome. I think. About this homicide, Odell. You just blurted out that this murder is the work of a serial killer! Talk about knocking me on my butt in the first few days of taking on this position."

Odell tilted his head a little and answered, "Sorry, Cap, I usually just blurt out things that are factual. My mind wanders around quite a bit."

"Okay, for that information. I think. However, a serial killer, Odell? What is with that? It is only one murder."

Odell looked up from the phone and blinked. He set the phone on the edge of the desk, shook his head, and explained, "I am sorry to say, but there will be more murders. This is a continuation of the rage of a madman who killed downstate, and then moved to Albany, and now, unfortunately, he has moved to Mohawk City. He will kill again in the next few days. Most likely a young woman. The daughter of a veteran. I wish that I could stop it, but sadly, I cannot. It is his pattern. Unfortunately, I need a blood trail. I despise that fact, but it is factual. This killer is cunning, super-intelligent and ruthless. I need to begin somewhere . . . now that he is here. I have nothing to go on from the murder from the other day. I am waiting for the crime scene reports, but I can tell it is a dead end. This madman targets veterans and if he cannot find any, then he kills their children and spouses. This one is a real sick one, but he is very skilled at what he does. He is a vet too. I hate to say it, but it is the truth. Many of us are screwed up. He goes after veterans of combat in wars or conflicts. The victim of the other night was a veteran of the Vietnam War. The slashed throat, the two bullets in the back, the letters v and w carved into the victim's back. It is all the same modus operandi as the unsolved murders of a few years back." Odell stood up from the chair a little, and mumbled, "Pants. Right side front."

Odell produced a rumpled-up section of a newspaper and he did his best to smooth it out, then he handed it to the captain.

"Here. This is from the Albany newspaper. From a few years ago. You can keep that copy, Cap Moore. You might want to show the chief. He might want to alert the state attorney general because all of this is gonna be messy. The Albany police detectives never solved the murders. Neither did Westchester County. I was hoping they would call me in . . . but they didn't."

Odell's eyes misted just a little as Captain Moore studied him, and then the police captain quickly glanced over the newspaper clipping.

"Maybe . . . I could have stopped the bastard. The killer took some time off, but now he is back. I am not sure what triggered his return. Whatever did so is a major clue. He is here. In our city. Sorry, Cap. Welcome home."

Odell stood up. He attempted to fix his hair; however, it was to no avail. Odell then adjusted his belt and tried to tuck his shirt back into his pants and finally, after those repeated unsuccessful attempts at gathering himself, he grabbed his phone and dropped it into his suit jacket pocket.

"Left side suit jacket pocket," Odell mumbled.

"He, Detective Odell? The killer is a male?"

"Yes. Definitely. The carvings are deep into the bodies. A powerful man did them. A big guy. Very muscular."

"I see. So noted, Odell."

"Don't worry, Captain Moore. I am on it. I will nail 'em. I always do. I will do my best to minimize the killing. My best, but, unfortunately, some things are out of my control. There is lots of evil out there, Cap. Mark my words that this guy is sick and evil. Very evil. It is okay. I will drown the clues and the facts in Irish whiskey tonight and find some answers. Tomorrow, I will set foot to get 'em. I need him to make seven mistakes and I will nail 'em. Seven mistakes and he will be dead and be history or in handcuffs. Please give me a few days to nail 'em. Oh, yes, you will have your report tomorrow."

"Why seven mistakes, Detective Odell? That seems so random."

Odell shook his head and then answered Captain Moore.

"It is not random. Including the homicide here in Mohawk City that makes nine homicides committed by this evil maniac so far over about six years or thereabouts. The crimes were until now deemed to be unsolvable by some very fine police detectives and outstanding minds. No clues. No mistakes. No errors. Nothing to go on. Until now. I am not counting this first one as an official mistake, but coming here to Mohawk City was a mistake. Because we are here."

Odell leaned in and spoke gently but forcefully.

"The killer is so good, so brilliant that I need a precise number of mistakes to solve the case. In my study of the case so far, I determined that exactly seven mistakes will do the trick. The first three mistakes that he makes will give me the background and direction that I need to get on his trail. The next two mistakes will identify the actual killer to me. The sixth mistake will confirm the killer's final intentions and victim for murder and the last mistake will be his final mistake. He will be dead or in handcuffs."

Captain Moore finally caught more of his words and he nodded and said, "Intense. Very intense and precise. Okay, thank you. Captain Tucker told me all about you, Odell. He informed me of your unusual methods and, frankly, your overall behavior. No offense, but you are rather unorthodox in your approach to detective work. You might say that Captain Tucker warned me, but he also told me that if there were a better detective on earth, or a better man, than Detective Lyle Odell, then he would be surprised to find one. Be careful, Odell. Do you even, ah . . . carry a weapon? I mean, I don't even see your police badge."

Odell looked down; he slid his hand along his belt and then shook his head.

"Captain Tucker is a class act. He is a good drinking buddy, too. He is a chowhound too. He loves grilled cheese sandwiches. Do you drink alcohol, Cap?"

"A little. Generally, no whiskey, except on Christmas Day. We have a special drink of cheer for Christmas. A little wine with dinner or some beers at the ballgame." Captain Moore held his hands up in a display of self-defense. He sensed an invitation, and Odell's reputation preceded him.

"Ok. You are better off. We can have a few beers together. It helps with my clarifying cases. We can grab Sergeant Grundy too. I talk aloud and bounce ideas off you guys. Anyway, thank you for the compliment and for the faith. I am severely flawed. Admittedly, at his point in my life and my career—it is way too much whiskey, too many dark shadows, too much evil that I have stared down, too many phantoms chasing me and that I have chased, but I do my best. It wears you down. The blood. The evil. The malice and the pain. Please stick with me, Cap. I know that it seems that I am a mess. On the surface, I am, but beneath the surface mess, I am good at what I do. I have a strong feeling that you are following in large footprints, but you more than fill them. As far as the badge goes, ah, sorry, Captain Moore. I forgot the badge. As far as the weapon goes, well, I seldom carry one. Usually, by the time that I corner the bad guy or guys, they surrender without any problems. Not always. Usually."

Captain Moore nodded and forced a smile while saying, "Your reputation precedes you, Detective Lyle Odell. I have reviewed your records. It is breathtaking. As far as the surrenders go, for your sake . . . I hope so."

Odell waved in the window's direction of Captain Moore's

office and said, "It sure is hot out there, huh, Cap? I mean, you can hear the hiss of summer. The dog days of August are finally here in upstate New York. Winter seems like a dream."

"Yes, it is a scorcher, Odell. Very hot. Please take care."

Odell waved, and with a quick turn on his heels, Detective Odell walked out and exited out of Captain Moore's office.

When the door clicked shut and Odell was gone, Captain Moore took a deep breath; he shook his head and mumbled, "Good Lord. What have I gotten myself into his time? Captain Tucker was correct. This man is a genius. A mess, but he is a genius." Captain Moore folded his hands and lifted his eyes to heaven.

He was a praying man.

"Lord in Heaven, protect him. The man is a mess. Guide him and be with him. There are so many people counting on him . . . me included." No sooner had Captain Moore finished praying and speaking aloud, there was a gentle knock at the door of his office. Even before he could answer, the door swung open and Detective Odell appeared in the doorway. He was attempting to tuck his shirt into his pants. It was to no avail.

"Sorry, Cap, for the interruption, but do you?"

Captain Moore's eyes studied the chaotic Detective Odell. Moore's face displayed how puzzled that he was at the nature of the question.

"What, Detective Odell?"

Odell smiled a weak smile when he realized that his question made little sense.

"Oh yes, sorry. Do you like grilled cheese sandwiches?"

"Yes, of course. Who doesn't love grilled cheese sandwiches? The ultimate comfort food," Captain Moore answered with a wide smile and wave of his hand in the air to emphasize his preference.

"Okay, great. Gulliver's Bar and Grille on Fifth Street and Main Street. Downtown. Best damn grilled cheese in the world. Grundy and I will treat you. Plan on a Saturday afternoon. That is Grundy's usual day off. There is this gal there that works at the bar every Saturday afternoon . . . she is ancient. Even older than Grundy and Odell are. Annie is her name. She knows how to sling 'em and pour 'em. You gotta go before the young crowd jams the joint up and makes all that noise. I love old time rock and roll, but the live bands there play that new stuff. It is too noisy. So, Sarge and I, we usually leave early. We will take you there and you'll see that it is the best damn grilled cheese sandwich in the world. All gooey cheese that the heat of the grill burns along the edges. Believe me—I investigate things. Everything. Even food. Food clues helped me solve a few cases over the years. I am a detective."

Odell smiled and waved in the air.

Captain Moore smiled and waved in return, and answered with, "Okay, sounds great. I am looking forward to it."

"Great. By the way, we will make Grundy pay," Odell said while he winked and the door closed once more.

Captain Moore sat at his desk and smiled. He was not exactly sure of what had just happened, but he was sure of one thing. He sure was happy that Detective Lyle Odell worked for the Mohawk City Police Department. The man was eccentric, but utterly brilliant. In fact, Captain Moore was very sure that his predecessor was correct in his analysis of Lyle Odell. He was a genius. A brilliant, eccentric, genius. The bad guys did not stand a chance.

Sergeant Grundy answered the cellphone call on the second ring.

"What's up, Odell?"

"Gonna need your help, George. After you hear the call about the homicide tomorrow morning . . . come on by and pick me up . . . okay?"

The old patrol sergeant sighed and his eyes wandered around the interior of his patrol car. The sergeant knew Detective Odell for close to thirty years and he might be the closest person to be considered a friend to Lyle Odell if there was such a thing. Other than a bottle of his favorite Irish whiskey.

"Is it gonna be a rough night, Odell? Another homicide. I know it would be a dumb-ass question, so I will not ask if you can stop it or not. I guess this has something to do with the murder from the other night."

"Yupper. Nothing to go on yet. I feel awful about it. Sick to my stomach, but I can't do anything. Yet. Nothing until he kills some more. It's a big city. No way to narrow down a potential victim in time. Too many variables and too many options. This is the same nut job that was killing in Albany and downstate about five years ago."

George Grundy sighed again. The pain was deep from his years working in Sin City, and he knew that the old city needed Lyle Odell more than ever now. A serial killer. A serial killer that just met his match. He was about to lock horns with the best of the best. Homicide Detective Lyle Odell was good at his job.

Very, very good.

"Dear Lord," George mumbled. "Nothing to go on, so you are going swimming in Irish to dive for clues, huh?"

"Yupper. Need to probe my mind. Gonna be messy, George. I will need your help."

"Okay, Odell. I am here for you. You know that tomorrow is my day off."

"I knew that, George. You don't want to take the day off. Too damn hot to work in the yard. Let the grass burn. Stop wasting your time by watering it. It will come back in September. Anyway, thanks, George. Use your key if I don't answer. Try to respond to the murder scene when you hear the call come in. Follow the same routines that we always do. Call in the crime scene guys. Then come get my drunk ass. You know the drill. It's gonna be awful. Another disturbing scene. The killer's patterns are until now consistent and obvious. How I wish and pray that it could be different and we could stop him now. But we cannot. That is a torture that I will have to live with . . . to know his next step but be helpless. This next victim will be a young woman.

Evil stuff. Very evil. Thank you, George, for being George."

"Click."

The line went dead. Sergeant Grundy reached for the cup of coffee perched on his dashboard and took a long sip. It was lukewarm now.

Sergeant Grundy despised lukewarm or cold coffee.

CHAPTER TWO

The cellphone perched somewhat precariously upon the upturned plastic milk crate that was sitting on the floor next to the chair. Suddenly, it rang loudly. The ringer on the phone was on the loudest setting. On purpose. Detective Lyle Odell opened one eye to look at the number on the screen. He groaned and moved in the reclining chair and strained his neck to read the number of the screen. He pushed in on the leg rest of the chair and reached for the phone, and when he did so; he knocked over the Irish whiskey bottle that sat on the floor next to the chair.

It did not matter because the whiskey bottle was empty.

It was difficult to grab the cellphone since it hung on the end of a charger. The battery was usually dead. However, before Odell wandered into the bottom of the bottle of Irish, he plugged the phone into the charger. He knew what this night would bring.

The caller was persistent. Odell did not pick up the call, and it went to voicemail. However, they called right back. Odell's head pounded, his eyes could not focus, and the Devil danced on his brain but also poked his stomach with his pitchfork. It was a tough night. Difficult, to say the least. Now, Odell focused his eyes enough to read the number on the screen and the time. Odell recognized the number. Sergeant George Grundy.

"Shit. Sometimes, I wish that I were wrong. Dead wrong."

A few seconds later, Odell looked over at the front door of his house as he heard a key enter the lock and then turn, and the door swung open. The enormous figure appearing in the doorway, in the darkness, did not alert Odell to any danger. It was his friend, following his request.

"C'mon, Lyle, get your old ass up. We need you. Badly. Sober or not, we need you. In fact, you are better when you are drunk, so get up," Sergeant Grundy growled as he closed the door behind him. Detective Odell could see Grundy's eyes peering at him even through the darkness of his living room.

"I'm up, George. I heard you calling, but I could not get to the telephone in time to answer it."

"Oh. Well, I figured that the battery was dead. You usually forget to plug it in." Odell reached over for the switch on the only table lamp sitting on the only table in the room, and he switched the light on. A dull, aching light bathed the room, just above the gloom level. Grundy studied Lyle Odell as his eyes went up and down the detective and then he studied the whiskey bottle on the floor, the milk crate and an empty pizza box perched on a plastic waste bin sitting next to the end table. Odell ran his hand through his hair and, even though the light was hardly bright, Odell squinted a little while his eyes slowly adjusted to the light level in the room.

Odell was still dressed in a white shirt, a necktie wrapped around his neck, and he had his suit pants and shoes still on his feet. His suit jacket hung from the doorknob of the only closet in the room. There was nothing much in the entire living room and, in fact, in the adjoining dining room, either.

Grundy took a few steps toward Lyle as the detective slowly rose out of the chair, kicked the whiskey bottle with his foot, and groaned as he stood up.

"You are worse than you usually are when you go off on one of these benders. Are you gonna puke, Odell?" Grundy asked as his eyes went to the waste bin next to the chair. George determined that the bin might be a potentially handy item in a disastrous situation.

"Nah. As you know, I never puke, George."

"Well, you might when you hear what I am gonna say."

Odell stopped tilting and wavering, and his shipwrecked eyes focused on Sergeant George Grundy.

"Damn, I was right . . . a young woman."

"Yes. Officer Phil McNally's daughter."

The words and news of the identity of the victim hit Lyle Odell as if a sledgehammer knocked his skull in. Odell grabbed his head with both of his hands and he flopped back into the chair, wrung his head in his hands, and moaned. George Grundy walked over and gently put his hand on his friend's shoulder. A few moans turned into sobs and George Grundy felt the tears brimming in his eyes too. Even for two battle-hardened police officers who had seen and experienced many wretched things through their long careers, this was difficult to take. The young daughter of a fellow police officer's daughter. One of their own families.

"C'mon, Lyle. Hold on, buddy. We need you. Don't be too hard on yourself, old friend. You said it yourself . . . there was nothing that you could do."

"Yes. Perhaps. Regardless, I have to do better. Much, much better. I have just a little more to go on now than I did before last night. The whiskey gave me some clarity and a few answers. Not many, but some. I . . . we . . . will nail this bastard, George. We're gonna nail 'em."

Odell looked up and George patted his shoulder.

"I know *you will*, Odell. I will help. C'mon, get up on your feet. Let's get you put together a little and go get 'em."

Odell nodded, and Grundy looped his arms under the shoulders of Detective Lyle Odell. Grundy was amazed at the intensity of the whiskey odor emitting from the breath and body of Lyle Odell. George had seen him in rough shape before, but this was a classic.

"George," Odell said, as he steadied his legs under the careful watch of Sergeant Grundy, "McNally is a veteran of the First Gulf War. Right?"

Grundy let go of his friend, as suddenly, the foggy look left Odell's eyes. It was as if Odell flipped a switch on, and his drunkenness left and the keenness reappeared.

"I think so. Air Force. I think."

Odell blinked and said, "The bastard carved a letter g and the letter w in her body. Right?"

"Correct, Lyle."

"Shirt pocket," Odell mumbled; he nodded, and he tapped his shirt pocket and realized that his cigarettes were not there. His eyes spotted them on the end table. "Okay. There are some clues and confirmed patterns to previous homicides by this lunatic. I need to wash up, have a cancer stick, some coffee, and we can get on with it. I will make some coffee for us." Odell took two steps to the kitchen, turned to Grundy and asked another question. "What day is it, Sarge?"

"Friday, Odell. It is Friday."

Odell nodded. He held onto the wall to catch his legs and with his free hand, he ran his hand through his hair and then tried to smooth it back down.

"Day five," Odell mumbled, while he once again tried in vain to smooth his hair down on the top of his head. Sergeant Grundy stood in silence and studied Odell. He knew his friend very well, and they worked together on many cases, therefore; Grundy knew that the genius wheels were now spinning within Lyle Odell's head. Silence was in order. Careful silence.

"Is it still ghastly hot outside, George? I actually turned my air conditioning on here last night. I seldom run it. Costs a damn fortune to run."

"It is still very hot, Lyle. It sucks. Hardly cooled off at all last night."

Odell shook his head and said, "Son-of-a-bitch kills in the hiss of summer. He killed during a heatwave years ago. Are there five bullets in her back, George?"

"Yes. Correct. Five."

Odell held onto the wall tighter.

"Gotcha. Five on the fifth day. Two on the second day. Another clue and confirmation. She is beautiful. Right? I used the present tense on purpose. Beauty never ends. It perpetuates forever. Death does not stop beauty, George. Poor McNally and his wife. Lillian is his wife's name. I met her once at a holiday party for the police force a few years back. Maybe eight or nine years ago. McNally is a handsome guy and Lillian is lovely, so I imagined that their daughter is beautiful too. It is a shame. They will never recover. How could you ever recover from such pain?"

Odell's eyes grew heavy with the burden.

Grundy correctly sensed that the inspiration ended.

George's voice grew softer. "She is beautiful. Yes."

"We need this evil son-of-a-bitch to make seven mistakes, George, and we will nail 'em. Seven."

George stared at Odell and nodded his head at his friend's emotions and words. Grundy's eyes were full of tears, as he too felt the anguish.

"Okay, Lyle. That seems random, but I know that you are correct. I think that I am better off not knowing too much right for now. I am here for you, though. Say, Odell, let's get coffee on the way from Mille's diner. Okay? Get washed up and let's roll. The crime scene guys are waiting for you. We need you, Lyle."

Odell nodded. He stood up tall and tried hard to search for soberness within a vast world of alcoholic haze.

"Yes. You are correct. Let's go, George." Odell wiped at his lips and forced a smile while adding, "You had better drive."

It was a pleasant apartment on a quiet side street off a major road on the east end of Mohawk City. Two up and two down. Side-by-side, a brick front, upgraded windows. This was a rental property close to the campus for Mohawk City University. Odell stopped short while walking up the front walkway to the door of the apartment house. His bloodshot eyes wandered across the entire home. He captured every detail. Odell, even while recovering from his night of hanging out with the Irish whiskey bottle, remained very sharp. Lyle Odell turned to George Grundy, who followed behind the detective, and he pointed to the lawn in front of the home.

"This lawn and the property are very well kept, George. The

turf is green and lush . . . even in this heat. It has the proper levels of fertilizer and of water too. Very important. Turf is very difficult to grow. It is a very demanding plant."

"I can't grow a lawn for shit, Lyle. Mine is a mess. It is all weeds and stuff. I set my mower low and as long as it is a kind of green, I don't really care. Right now, in all this heat, it is a burned-out mess."

Odell nodded and pointed at the lawn and explained, "Mine too. I don't care. At least, when it burns up, I don't need to cut it. But lookie here, they have automatic irrigation. Keeps the turf from burning up . . . at least from completely burning up. It still gets brown edges here and there," Odell finished his observation. He bent down on one knee, set his coffee container next to him and he ran his hand along the blades of grass while Sergeant Grundy observed him. "See the irrigation heads buried within the grass? The grass is still a little wet. During the hot days of summer, it is best to water at night or early in the morning. Otherwise, the heat evaporates the water, and it is a waste of water and money. The grass was recently cut. The maintenance person cuts it high to prevent burning in the heat, but they do not bag the cuttings. They use a mulching blade so the cuttings do not clump up and it adds free nitrogen to the turf. However, they do stick to footwear and then track off. Especially when wet. Even on the driveway there. We might find the cuttings. It could provide us with some clues, George."

Sergeant George Grundy nodded, and he leaned in to observe what Detective Odell was pointing out to him. He was not sure why Odell was focusing upon the lawn and the irrigation system, but from working with the man for all of these years, he knew never to discount anything that Odell points out during an investigation. And even when he was not investigating a case, Grundy knew to listen and watch Odell very carefully. Then again, it seemed as if Detective Lyle Odell was always investigating.

Odell went to stand back up, but the remnants of the whiskey appeared and he stumbled a little in his effort.

"Woah, easy there, Lyle. Here, let me give you a boost," George Grundy caught Odell in his armpit, steadied the detective, and then helped pull him to his feet.

"You okay, Lyle?" Grundy asked while studying Odell's face and measuring his steadiness. Odell ran his hand through his hair, tried to smooth it out, and then he quickly gave up.

"I am okay, George. Just a little rough and rocky, but I will be fine. Say, George," Odell said with that wandering look in his eyes that he usually got when his mind was whirling with ideas, "The victim, ah, ah, Allison was not a college student. Was she?" Odell asked.

Grundy bent down, picked up Odell's coffee and handed it to him while saying, "Honestly, I do not know, Odell. In fact, I am ashamed to say that I didn't even know her first name was Allison until you just mentioned it. I ignored those details when I arrived at the crime scene with Officer Taylor."

"Gotcha, okay, well, let's go take a look now. We are gathering a crowd and I want to avoid the media. They should be here any second now. Especially with all these police and official vehicles around."

Odell waved to display the multitude of cars parked every which way on the side street and the growing crowd of neighbors and curious on-lookers now huddling in front of the house to figure out what was going on in what appeared to be a usually very quiet neighborhood.

"Officer Taylor. A good man. Young, but seasoned. No more rookies, George. That rook from a few years ago was not a ton of fun. Now that I think about it, a little more, I think she worked as an accountant downtown."

"Is there anything you don't know, Odell?" Sergeant Grundy asked as he held the front door to the apartment open for Detective Lyle Odell to enter.

"Yupper. Right now, I don't know the most important thing in the entire world. That is who this damn evil bastard of a killer is."

Detective Lyle Odell nodded to Officer Brendan Taylor as he

surveyed the horrific scene in front of him. Odell only took a few steps from the hallway, through the doorway and into the bedroom, where the dead body of Ms. Allison McNally lay sprawled across the bed, with her blood spilling out onto the linens. Odell stopped in his tracks after taking those few steps. The detective remained a few feet or thereabouts into the bedroom, with Grundy standing behind him. Odell glanced quickly at her body, blinked, and then his eyes wandered all around the room. While seemingly on purpose, avoiding the body on the bed, he took in every detail of the room, and although, Lead Crime Scene Investigation Officer Oliver Crump, Officer Taylor, and Sergeant George Grundy were in the room along with Odell, no one moved and no one spoke a single word. Everyone there in the room had worked with Detective Odell before. They knew his methods well and his reputation for greatness surrounded him as if it was an aura of light.

After scanning the room and making a careful study of the details, Odell mumbled, "Right suit jacket pocket."

After speaking those words, he handed his coffee to Grundy then he reached into the pocket on the right side of his suit jacket, pulled out a pack of cigarettes that looked as if a freight train had run over them, he struggled to open the pack, and then while everyone stared at him, Odell finally shook a cigarette free from the pack, and he stuck it in his mouth.

While once again mumbling, "Right side suit jacket pocket," Odell jammed the pack into that specific pocket. He waved in the air and said, "Don't worry. I just need to taste it. I won't light it. Everyone is so sensitive these days. We live in a world of cupcakes. Present company excluded."

Odell stuck the cigarette in his mouth and the butt hung on his lip as if it was glued there. Grundy handed the coffee back to Odell, after he realized that Odell did not set it down anywhere that might disturb some evidence.

Odell nodded to George, took a sip of the coffee with the cigarette stuck sideways in his mouth, and growled, "Hello there, Officer Crump. Someday, I am gonna buy you a beer and we can meet under better circumstances. I never see you unless we are staring at dead bodies. It sucks. Anyway, I am still a little wobbly here. It was a rough night until Grundy got my drunken ass up outta of the rack, but I am sobering up. Even in the state that I am in, let me take a guess. You combed the hell outta of the room and you got nuthin' significant to go on. I know that I look like Hell, but I am gaining. Slowly. The whiskey keeps the phantoms away for a little while and it helps me to think and hopefully, even if my liver takes a few hits, it will be worth it to nail this son-of-a-bitch."

Odell knew CSI Officer Oliver Crump very well. They had worked together for many years and had just been together earlier this week on the first murder in the city. Officer Crump shrugged his shoulders, shook his head, and with a low voice filled with a hint of sorrow, he answered Lyle Odell.

"We are with you on the nailing part. Not sure about the liver. I would love a beer and better circumstances, Odell. I would love it and look forward to it. Sorry, Odell. We have very little. Just like the other night. What was it? Tuesday? Practically nothing. You are right on. This bastard is good. As in bad for good. Terrible. Whoever it is, they are a pro."

"Yeah, bad for good. Sort of correctly phrased but a twisted set of words. Anyway, Officer Taylor, has the medical examiner been here?"

"Yes, he was here and left about one hour before you arrived."

Odell took another sip of the coffee, pulled the cigarette out, and stuck it in his right-side suit jacket pocket.

"Get in there with the rest of the pack. Gimme whatcha got, Taylor, because I see very little here to go on. Give me the time of death first, according to the doc. However, do not give me the details of the medical examiner's examination. Please. I need to examine the body on my own and make my own determinations without prejudice or influence. No details of the gunshots. Only the time of death, any signs of sexual assault, and whether the carving of the letters g and w were done after she died of the gunshot wounds, during or before. Oh yes, was the examiner,

Doctor Kent?"

Taylor nodded, pulled his notepad out of his uniform shirt pocket, and studied his notes.

"Yes, it was Doctor Kent."

Odell dug his feet in a little on the hardwood floors and repositioned his stance. He was now sobering up, and he was feeling the details of the case. His eyes quickly darted to the body, which was lying face down on the bed with a visible gunshot wound through her thin nightgown and visible wounds to the back of her head. Yet, his eyes did not linger on the scene.

"There are the letters g and w carved into her body, correct? On her stomach?"

"Yes, that is correct."

"Please go on. Thank you, Taylor. Thank you."

Odell ran his hand through his hair and closed his eyes while Officer Taylor spoke the details of the case so far. Odell's hair stood up in all directions from the top of his head.

"Time of death was around two in the morning today. Doctor Kent feels that she died of the gunshot wounds before the carving and mutilation. She was asleep in her bed. No signs of sexual assault. It appears to be an ambush of sorts. According to Crump and his team, this much we can tell so far. The killer picked the front door lock with professional tools. No deadbolt on the door. As of your arrival on the scene, about," Taylor glanced at his watch, "sixteen minutes ago, the crime scene techs are still scouring the house for evidence. They finished up here about thirty minutes ago and are downstairs now. The victim is Allison McNally, twenty-six years of age, lifelong resident of Mohawk City. She worked as an accountant in an agency downtown here. She graduated from the local university a year or so ago. No current boyfriend. Her roommate is away for the summer. The roommate is living in New York City with her parents, trying to find a better job. We spoke to the landlord, Mr. Guy Travers, to get much of this info. He found the body when he came to do some lawn and yard work. He noticed the front door open and Alison's car here. He thought that was unusual and after calling out for her, ringing the bell and knocking, he entered to investigate. Mr. Travers said he touched very little, but I made a listing of what he recalled touching and doing and I gave it to Officer Crump. Mr. Travers broke down emotionally while telling us the story. He gave us some details about the victim. Apparently, she rented here from her college days, and had now stayed on, so the old man knew her fairly well. The old man seemed very sincere and upset. His wife came and picked him up because he was so terribly upset. So far, in our interviews, the close neighbors that we spoke with to this point heard nothing. Saw nothing."

Officer Taylor looked up at Odell. Taylor remained stoic and his facial expression was blank. He folded his note pad up and replaced it neatly into his uniform shirt pocket.

"She is the daughter of our own, Phil McNally." Taylor announced, and then he swallowed hard and his eyes went over to the dead body on the bed. "Our chain of command notified Officer McNally of the news. He did not come by the crime scene. We have very little. Nothing. As CSI Officer Crump said, his crew is almost wrapped up and they have very little to go on, too. We were waiting for your arrival until we called the coroner for removal of the body."

Tears welled up in Officer Taylor's eyes. He spoke in a quivering voice, while watching Odell reach back into his right-side suit pocket and he dug out the same pack of cigarettes. The pack was squished even more than before and they appeared flattened now.

"It's a shame, Detective Odell," the young police officer lamented while glancing at the dead body of the woman sprawled out and riddled with bullets and surprisingly little blood traces, "she was so stunningly gorgeous."

Detective Odell downed the rest of his coffee and handed the empty container to George Grundy. "Please, George, hold my coffee. It's empty, but please don't toss it away in that red wastebasket there. You can use the wicker one near the door.

That one is unimportant."

George's eyes traveled to the wastebaskets, but he instead held on to the empty container. It appeared as if he wanted to play it safe and not risk making an error.

Odell shook a cigarette loose from the pack, stuck it in his mouth, but did not light it. Instead, the cigarette dangled from his lower lip as he spoke, once more as if it was almost as if he glued it there.

His voice came out as a growl, "Yeah, she was. You know sumthin'? Appearance and skin are simply a shell for hiding what really counts. It means very little. The soul that lies within is what truly matters. Thank you, Taylor, thank you, George and thank you to you, Crump and your entire team. Great work on the notes, Taylor. What time did you get the call and arrive on the scene?"

"I received the call at six-fifty this morning. I was only a few miles away. I arrived around seven ten."

Odell nodded and said, "The landlord, the old man, this Travers guy. He made the call a few minutes earlier, and the paramedics followed shortly thereafter after you made the call. But you and everyone else could tell that she was dead."

"Correct. Detective Odell."

"And the old man was here early to do the yard work because he did not want to deal with the heat. Correct?"

Taylor did not react to the precision testimony of Odell. He knew how good the detective was. The young officer simply answered the questions efficiently.

"Yes, correct. The heat today is supposed to be unbearable. He is an old man. He wanted to get done with the work very early."

"It makes sense. The landlord might be old, but he does a helluva job. The place is beautiful. The turf, flowers, and landscape are top-notch. Old man. Old time work ethic. Get your ass up early and get the job done. Relax and drink beer later. Travers most likely retired from a factory job. He was used to being into work at the ass-crack of dawn."

For one of the first times, Odell's eyes turned their attention to the victim's body for a long stare. Odell studied the victim from a few feet away, tilting his head, and then he took a few steps closer until he was at the foot of the bed.

He spoke in a low whisper, "Left side back pocket."

Odell dug around in the back pocket of his pants and he pulled out some rubber gloves. He slipped the gloves on his hands and then dug around in the same pocket and produced a small folded magnifying lens and he unfolded it. Then Odell used the glass, peered in over the dead body, and studied all the details. Remarkably, the unlit cigarette still hung like an icicle in winter from a gutter line to Odell's lower lip. It clung and did not move even as the detective moved all around. First, he hovered over the body, and then he gently rolled the body over and studied the wounds on her stomach with the carved letters. After rolling the body back into the same position, Odell stepped back and seemed to frame the scene by making a box with his fingers, much as an artist or a photographer would do when studying and framing a scene. Then Odell studied all the linens and bed covers while he peered over the top of the bed, then around the bed, and then, with a moan and groan, (but no unsteady waver as was the previous case when he bent down) Odell even studied the floor and under the bed. No one spoke as he worked. Everyone remained motionless and silent.

While still on his knees and peering around on the floor, Odell spoke, "Too bad or too good. It is a hardwood floor. It depends upon your point of view. Crump, where on the floor did you find most of the blades of grass? Were they mostly by the door or here on the side of the bed?" Officer Crump blinked, but he did not seem too surprised that Odell knew of the blades of grass. Everyone looked at Crump, but everyone in the room already knew that Odell was correct, that his team had found blades of grass.

"Ah, mostly right in the doorway. Five or six wet blades. I assume they are from the old man from walking in the room. We only found two there by the bed. Where you are right now."

"Yes, outstanding work, Crump. And how many are on the

stairs coming up here?"

"Quite a few on the lower part, maybe six to eight and only one or two on the upper part of the stairs. However, the stairs have carpet coverings. The rest of the apartment has hardwood floors."

Odell nodded. He took the cigarette out of his mouth and jammed it into his shirt pocket under his suit jacket. He then used the bed as a support and pushed himself to his feet.

"Did you keep them all separate and label them as to their locations?"

"Yes, we did, Detective Odell. Of course, we did."

Odell seemed very pleased. He removed the rubber gloves and handed them off to Crump. Crump dropped them in his disposal bag to join the rest of the spent crime scene tools used on the scene. Odell then folded his magnifying lens up and returned it to the left side back pocket of his pants while mumbling the location and then tapping his shirt pocket, where he placed the cigarette.

He opened the top of the pocket and peered in as if he needed to confirm what was in there and then with a puzzled look on his face; Odell looked at Crump and said, "Great work. Crump, you are the best in the business and I know this goes without saying, but I need you and your team to be on top of your game on this one. This killer is a pro and with this death, and the others both here and in Albany and Westchester years ago, this makes ten victims in total. You do know that we are dealing with a serial killer?"

Crump nodded and blinked while answering, "Yes, I heard and don't worry, Odell . . . we won't miss anything. Not even blades of grass."

"Good. So, other than what you surmise are the fingerprints of the landlord and the victim and possibly the roommate, you found nothing other than the blades of grass? Hence why you and Officer Taylor reported that you have very little to go on."

"Correct, Odell. Correct. Very little. Just little things here and there. We will confirm the identity of the prints, but because of the amount and consistency of them, yes, we feel that we know whose prints they are."

Odell tugged at his pants and tried to tuck his shirt into the waistline, but he quickly gave up. His eyes wandered around and then he spoke as he pointed out various observations of his initial investigation.

"Gotcha. Let's not be discouraged, men. I don't allow all the little clues that come along in a homicide investigation to distract me. Instead, I take all the little clues, pack them into one helluva huge basket of clues and then I begin to blow shit up. I find it to be a more efficient approach to homicide crime solving. Right now, these little things are what we need because I do not want to quibble about the facts, but we do have some clues and items to go on here."

It appeared as if Odell almost smiled, but the impulse quickly faded as he went off exploring his thoughts aloud to the group, "I am pleased with what we have. I am not discouraged. I know it seems as if it is another dead end, but not really. The blades of grass are our first piece of evidence to go on in an otherwise huge void of evidence. The murder from earlier this week had zilch. At least we have something. Grundy and I admired the perfect turf when we arrived. Perhaps the killer cut across the turf at some point, and he made a mistake in doing so. The lushness of the grass and the wetness caused some issues of track off with the grass blades. We need to check out the irrigation time clock to find what time the system activated. It could be a key in a timestamp for us. The blades of grass on the lower part of the stairs and there on the side of the bed are from the feet of the killer. The upper part of the stairs and there in the doorway came from the old man's shoes. I think he had work boots on to work in the yard. We will need to speak with Mr. Travers at some point and confirm his footwear and some of these other points that have and will come up during this initial investigation. Maybe we can arrange that fairly soon."

None of the officers spoke because Odell launched back into his own explanation.

"The killer wore sneakers. There is a slight imprint of an old wet mark underneath the bed, right there on the edge. It looks to me to be a sneaker imprint. Crump, you and your team need to check it out carefully. The old man, having deeper treads on his work boots, had the blades of grass only dislodge after he took many steps. When he reached the top of the stairs, a few came off, but here," Odell walked closer to the doorway of the bedroom and he pointed at a location on the floor, "here, when the old man flipped the light switch on and saw the horrific scene, he turned and fled. His quick spin caused more blades to dislodge as opposed to the smoother finish of the sneakers of the killer. The old man is innocent. His reaction to the horror proves it. Crump, please, grab that tissue in the red wastebasket here. I think that might have some blades of grass inside of it, pulled from the shoes, or sneakers or feet of Miss McNally here. Please find her shoes and check. Also, please scour the turf areas of the front yard. Do not miss anything. We need an imprint. It could be vitally important. If the turf was wet, as I suspect it was, there could be another, or a better-quality imprint. Then we can determine sneakers, foot size and so forth. Or maybe the killer finally slipped up for once and dropped something on the property in a hasty entrance or retreat."

"Roger, Odell. We are on it. Please let me call the team now and I will be right back," Crump said while he held a finger up, nodded, and grabbed his radio off his belt to direct his team. He stepped out of the room and his finger showed that he meant to listen after the call.

While waiting for Crump, Detective Lyle Odell messed with his hair, tugged at his belt, and then, when the radio call finished, and he had Crump's full attention, he continued, "The victim has five gunshot wounds. Two were lethal. One in the back of the head and one directly through the heart. They are twenty-two L-R calibers, fired at close range from the handgun. The hit man's weapon of choice. Quiet and lethal under the correct circumstances by the correct shooter. Very little blood. The other shots and wounds are symbolic to signify the day of the week. The killer will skip a day and kill again on this Sunday. This is his sick pattern. The same as it was years ago in the other locations. To our killer, Monday is day one of the week. There will be seven gunshots on Sunday. Unless we stop him before that."

George Grundy cleared his throat; the big sergeant tugged at his gun belt, looked at the empty coffee cup in his hand and tossed it into the wicker basket.

"What are the odds of that happening, Lyle? I mean, of us stopping him. You used him as a pronoun, so I am guessing it is a male."

"It is, Sarge. A powerful male. A military man. He used a SOG knife with a serrated edge to carve up the body. Usually that is a United States Navy issued knife. With this damn nutcase, I think he just likes the feel. Of course, the g and the w are for the Gulf War. As far as stopping him goes, sadly, we have a very poor chance. I am afraid he will kill one more time before we can nail 'em. Lord in Heaven, I hope that I am wrong and with the help of some Irish and quiet time, I will retreat to study the facts once more and we will do everything in our power to prevent another murder by this lunatic. I will pray for that to be the case."

Odell looked around the room and studied the reaction of the team before explaining, "Officer McNally is a Gulf War vet. Combat. The first Gulf War. Desert Storm. The killer is a vet too, but he has some sick vendetta to carry out on veterans of combat, their family members or friends. Especially so of military veterans now serving as civilian police officers, or in government positions, or civil service positions. Positions of authority over others."

"So, the killer is not a Navy vet? He just likes the SOG knife?" Sergeant Gundry asked.

"Oh no, he is a Navy veteran. A combat vet too," Odell said, while tapping all the pockets of his pants and his shirt and pausing to answer Grundy's question. Grundy knew his old drinking friend rather well, and he realized that Odell was searching for his cigarette to stick in his mouth to, as he always says, "Just to taste it."

"It's in the top shirt pocket, Odell. You forgot to tell yourself where you put it."

Odell's eyes narrowed, and he mumbled a thank you while digging into the pocket, plucking the wayward cigarette and sticking it into his mouth.

"Thank you, George. I lost track of that one. Anyway, yes, the killer is a Navy veteran. A Corpsman. He understands the human body. He has medical training too. He knew where to shoot with the twenty-two to kill. If you study his past kills, they all follow the same method. Lethal shots, then symbolic shots. He uses a knife with skill. He also is an artist, either in photography or in painting. On the other hand, if he is not an artist, then he appreciates the arts or some training thereof. Perhaps just some classes in a local college or such. He appreciates the human body because of his medical training, but he also studies the structure of muscles, tissues and bones and of the human frame. The exact placement of the bullets is precise, keen, and measured. Expert marksmanship. The killer has great eyesight. This nutcase might be a killer, but he is highly intelligent. He admires nude painting or photography. Art. No lewdness, because he appreciates the structure of the body. That is why—he posed the body so beautifully after killing her. She is a gorgeous woman. He posed her body. He killed her, carved her, and then . . . he had the condescension to stand there and admire the scene and touch her, and the. . .." Odell's voice quivered and he stopped speaking. His eyes traveled around the room while he studied the faces of the men there with him. Grundy, Taylor, and Crump. Good men. Solid men. Men who Odell now knew were all on the same team as he was. A police officer's daughter ruthlessly murdered because of one thing. Because the officer served his country. A gorgeous young woman in the prime of her life. A woman with everything to live for. Lost. Odell caught his voice, the cigarette danced on his lips, and the words finally arrived.

"The bastard posed her. We need to get his evil bastard. Men, I need your help. Can't do it without everyone."

"You know you got us, Odell. I will be glad to put a bullet in this son-of-a-bitch myself. Let's saddle up and go get 'em, Lyle. Whatcha need?" Sergeant Grundy asked while the other men nodded in agreement.

"I need . . . some more bottles of Irish. This is going to take some pondering and some sippin'. Can you drive me, George? I think we are off duty now."

Grundy looked at his watch and he turned to Officer Taylor and said, "Taylor, please, go ahead and call for the morgue wagon, do the paperwork, and tidy this all up for me. Will you?"

"Gotcha, Sarge. Go get Odell, what he needs," Officer Taylor said with a wave.

Odell took a few steps to leave the room, and he stopped and turned and looked at Crump, and then at Officer Taylor.

"Oh yes, one thing that I almost forgot. Please don't text me the info or call me on my cellphone for any updates or alerts on what you find here. Best to go through Sarge Grundy and he will track me down. Chances are the damn cellphone battery is gonna be dead. That cellphone and I have to come to terms. Thanks."

Despite the dire circumstances and the sadness surrounding the scene, Crump smiled and waved as Odell and Grundy left. Crump knew that Detective Lyle Odell might have some demons chasing him, but he was a genius.

Odell was good at his job.

Very, very good.

Exceptional.

CHAPTER THREE

"Sarge Grundy not coming in to stock up?" Danny Clark asked Detective Odell as he placed two bottles of Odell's favorite Irish whiskey on the counter of the liquor store. "Saw you coming, Detective Odell. My feet are killin' me. Been humpin' cases and kegs of cold beer all day long. Those cases are no joke. Weigh a shit-ton. Good thing that I wore my sneakers today. Been on my feet all day. You are, the first customer buying whiskey, rather than beer today. So damn hot," Danny said with a hint of a smile. Odell looked at Danny as he reached around in his pants pocket and fumbled to find some cash. Odell always marveled at how Danny Clark had never aged. Danny was the daytime clerk in the store; his uncle owned the place. Odell had known him for at least ten years. Danny worked here on and off over the years. About five years ago or thereabouts, Danny went away for a few years and then he returned. Odell had heard that his uncle owned stores in other locations, a few here in the area, a few down in Albany and some downstate somewhere. The uncle asked his nephew to work at the various stores, as he needed him to do so. After another stint working the counter here in Mohawk City for a few years, he went away again and then he returned about six months ago. Odell surmised that he was finding his path, but he never seemed to progress much from being a store clerk. Odell always thought there was nothing wrong with that job. It sure was a lot less stressful than the madness of a career that Odell picked for his life. Odell's house was right around the corner from the store and in all those years of visiting the store; other than now wearing eyeglasses, it seemed as if Danny Clark never aged. He was a big, powerful guy, who lifted cases and kegs of beer with ease. He had hair that looked like a pile of black steel wool on his head, thick eyeglasses, and a small nose and mouth. Yet, the steel wool hair was just as black as it ever was . . . not even a lick of gray along the sides or edges.

"Nah, he wanted to get home and do yard work before it became too hot. In theory, it is a day off for both of us. We just had to respond to a situation. I told Grundy to take off. I can walk a little, even in the heat. It will help me sweat out the horribleness inside of me. Damn, where is that cash?"

Danny pointed at Odell's front right pants pocket and commented, "Grundy's too late. It is already too hot. Usually, you put it in that pocket there, Odell. Usually. Not always. And you never seem to wear your shoulder harness with your weapon in it these days. If I might be a little rude, you look awful."

"I seldom carry my weapon. Seldom. Not never, but seldom. Do I ever not look awful, Danny?" Odell asked as he dug around in the suggested pocket and produced some wrinkled bills out of the depths of it.

"Sometimes. I mean . . . today you look aw-full-er. I am sure that is not a word. How about extra awful? But then, again, my eyesight is poor even with my eyeglasses on.

"I understand. You are getting old, Danny. Join the crowd of us old geezers with old people's troubles. I 'member a few years back when you did not wear glasses. Just when you returned here to the store here on this latest tour. Here, I am not sure there is enough money there, Danny. Let me have two packs of my cancer sticks, too. Please check it for me." Odell handed the unruly roll of paper bills to Danny and after Danny straightened them out and counted them, the clerk reached behind him, pulled two packs of Odell's brand of cigarettes from the store display, and dropped them on the counter.

"Need matches?" Danny asked as he plucked a book of matches from a bowl on the counter that overflowed with matchbooks and held them in the air.

"Nah, I have a fine collection of matchbooks from here in my kitchen drawer at home. I need to use them up. Thanks."

Danny nodded, and he thumbed a thumb toward a television mounted above the rear of the front counter. The television sat on a dusty shelf in between small liquor bottles, and it had a dusty screen and worn knobs. Odell lifted his eyes, and they traveled from some dusty liquor bottles on the upper shelf above the counter, to the wall above the shelf where there hung, some framed black and white photographs of landscapes and a few pretty girls sitting on the hood of classic cars, and a few antique tin signs of liquor and beer companies. There was a picture of a rustic hunting and fishing cabin at a lake and a picture of Danny proudly posing for a picture at the same lake, while holding a large lake trout in his hands, his fishing pole standing by his side and a trout net and knife strapped to his belt. A lucky fisherman. Odell recognized the lake in the photograph as Piseco Lake, a nearby haven of adventure for outdoor enthusiasts. Odell recognized everything. He was good at his job. Very, very good. Odell's eyes lingered the longest on a woodcarving. His focus remained on a carving of initials hand carved by a knife into a piece of oak. D-w-c and then the carver applied a few polished coats of lacquer over the wood. It was rustic and fine work. Odell surmised they were Danny's initials. It appeared as if he was a creative guy. Finally, his eyes landed on the television set. Odell did not linger too long there.

"I imagine the awfulness has something to do with the news there. It is all over the news now. I am sorry, Odell. Very sorry. Sometimes this city is just too sad for its own good any more. A friggin' serial killer. Unreal. Here, you gave me extra," Danny said as he handed a twenty-dollar bill back to Odell.

Odell's eyes had carried to the items on the shelf and to the television screen, but somehow, he also watched Danny count the cash. Danny had removed his eyeglasses and placed them on the counter to count the bills. Odell noted that he left the eyeglasses there.

"Extra. Nah. You counted wrong, Danny."

"I gave you the homicide detective involved in a horrible

murder investigation discount, Odell. Two for the price of one. You need the inspiration to catch this crazy bastard. I am just doing what I can to help. I hear that you have got a new boss, too. Oh, my. Ha! The pressure is on. Saw that on the news last week. Decorated combat hero guy. An officer in the Army Reserve. Stiff. Guys like that deserve to be stiff. He looks uptight. I bet you wish ole Cap Tucker was still around."

Odell blinked and forced a smile while he watched Danny ring up the sale, and then placed the two bottles into a paper bag.

Odell admitted to Danny, "I dunno. The jury is out on the new captain. I really don't know him very well. Yet. You gave me the homicide detective involved in a horrible murder investigation discount. Wow, that was a lot of nouns. Thanks for the confidence, Danny. This one is a toughie. He killed a few years back down in Albany and downstate in Westchester. They did not catch the evil bastard then, and now he is back."

Danny nodded. He glanced at the television screen, where a news reporter was reporting live from in front of the house where Allison McNally was murdered and the reporter stood just outside the crime scene with a string of yellow tape surrounding the property.

"They didn't have you, Odell. But remember, even Derek Cramer struck out. You can't hit a homer every time. Sometimes the pitcher wins. The fastball, then a curve, you know. One of those big hooks that slid across the plate and it would catch Cramer sittin' on his heels."

Danny spoke and simultaneously made a baseball demonstration swing behind the counter as Lyle Odell watched his eyes and his motion and listened to the words of the analogy. Something in Danny's tone stuck in Odell's mind. He loved Derek Cramer. He was Odell's favorite baseball player, who played on his favorite team, the New York Clippers. Odell loved Derek Cramer mostly because he had great admiration of Cramer's commitment and his character. Odell shook it off and concentrated on Danny and his actions . . . and his words.

Danny finished his mock baseball swing and then leaned in a

little and said, “Anyway, good luck, Lyle.”

“No, they didn’t have me, Danny. For what that might be worth. That and a buck two-fifty gets me on the bus round trip to downtown and that is about all. See you around. Thanks for the discount. I have a feeling that I will be back. Soon.”

Odell gave a wave, he picked up the paper bag and tucked it under his arm and within a few strides, Odell, turned around and looked at Danny and said, “But you gotta ‘member that sometimes, Cramer waited on that big slow hook, sat back and hit that sucker to the moon. Upper deck. He had deceiving power. Cramer hid it well.” Odell then pointed at Danny to emphasize his point.

Danny nodded, but he did not comment as Odell turned and fiddled with the door, opened it and the good detective was back out in the stifling heat of the day. He walked into the hiss of summer.

Odell took two steps toward his home and heard a soft female voice. The voice was crisp and her voice was sweet.

“Hello, Detective Odell.”

Odell stopped and turned in the voice's direction, and for a fleeting second, he realized that, as usual, he did not have his service weapon with him. In fact, he did not even have his police detective’s badge clipped to his belt. However, he had a paper bag with two packs of cigarettes and two bottles of his favorite Irish whiskey inside. When Odell spotted the woman from where the soft voice emitted, he immediately defused his stance. Odell was used to a lifetime of snapshots. He took snapshots of everything, everyone, and the entire world within seconds and filed them away in his complex mind. Odell captured every detail. He took a snapshot of the young woman standing in front of him. Just a few feet away on a sweltering hot summer’s day. The snapshot came back with a label.

She was soft, very soft. She was very pretty.

No, in fact, after another careful examination; Odell determined that she was beautiful. Stunningly beautiful. Odell swallowed, but the lump that suddenly formed in his throat remained.

The woman was young. Only forty at the most. Short, rather curvy, with long black hair, large framed glasses surrounding her eyes, a gentle slope to her nose and slightly round cheeks. She wore prescription eyeglasses; they were the type of eyewear that changes colors automatically according to the level of light. Her dark eyes flashed underneath the lens of the eyeglasses and Odell admired how her summer blouse hung to her generous breasts rather nicely and the rather tight shorts that she wore clung to her hips rather nicely too. Despite the heat, she wore work boots on her feet, with socks pulled up rather high onto her ankles. She tightened the bootlaces in generous overlaps, working them around the top of the boot and tying them tightly in the boot's front. Odell noticed the dried licks of dirt on the boots. Black dirt. Onion fields.

Odell thought, 'This young woman lives and works on a farm.'

Over her shoulder hung a leather bag. It was a much-worn leather bag. She smiled as Odell studied her and she tugged on the leash that she held in her hand. A leash that held back a pig. A pig that looked just as hot as Odell felt. The pig stared up at Odell in a slightly disturbing manner, and Odell locked eyes with the animal and then shook his head a little in disbelief. The pig acted much as a faithful dog would act. He stood faithfully by the young woman's side and watched and listened. Following her lead.

"Do you know something? There are days, and then there are *days.* Here it is hotter than seventeen Hells, humid as a tropical rainforest, I just left out of work, investigating the latest wretched act of a deranged killer, and now, a rather cute young woman, who knows my name, meets me outside my favorite local liquor store, while I am carrying two bottles of my favorite Irish whiskey and two packs of cigarettes. Just to add a fresh strawberry on top of this sundae of madness, the cute young woman is holding a leash with a pet pig on the end. A Yucatan pig. A male about sixty pounds or so, and he is hot. Very hot. Yucatan pigs are super-intelligent and, unfortunately, are used in lab work because their skin and organs are very close in composition and type to humans. You and your faithful friend here live and work on a farm. A black dirt farm growing sweet onions. That is why you have it all dried on your boots. New York State not only has black dirt down in Orange County, there are a few in and around here, too. I suspect it's near Greenfield. Yet, meeting you and the pig here, in the hiss of summer, is just another cog in the weirdness wheel for Detective Lyle Odell. This is another example of the reasons that I need to drink so much."

The pig tugged on the leash, snorted, and clawed at the sidewalk. The young woman tugged at the leash and smiled at the pig. The young woman bent down, and she spoke to the pig in a whisper. Then she stood up and pushed at her eyeglasses to push them farther up to the top of her nose. After the whisper of words that seemed bent on convincing the pig that there was a purpose to this visit, the young woman spoke again to Detective Odell in her soft and rather captivating voice.

"I just told Doodlesticks that you do not yet know his name and we will bring you up to speed on our likes and dislikes. He does not like when people call him by the common swine identification word. Right for now, he understands. Ha! Your reputation for genius is dead on. Brilliant. There are many reasons that you drink and I understand. Totally. Many bad guys would have escaped without you drinking, Detective Odell. Regardless, I know it is terribly hot and I beg your pardon for the interruption, Detective Odell. I am a huge admirer of you and your work, and I am here to offer our help."

Odell lifted an eyebrow and asked, "You actually admire me? You are amongst maybe two people in the entire world. Anyway, you used the rather puzzling word of help. To add to the intrigue, you added the word our in front of the word help. You and who else?"

"Doodlesticks and me. Of course," she answered without hesitation.

Odell shifted his feet uncomfortably, and he tucked the paper bag with the bottles under his arm just a bit more.

"Doodlesticks is your companion's name. I get it. Very cute. Of course. Once more, this is why I need to drink so much. Look, honey, you are beautiful and all, but it is very hot. Your companion is uncomfortable because he cannot sweat, so he needs some mud and cool water to wallow in and I need to drink. Therefore, please go inside where it is cool. Please go and find some mud for Doodlesticks and we will see you down the road. Wherever. Whenever. Thanks for the admiration. Stay cool, honey."

The young woman promptly produced a spray bottle of water from her leather bag; she unscrewed the tip of the bottle, aimed it at the pig and sprayed the pig down with the cool water. It was easy to see that the pig enjoyed his shower, and the water instantly revitalized his behavior.

"Doodlesticks is fine. I know that he will enjoy some cooler water from a hose. Perhaps in your backyard. But for now, he is fine. Your house is just down the road there. There we can hose down Doodlesticks and we can discuss how we can help you. I even enjoy Irish whiskey." The young woman smiled and blinked as she slowly replaced the water bottle in her bag.

"I work alone . . . ah . . . ah . . . I did not catch your name." Odell ran his hand through his sweaty hair. This time, because of the heat, his hair did not stick up in all directions. The humidity forced it down onto his scalp.

With a wave in the pig's direction, Odell added, "I have your companion's name down pat, though."

"Ms. Marlin Santini. The only non-Irish chick within thirty-five miles of Mohawk City. Although in full-disclosure, my mum was an O'Hara and my middle name is Maureen. Named after the movie star. How I wish that I looked like her." Marlin rolled her eyes, and Odell carefully studied every move and hung on every word of Marlin Santini. She had caught his attention, and Lyle Odell was perceptive beyond any normal human being. He knew intelligence, and he sensed when a person or a situation would or could be used to his advantage. This was that type of situation and that type of person. And animal too.

"Marlin, huh? Interesting first name."

"I guess. It has served me, so far, rather well for interest, so yes. You are correct. Dad was Italian. He is gone now. Four years ago. Next month. Doodlesticks and I live in Greenfield. You were correct, as usual, with your brilliant observations. I rent a small room on a farm there. Doodlesticks gets his mud. I get my peace and solitude to study crime fighting. An amateur crime buff, yes, dumb-ass chick with nice breasts and a pretty little ass, no. I was a criminal science major at Mohawk University. I attended a long time ago, but a silly romance and time and money got in my way. Now, I take courses here and there and crawl to a useless degree of some sort. Anyway, one of the professors there often lectured on your cases. He seemed quite intrigued by you. Almost unnervingly so. He said that you were a genius. Usually you work alone, yes, but it is not unheard of for you to enlist some help. Sergeant Grundy assists you, mostly as a drinking buddy and driver, but at times, he lends you his experience and his help. And you recruited Officer Dennis Baker to assist you in the Murdock homicide case, but that was because you knew he was a bad guy right off the bat."

Marlin stopped speaking for a second and studied the face of Lyle Odell. She knew that she had captured his attention as she launched into further explanation without undue pause.

"Right now, since I never cracked into any police jobs, and I am now too old to do so, I work as a server in a restaurant and I shovel cow pies and dig onions out on the farm for reduced rent, but I have to tell you that my younger sister went to school with Allison McNally. I sort of, kind of, knew her and she was a wonderful person. I was out at the house this morning. You need Doodlesticks. You need me. This killer is no joke. Even for your genius level, this dude is no joke."

Odell peered at Marlin with deep intent in his eyes. "Why do I need Doodlesticks and you?"

Marlin's eyes quickly darted to the pig sitting at her feet. The pig moved and snorted a bit and wiggled his backside around in a display of recognition of his name.

"Doodlesticks likes that you call him by his name. You need us because your crime scene dudes are combing over that front lawn like twenty friggin' Sherlock Holmes and ten Doctor Watsons would. It is obvious that you told them to do so. You are looking for imprints, or footprints, or something the killer dropped as he cut across the lawn. The killer made the first mistake he ever made in all of his sick ventures. And the genius Detective Lyle Odell picked up on the mistake. Maybe a blade of grass inside the house? I dunno. Just a guess. No doubt that he cut across a wet lawn. In haste. Perhaps someone was lurking about, or he picked up on something. Time will tell. Doodlesticks can smell things twenty feet underground, and he can detect odors and distinct smells from five to ten miles away. I trained him to track and obey my commands. Yes, he is a Yucatan Doodlesticks, and he is super intelligent. More so than most humans are. He just needs water, mud and food and drink. He gets a little vocal when he wants for those things."

Odell nodded and said, "Don't we all? Except for the mud. I will skip the mud. Super intelligent and super smell, huh? You trained 'em in scent tracking, huh? From Central America, huh?"

Marlin nodded.

"And most likely a helluva lot more likable than most humans are, too. Here . . . can you please hold this paper bag of inspiration while you hold the leash too? Don't drop it. In theory, your future hangs in the balance," Odell said as he handed the bag over to Marlin.

"Got it."

Marlin grabbed the paper bag full of whiskey and cigarettes and she watched while Odell tapped every single pocket on his body, in his suit jacket, in his pants pocket, and in frustration, the good detective screwed his face up like a corkscrew.

"Detective Odell, try your top shirt pocket. That is usually where you keep them. You didn't remind yourself that is why you lost track of them. Your brain is going a million ways to Sunday. Thinking of solving the crimes and catching this evil man. You have no need to recall small details such as where your pack of cigarettes is. Do you need a light?"

Odell nodded, checked the recommended pocket, and pulled out the ramshackle pack of cigarettes. He tapped one out and stuck it in his mouth.

"Yes, please. Do you have one?"

Marlin nodded, she juggled everything while she deftly reached in the leather bag and pulled out a lighter. She flicked it to life with her finger and Odell leaned into the flames. Odell took a long drag on the lit cigarette and he exhaled in a relish of the taste and the enjoyment of the flame and nicotine.

"I know there is something to find on that front lawn. Maybe the killer made a mistake. He cut across that lawn. I can feel it," Odell said, and then he allowed his eyes to wander. First to the sky, then to the faithful Doodlesticks, then to Marlin's face and then the curves of her body. Odell felt her eyes following his, but he was trance-like and Marlin knew that his mind was pondering every aspect of the case. She also did not move or say a word. She enjoyed when his eyes lingered on her curves.

After the pause and another drag on the cigarette, Odell asked, "How do you know it is a he, Marlin?"

"I read as much as I could find about the previous murders by this nut job. I am a crime buff and a serial killer is one of the ultimate crimes. Like a diamond heist. As far as if the killer is a male, well, duh, there are many telltale signs. This guy is a vindictive and bad-ass bastard. Strong. Physically. Not so much emotionally. A woman most likely could not carve so deep into muscle and bone with the knife. Yes, indeed, I suspect a man. Super-intelligent but evil as all of Hell is. He put it all aside a few years ago, but something triggered his sickness a few days ago. Or weeks. Who knows? Regardless, he is sick and nuts, too. Bent on revenge for some military bullshit. Women are only vindictive when love and stupid men decide to cross them."

Odell nodded. "Are you vindictive because of a stupid man, Marlin?"

"No. Why would you ask?"

"I always pay attention to every word that a person says,"

Odell said, while blowing out the smoke from another long drag, "you mentioned a silly romance. It interrupted your education and also your career plans."

Marlin worked a weak smile across her face. The memories hit home. She motioned for Odell to hand her the cigarette, and he did so. Marlin took the cigarette with her free hand while still holding the bag with a tuck of her other arm and hand. Odell studied her face and especially her eyes while she took the cigarette, took a long drag on it, blew the smoke into the humidity, and then handed the cigarette back to Odell.

While remnants of the long drag from the cigarette continued to escape from her mouth, Marlin explained, "He went his way and I went mine. We are cool to this day with our decisions. I am climbing closer and closer to forty years old now, and I am comfortable in my life. With a man or without a man. You see, Odell, you and I are much alike. We both demand honesty from people. I do not ask for much else. That is why Doodlesticks and I get along so well. He is very honest. Deception is not only displayed in words and actions. Humans are immensely flawed. They display deception in emotions. Romance is for chumps. It is like beating your head on a wall. Eventually, you stop because it hurts too much. Just share some quality time together, some intellectual discussion, share some culture, have a little physical roundabout and interaction or two or three or so, laugh a lot and enjoy the company. Good luck with all the other stuff!"

Odell did not comment on her words or explanation.

Instead, he narrowed his eyes, took a short drag on the cigarette, and asked, "How did you know to stake out the liquor store?"

"Duh again, Odell. You are perplexed. This madman has killed for years. How many people? Ten now. I am not sure of the exact count. He gets away with it. His power grows with each murder, and he already has another victim in his sights. You feel the victim's burdens. It weighs you down. The whiskey brings the answers. Everything haunts you, Odell. Evil haunts you non-stop. The whiskey chases the pain and the evil away so you can find the answers."

"Your professor said that I was a genius?"

"Yes, he did."

"Did he say you were a genius?"

Marlin smiled widely and answered quickly, "Not at all. I barely passed his class."

"Interesting. Huh? You are an amateur crime buff. An amateur built the ark and professionals built the Titanic. Which one do you wanna ride on? Look, Marlin, I am super-flawed. I am nothing more than a functioning alcoholic. Your professor said that I was a genius. Maybe. Maybe not. My old man used to say that behind every supposed successful man is a more brilliant woman. A beautiful woman, smarter, more capable and more dedicated. It is just the way it works. The successful man ain't anything without the amazing woman standing behind him. My old man was talking about my mother. His wife."

Odell paused within his words. He reached out for the paper bag, nodded his head in indication, and Marlin, in understanding, handed the bag off to Odell.

"Thank you. Honestly . . . Marlin and Doodlesticks . . . I usually work alone. Just a little side help from Grundy and Crump and his team of genius techs, occasionally Doctor Kent for medical advice and information, and on even rarer occasions, my commanding officer."

"Agreed. Usually, you do. This case isn't usual."

"Yes, spot on. I agree with you. Perhaps we can speak some more about this case. Perhaps Doodlesticks and Marlin came along because of fate. It is rather intriguing and interesting. The timing. This situation. I see that you drove a pickup truck here, because I see the keys for the vehicle hanging from the carbineer clip on your shorts there. They are quite distinctly keys to a pickup truck. An older model, in and around ten years old. Before the manufacturers went to those stupid chip things at the end of the keys. Despite my recognition of the keys, your vehicle has to be a pickup truck to haul Doodlesticks around in the bed of the truck. You parked your truck at my house.

Doodlesticks and you walked here. I propose that we walk to my house. We will get the hose out and make some mud in the yard for Doodlesticks."

"You are correct in all of your statements, and I agree with your proposal, Detective Odell."

"You like Irish, huh?"

"I do."

"I don't have any fancy whiskey glasses, and no faceted, cut-glass bullshit, and my house is kind of lean and mean. I pour the Irish whiskey neat and tall. My house is clean, but it ain't fancy. I seldom, other than Grundy, have any visitors. As of late, I have improved my housekeeping duties. It helps me think when I clean."

"Do I look fancy, Odell?"

"Nah, I guess not. Cute, yes. Fancy, no. Although, you most likely clean up fancy. You will need to take a few gentle sips for now of the Irish. Gonna need you to drive us to the crime scene. Doodlesticks and me, that is. Afterwards, then we can tip 'em hard. Grundy is working on his lawn, so I can't bug him for a ride."

"Bullshit. Grundy is sitting in his house, in the air-conditioning, sipping a cold beer. He is not working on his lawn."

Odell almost smiled. "You are correct. Anyway, let's go put our heads together, put Doodlesticks to work and we can talk. Weld our minds. I say, let's go get this bastard."

"Yes, let's go get him, Odell. Let's go get him."

Odell commented as the pickup truck glided to a stop in front of the home where the crime scene investigation was still ongoing.

"Damn, I am glad that Doodlesticks is happy because I am buzzed. Big time. Irish on an empty stomach ain't workin' out too well. At least he had the mud and the water."

Marlin put the gearshift for the pickup truck into the parking gear and she shut off the engine. First, she glanced over to Officer Oliver Crump as he looked up from directing his team combing the front lawn of the apartment house where the homicide occurred to glance at the pickup truck, and then she pulled the key from the ignition.

Marlin listened to Odell's comments and replied, "Mud and water are grossly overrated. Unless you are Doodlesticks. I took your advice and only took a few sips, but I assure you that I will be right behind you once we find something here and get back to your house. I don't need any fancy glasses. It is obvious that your elite crew of techs have nothing at hand. They are still wandering around. They are still in the same spots as I left 'em. As I said, Detective Lyle Odell, you need Doodlesticks and you need me, too."

Odell opened the door of the passenger's side of the truck and he stepped out and landed on terra firma. He was wobbly. Immediately, the good detective faced the puzzled look on the face of Oliver Crump. When the curvy and attractive Ms. Marlin Santini exited the truck and worked her way to the rear bed of the truck and to the cage that held Doodlesticks captive, Oliver Crump stood up tall and put his hands on his hips. He was used to working with Detective Lyle Odell and his eccentric ways, but this one was a bit of a stretch. He was not sure what he was working with now.

There was no way to tell. . ..

Odell's eyes scanned the entire scene. He took in the technicians working; then his eyes went to the house, to the driveway, to finally, where the yellow crime scene tape was haphazardly flapping in the scorching breeze of the day. Odell also pointed to five or six people standing on the edge of the property line on the other side of the tape.

"Good. No media around. I guess they got bored. Just some neighbors. Wait until one of them earns the twenty bucks that one of the news reporters offered them to drop a dime if anything happens. They will be here in fifteen minutes, or maybe even less than that. I guess." Odell tapped his suit jacket pocket and mumbled, "Maybe I better let the captain know. Nah. Left that stupid cellphone at the house. The battery is probably dead." Odell took a few wobbly steps up the driveway. With some effort, he bent down and slipped under the crime scene tape and then he stopped; he turned to face Marlin as she tucked her arms underneath the belly of Doodlesticks.

Odell asked, "Do you need a hand with Doodlesticks?"

Odell realized that the pig weighed a few pounds.

Marlin answered Odell with some sass in her voice, "Nope. I put him in here without your help. No prissy ass bullshit over here, Odell. A nice ass, but it ain't no fancy ass." She paused and with a little chortle in her voice added, "Well, it can be. I guess."

Marlin deftly lifted the big guy up and gently placed him on the ground, pulled out his leash and snapped it onto his body harness as she leaned in, mumbled something in his ear, and then gently patted him and she smiled. Doodlesticks wiggled his backside; he snorted and choked out some noises. The two of them were best friends and had a communication language that was all their own. Marlin smiled and tugged at the leash, and the big guy turned and happily lumbered along next to her as they approached the front lawn. Marlin bent down and slipped under the crime scene tape and when she did so, every man on the crime scene crew studied her toned body as her tanned and toned legs rippled with muscles and her blouse slipped down to reveal a touch of impressive cleavage. Her tight shorts clung to her body and displayed her perfect female curves. While she stood up and walked closer, Officer Crump ran his hand through his hair, turned to his crew and waved at them to continue in their work. There were now six technicians working the scene. Officer Crump was doing everything that he could to find a clue, a telltale sign, a fact . . . or something. Anything. Four of the crime scene technicians quickly returned to work while on their hands and knees combing the blades of grass, while the two other technicians went back to combing the foundation plantings of juniper shrubs running along the front of the apartment house.

"Ah, hello there, Crump, do you have anything?" Odell asked. He then tapped his shirt pocket underneath his jacket and mumbled, "Top shirt pocket and Marlin has a light." Odell pulled out the same flattened cigarette pack, tapped one cigarette out, and stuck it in his mouth. Marlin nodded. She reached into her ever-present leather shoulder bag, produced a lighter, snapped it to a flame and Odell leaned into it. There was a long, powerful pull and then some gentle smoke blown into the air.

"Nothing, Odell. Sorry, we are doing our best. But, not a thing so far out here. There are a few imprints—they seem to be work boots. Therefore, we are thinking it is Mr. Travers walking around while checking his beloved lawn areas. Just a guess, but in reality, who knows whom they belong to? It is impossible to tell. Once Mr. Travers recovers, we need his boot imprints. The turf is so lush," Crump said as he glanced and pointed to the front lawn and then turned his attention to Marlin and Doodlesticks. Odell watched Crump's eyes while he blew a long puff of smoke into the air.

"Ah yes, sorry. Officer Oliver Crump, please meet Ms. Marlin Santini and Doodlesticks. They are here to assist us."

Doodlesticks wiggled his backside, pawed at the asphalt surface of the driveway with his front hoofs, and snorted in response to his name and introduction.

"Ah . . . well . . . okay. Gotcha. I think. Nice to meet you . . . both," Crump said as he reached out and shook hands with Marlin, and she smiled at his awkwardness.

"You can pat Doodlesticks on his back or scratch his neck as a greeting. He likes you. He knows that you are a good guy," Marlin said as she pulled on the leash a little to lead her faithful friend closer to Officer Oliver Crump.

Crump nodded, and he reached down and gently patted the back of the pig and gave him a scratch behind his left ear.

"He is quite friendly. Almost acts like a dog does," Crump said while he stood up as Doodlesticks snorted and nuzzled his back into the leg of Crump's uniform pants. "You were here before. You stood on the curb line and watched us working on the front lawn. You stood behind most of the media and the reporters," Crump said while studying Marlin's face for her answer.

"I was. I saw where the area of focus was and knew that we could assist. I saw the news of the homicide on the television this morning. It was non-stop. As I explained to Detective Odell, my sister knew the victim. They went to school together. She was a nice woman. It is very sad."

"It is. Very sad," Crump said as his eyes continued to study the lovely face of Marlin Santini.

She felt his stare, and she tested the waters.

"I thought that I blended into the crowd."

"Chicks that look like you . . . don't blend. It ain't only the weather that is hot. I am trained not to miss a trick," Crump said with a wink of his eye. After the quick sideline flirt, Crump went back to business, "So, you have a pet pig here. . .."

Immediately, Doodlesticks protested the classification with some loud snorts and a forceful bump into the leg of Crump. The pig was strong, and Crump stepped back in surprise at Doodlesticks's reaction.

"Geez, wow! What the hell was that for?"

Officer Oliver Crump rubbed at his shinbone.

Odell blew a long puff of smoke into the air, pulled the cigarette out of his mouth and explained, "Don't call Doodlesticks anything but a Doodlesticks. Call 'em by his name. As you can see, he gets a little cranky."

Crump nodded and shook his head a little while mumbling, "Sorry."

Odell jumped back into the conversation.

He stuck what was left of the cigarette back into his mouth and there it hung from his lower lip as the detective explained, "Lookie here. Now that you know the inside scoop and the rules, let's get into this because it is only a matter of minutes before the media comes flying up here. I saw one neighbor run back to the house as soon as they spotted Marlin and Doodlesticks. The guy wants to earn his side cash. He looked like a beer drinker, so he can sneak the dough for a case of beer and not have his wife squawk at 'em. Captain Moore will flip his captain bars when he sees this on the news. Doodlesticks can smell things twenty feet underground, and he can detect odors and distinct smells from five to ten miles away."

Odell took the cigarette out of mouth and the butt continued to burn down, almost to his fingertips as he waved it toward Doodlesticks, who stood and watched and listened to Detective Odell.

"Did you know that in England, a bloodhound's testimony can convict a criminal?" Odell did not wait for Crump or Marlin to answer, "Doodlesticks can smell about a thousand times better than a bloodhound can. Remarkable, huh? But he cannot hold the scent in the folds of skin like the bloodhound can. He needs to stick his snout down and go for it. He is also a pretty cool dude. Smart as a whip, too. He better not come around and sniff around on me late on a Friday night after a night of wrestling with the phantoms and kickin' Irish bottles. He will catch a flight back to Yucatan." With those words, Odell stuck the cigarette butt back into his mouth, drew the last puff, took it out, kicked up the sole of his shoe and ground out the flame into his shoe. Odell looked at it, then stuck it in his pants pocket while mumbling, "Left front pants pocket. Marlin, lead onward."

Marlin nodded. She leaned down and whispered some words into Doodlesticks's ears and then she stood up.

"First, please, we need to let Doodlesticks smell each of you. Not Odell," Marlin winked and smiled, "we don't want Doodlesticks becoming intoxicated on whiskey fumes and heading for the Yucatan. Seriously, he already knows his scent. Can you line your team up, Officer Crump?"

Officer Crump screwed his face up as if he was not keen on any of these plans.

He looked at Odell, then at Marlin, and turned to his crew and said, "Hey, guys. C'mon over now. Please only walk in the areas we already searched. C'mon . . . we have a tracker here. An expert scent tracker. Warning, his name is Doodlesticks. Don't call him anything but Doodlesticks."

A few grunts and happy snorts filled the air.

The team lined up and stood in a line as Marlin whispered more commands to Doodlesticks, who grunted and moved in to sniff each of the men, with Marlin patting his back and the pig wiggling and grunting along.

Doodlesticks sat down and looked up at his leader and Marlin proudly stood up and announced, “Doodlesticks is ready. Since we discussed the details of the case over a few sips of Irish whiskey, and both Odell and you gave me the high-altitude scoop, I suppose you want us to start on the front steps and then work our way into the house and to where the killing occurred? Doodlesticks needs to catch a scent of Mr. Travers, and whoever else was here, but if he can find one specific scent, other than someone he now knows of, then he will lead us in that direction. Doodlesticks understands the mission.”

“Damn, this Doodlesticks is smart and trained too,” Crump mumbled.

Odell ran his hand through his hair and pointed in the direction of the front steps of the home.

“Correct. I think the killer cut across this front lawn somewhere, somehow. He picked the front door lock, so he stood for a long time in front of the door. Once inside, he crept up the stairs, murdered the young woman while she slept, and then made his way back down.” Odell paused in his words. He closed his eyes and then turned to look at the street in front of the house, and then he quickly turned to Oliver Crump and his men. No one said a word; even Doodlesticks sat in silence. His snout was up in the air, sampling scents but in silence. No grunts or snorts. Not that anyone other than Marlin understood and spoke his secret language.

Everyone could tell that Odell was deep into one of his thought sessions.

“Wait. No, no, no. Hold on, now. Crump . . . you have very little out of the front yard, huh?” Odell asked. He then turned and stared at Crump and each of his team members.

“Roger that. Nothing, really. And very little else that we found anywhere. We have some work boot imprints, which we believe are from the landlord. We have a few blades of grass that led you to believe that Mr. Travers is innocent, so I guess that is something. And we also have the very weak sneaker imprint that you found on the floor near the edge of the bed. The imprint sucks. Not much there. I don't even know how you saw it."

Odell closed his eyes and nodded. He opened his eyes, turned and looked at the front porch and then to the side of the porch and then closed his eyes once more.

With his eyes closed, he held his arm and hand out to his side and when he spoke, his voice came out just above a whisper, "Please, Marlin. The flask."

Marlin did not say a word; she reached into her leather bag and pulled out a small whiskey flask, unscrewed the cap and placed it into Odell's outstretched hand. Odell tilted the flask over and took a long sip and, still with his eyes closed, he handed the flask in the air to Marlin, who took it, screwed the cap back on and replaced it into the bag. Still, no one said a word.

Odell opened his eyes and looked at Officer Crump. He ran his hand through his hair once more and his hair stuck up in all directions.

"Damn, it is hot. We only have a few more minutes before the media assault occurs. Please don't judge me on the booze. I was off-duty when Marlin and Doodlesticks arrived in my life. Technically, I am still off duty. Crump, please, only the answers to these questions. I don't mean to offend you, but please, yes or no or minimum information. Please. I need to remain on track here. The work boot imprints are on the front lawn and they lead off toward the left side of the house, to the backyard and to the garden shed in the rear area of the property. Is that correct?"

"Yes."

"You found some fertilizer in the shed. Left over from a recent application, but we need old man Travers to come up for air before we can ask about the date and time and such. But we potentially have the chemical content that we could trace to boots and sneakers and footwear and such. If we find them and do some chemical take offs and establish some sort of link to the crime scene. In reality, that will not help us very much or be hard-core evidence. Common fertilizers . . . track-offs could be picked up anywhere. In a park, on any lawn. Yet, we will remain positive and we will prevail."

"Correct again. Yes, we will, Odell. No doubt that we will prevail."

Odell nodded. He closed his eyes again and Marlin reached in her bag, paused, watched, and waited. As did everyone, including Doodlesticks.

With his eyes remaining closed, Odell asked, "Did you check the time clock for the irrigation system?"

"Yes."

"The system waters during the night and early morning hours and besides watering the front lawn area, it even waters the backyard and the side yard, too. So, we can generally confirm Doctor Kent's timeframe of the time of death because of the wet blades of grass track off."

"Correct."

Odell's eyes sprung open, and he suddenly rushed to the front steps and studied the front porch and the cement steps leading to the front door. His eyes went to the iron railings on each side of the front porch, and then his eyes traveled to the right side of the steps and porch. He pointed at the large evergreen trees on that side of the house.

"The grass is sparse here because of the tree cover. However, the ivy thrives. Ivy is so damn shameless. It sprawls wherever the hell that it wants to. Takes over everything. Travers kept it under control. To an extent." Odell grew impatient and his voice rose because of his impatience. "What is on the next street over? Quickly, please. I mean, what is over this way . . . behind this property? I should know, but it escapes me right now."

Odell waved to show that he meant behind the property.

"Beyond the backyard here. Quickly. My mind is wandering, and the whiskey is fading."

A crime scene technician spoke up first, "Detective Odell,

it is mixed use. Some residential, but there are some small mills and factories behind here. One factory is directly behind this property and small houses are on each side of the factory. Another factory down the road. Near the main street. Abandoned lace factories. Like everything else to do with manufacturing around here. Abandoned."

"Thank you. Too much info, but thank you. I was wrong. Totally wrong. I need to do better and be better and I am so sorry for wasting everyone's time and effort. Officer Crump, my sincere apologies. I see why the grass blade track offs inside the home varies. Mr. Travers came across the front lawn. No questions about that. He will confirm his path when we speak to him later. He loves his lawn, and he puts a ton of work into it and he would walk across the lawn and check the irrigation patterns and the recent fertilization applications to see how the turf is holding up in this awful heatwave. The killer . . . however . . . took a different route."

Odell put his hands on his hips, tapped his front shirt pocket for the cigarettes, and then on a whim, he changed his mind.

He turned to Marlin and asked, "Please, Marlin. Can you focus Doodlesticks on the porch and the front steps and then . . . here?"

Odell broke into a little jaunt. The detective was on point. His mind was whirling in a specific direction; Odell was intentional. He was on a mission, and everyone understood the genius at work here. Odell ran to the front steps and then after reaching down and hovering his hands over the cement steps, he leaned to the side of the porch, turned, and pointed to the grass and some ground cover ivy scattered along the right side of the porch.

"I was so wrong. So stupid of me! Why would you risk parking in front of the house or nearby? This street is residential in nature. Potentially, far too many witnesses. If the killer parked at all. Maybe he walked. Regardless, it is a much better plan to work through the abandoned factories and mills, where there are few homes and potential witnesses. The killer parked or walked from the next street over behind the home. He cut across the backyard to the side yard, to this railing and jumped over it and worked the front door to gain entry. After the homicide, he jumped this railing and reversed his steps. Any imprints in the turf areas on the front lawn will be from Mr. Travers. I blew it. Please, Marlin, Doodlesticks," Odell stopped talking. His eyes blinked and everyone studied him carefully. His words caught in his throat, the emotions captured him, and it seemed as if tears rimmed the corners of his eyes for a very brief moment or two. "I need you both to help me here. I really need you. Both. Please."

Marlin nodded in understanding, and without speaking a word, she bent down and whispered to Doodlesticks. While everyone stood in silence, Doodlesticks grunted and snorted and he stuck his snoot down and headed toward the front porch. He wandered all around, sniffing and sampling along the steps, then as Marlin carefully watched and allowed his leash to extend, the amazing nose of Doodlesticks, worked every nook, every edge of the cement and then he worked his way slowly up the steps.

While the two of them worked, Crump wandered over to stand next to Odell and in a whisper, Officer Crump leaned in and spoke to the good detective, "Damn, she is gorgeous, Odell. This is kind of . . . surreal. I always heard that pigs have amazing scent capabilities, but damn, he listens to her commands."

"Yupper. Remarkably, this is not my first venture into using swine to help me in crime solving. I guess that is why she sold me on the services so easily." Odell turned to Crump. He smiled a faint smile and added, "Well, that and some other factors weighed into my decision. Just being honest here, Crump. We used Doodlesticks's friends in the Coast Guard for sniffing out drugs and trails. They can be stubborn, but it is obvious that Marlin trained Doodlesticks since he was a piglet. Hence the loyalty. Their scent detection is even better than dogs. They just need mud. Mud ain't always easy to come by."

"Gotcha. I understand. Do you trust her? Any blips of side motives or a little touch of evil on her part coming up on that incredible radar of yours?"

"No blips. I trust her. Without a doubt."

"I mean, damn, Odell, she just wandered into your life out of nowhere?"

"She ambushed me outside of my favorite neighborhood liquor store. Sometimes, Crump, it pays to be a lush. She knows my habits. She knows my patterns. Says that some professor at Mohawk U lectured on my methods. She is an amateur crime buff, but besides being a knockout looking chick, with a great figure, she is super-intelligent too."

"I might need to hang around those liquor stores too," Crump said as noises on the street in front of the home captured his attention.

He turned to face an onslaught of media vans, cars and trucks, sporting satellite dishes on their roofs and other equipment for live broadcasting as the vehicles slammed to a halt in front of the home. Handsome reporters with perfect hair and white teeth and beautiful reporters in tight dresses with makeup teams prepared for the heartless heat, and reporters and technical support teams and camerapersons dumped out of the vehicles and scrambled to set up in front of the home to capture the action.

"You really didn't let the new captain know that you recruited the cute civilian chick and her unusual assistant? Cuz, these media dopes are drooling at the mouth. This is hotter than hot is hot. And I don't just mean the weather."

"Nope, no time to let 'em know. It is what it is," Odell said with a shrug. "We are dealing with a crazed serial killer and time is of the essence. He will need to buckle his seat straps in and hold on tightly. Lookie there, Doodlesticks just sat down." The two men directed their attention to where Doodlesticks and Marlin stood on the right side of the porch, next to the bed of ivy near the edge of the cement.

Odell and Crump walked over as Marlin announced, "Doodlesticks caught a distinct scent here. There were many scents, but this scent keenly interested Doodlesticks. It went off in this direction. He tracked it to this bed of ivy. Do you want him to continue? He wants to sniff in the bed of ivy."

Odell stopped and shook his head, and said, "No. Please hold him back. For now. Too many spectators."

Odell turned and looked at the crowd of reporters and the cameras and he frowned.

"Crump, please have your team form a line here and do your best to block the view. Marlin, please you and Doodlesticks, too. They can all focus on your beauty and your unusual companion, and it will keep them busy for a few minutes. The killer is watching, too." Crump waved his team in as Odell fumbled through his pockets and mumbled, "Left side pants pocket. Front." He produced his magnifying lens and when the team of crime scene technicians, a pig, a gorgeous chick in tight shorts and Officer Crump formed a blockade, Odell dropped to his knees and peered into the ivy with his lens. The detective crawled all around on his knees in the bed of ivy, moving the leaves and stems, and he worked through the jungle of ivy carefully and methodically.

Odell called out, "Crump . . . just to confirm . . . you dusted all the railings for fingerprints?"

"Yes. I think that we only found what I think is the landlord's fingerprints because it is, from what I can tell from here in the field, the same print that we found on the garden tools. And the victim's prints and her roommate, and that is it. . . ."

"Of course, this guy is too good and too smart to do something as silly as to . . . ." Odell stopped speaking in mid-sentence and he dropped his lens and dug deep down into the ivy.

"Crump! Please, gloves! Please! And a bundle of the orange evidence markers and an evidence bag too!"

Crump waved to one of his technicians, who rushed to where the supply box was and grabbed a set of rubber gloves. He ran over, handed them to Odell, and stood by with the evidence bag in his hand. Odell put the gloves on and then returned to digging around in the bed of ivy. With a frantic reach, Odell plucked something from the bed and he held it in his hand. He fished around for his wayward lens and picked that out from the leaves and stems. A slight smile broke across his face and he held the prize in the air.

"Bingo. Second and third mistake, you evil bastard."

In Odell's hand, he held a paper book of matches. It was just a typical book of matches, yet to Odell it was as if he found the elusive Shangri-La. Odell motioned with his head and free hand to the crime scene technician to open the bag, and when the technician did so, Odell dropped the book of matches into the bag.

"Crump," Odell said as he wobbled to his feet and the crime scene technician reached out to help steady the detective, "you are going to want your team here in this bed of ivy. There is a deep imprint in here. A sneaker imprint. The son-of-a-bitch jumped the rail after the murder and landed hard and deep in the bed. In doing so, he dropped a book of matches. Maybe it dislodged from his pocket upon landing. He also sunk deep into the dirt underneath the vines. The dirt is soft, almost mud, but don't let Doodlesticks in here. It is soft because of the sprinkler system. The killer thought it was a dry bed of ivy and did not realize the mud underneath the maze of vines. Pay dirt. The killer now has this mud on his sneakers. I can look at this in two ways—unfortunately and fortunately. Unfortunately, because he is smart, he will ditch the sneakers rather than clean them. On the other hand, fortunately, because he is a smug bastard who thinks that he is untouchable, he will keep them and try to clean them. Time will tell. Left pants pocket. Front," Odell said as he folded his lens up and dropped it into his pocket.

Odell looked at Marlin and Doodlesticks and he smiled and said, "I think that I am in love."

Marlin smiled in return and she tugged on Doodlesticks's leash as her faithful friend sat down next to her. He looked up at her and then at Odell.

"With Doodlesticks or with me?" Marlin asked.

"Both. Crump, it is all yours."

Odell took some of the small orange markers from the technician and dropped them in place in the bed of ivy to mark the exact spot.

"Please, sir, let me have a few more of those." The technician handed Odell a handful of the markers and Odell dropped them in his front pants pocket while mumbling the location as a reminder.

Odell stood up; he rubbed at the dirt on his knees and pulled at his back. Despite the heat, Odell refused to lose the suit jacket. It was his storage locker for all the gizmos and gadgets that he constantly carried.

"Please, Crump—put some of your team on this sneaker print. Unfortunately, one or two techs need to remain in the front to hold off the prying eyes of the media hounds. Maybe set up a canvas around the entire staircase so the media cannot see our focus upon the ivy bed. I knew we would not beat them in time. I hope the beer money that the neighbor got for dropping dimes on us adds up to a good buzz for 'em." Odell brushed back his black hair as sweat ran down the sides of his face. A few strands of hair stuck out in all directions, and now Odell looked even more unraveled than he usually did. "This is going to take us a little longer than I expected. We are onto something now. I realize that is not their job here. Crowd control, I know. I know . . . so can you please call in for some uniforms? I ah . . . forgot my radio and cellphone and stuff." Odell flashed his eyes toward Marlin and Doodlesticks. Mostly at Marlin. "Something distracted me."

Crump smiled and nodded, and unclipped his two-way radio from his belt to make the call for some help on the scene. Odell stood and wobbled in the heat. The heat was pushing the whiskey out of his pores. You could smell the Irish whiskey and the cigarettes all around, Detective Lyle Odell.

The detective carefully stepped out of the ivy and then waved in the direction of the backyard. He spoke in a calm voice as though he was piecing thoughts and words together while speaking, "Marlin, please, we need Doodlesticks to lead us around the back here. Trail the scent all the way to the rear of the property. I think our killer worked his way across the rear lawn area, then jumped the fence behind here and made his way to a car parked in those old factories. If not a car there, then a car somewhere. Or he walked. He backtracked the same way that he arrived. Doodlesticks can tell us."

Odell looked up at Officer Crump, who had finished with his request, and Crump nodded to affirm that uniformed police officers were on the way to the scene to assist. Crump quickly directed his men, and the team went to work in the ivy bed as the other part of the team kept watch on the media. Odell steadied himself and Crump and Marlin observed him as he walked away from the bed of ivy, turned to study the side of the house and closed his eyes to think. He mumbled and, still with his eyes closed, fished around in all the pockets of his storage and finally produced a cigarette that he stuck in his mouth but did not light, nor did he request a light. The barely audible mumbling went on as he opened his eyes and walked a few steps on the side of the house and started down the side yard and into the rear of the property.

"Just need to taste it," Odell said as he stopped, then bent down and, not being able to squat without falling over, Odell dropped to his knees and studied the turf area carefully. After a careful study, the detective wobbled back upright, and he suddenly shouted, "Marlin! Doodlesticks!" The cigarette stuck like glue to his lower lip. It was marvelous how he did that trick every time, and he never dropped a cigarette from its perch. After realizing they both were closely following him, everyone jumped, except Doodlesticks, who sat down and looked up at Odell as if he was awaiting the orders. "Please, Marlin, have Doodlesticks track here, here and there and then lead us on as he detects. Front right pants pocket." Odell reached into the pocket, pulled out the orange markers, and tossed a few onto the ground as he pointed to some specific paths in the rather sparse turf along the side yard.

"We have you covered, Odell." Marlin said while bending down next to her faithful friend and while scratching behind his ears, Marlin whispered in his ears some directions. Her tight shorts clung to her body in the dampness, and both Crump and Odell stared at the scene. Not only was the entire process fascinating but also Marlin was an extraordinary woman. Her beauty almost melted the thick heat. Crump, who was around the same age or so as Marlin was, and like Odell was, Crump was not married or apparently attached to a steady companion, wiped at the sweat on his brow and narrowed his eyes in focus of her beauty. Odell made careful notes of Crump's attraction.

Marlin jumped to her feet, and Doodlesticks went to work. He stuck his snout into the ground and he snorted. He stopped, sniffed, and went on his way. Marlin worked the leash carefully, giving him gentle allowances and watching his lead. Crump and Odell followed along as Doodlesticks and Marlin worked the scent trail. First, from the edge of the ivy, then the pig circled around and stopped but did not sit down. Marlin bent down, mumbled something inaudible into his ear, and patted his back. Off Doodlesticks went, and he ended up right on the worn path of sparse turf that Odell had pointed out when instructing the team in his theories.

Marlin turned and smiled a wide smile as she ignored Crump's gaze and instead focused on Odell.

Marlin pointed to the path and said, "He has it. Off he will go now. Please follow along."

Odell nodded, wiped at his brow, readjusted the dangling cigarette, and gave a brief wave of acknowledgement and off he went, following the team. Crump nodded and also followed along, however; his eyes seemed to look more on Marlin's wiggling backside than on the detective work by the Yucatan Pig.

Crump mumbled so low in volume that only Odell could hear, "Gladly."

Off Doodlesticks went across the lawn at a quick pace, his snout not lifting more than just barely over the top of the blades of the turf.

"Crump, please, make careful note of this path. There could be more clues along the way," Odell said to Officer Crump, as Crump nodded and reached into his uniform pocket and dropped some of the small orange markers on the lawn where they were following the trail detected by Doodlesticks. Odell did the same, as he also dropped the markers along the way until they reached a small chain-link fence at the rear of the property. The factories loomed on the other side. Abandoned, with sad weeds growing in all directions. They were rudely unkempt reminders of the economic change and related despair of the old city. The abandoned properties were in stark contrast to the tidiness of the property maintained by Mr. Travers. Doodlesticks snorted and pawed at the turf and banged into the fence in a display of the trail.

Marlin explained, "He wants to continue on the other side. We will have to lift him over. It is only three feet or so. . . ."

Crump very willingly met Marlin and offered his help as Odell smiled at his ambitions.

"No, it is fine. I have him. Doodlesticks will only allow a person to hold him in a certain way, and only by certain people. He is like me. I am the same way," she said, and her face reflected the duality of the meaning of the statement. Now, as the heat burned off the alcohol at a rapid pace, Odell surprised everyone as he nimbly grabbed the top of the chain links and, in one graceful leap, jumped over the fence and landed on his feet. His feet touched nothing but ground, air, and then ground. It was graceful, athletic and surprising. It caught Marlin's attention and her eyes flashed in surprise and a hint of admiration, while Officer Crump not only caught the move by Detective Lyle Odell but also the flash in Marlin's eyes. He might suck down gallons of Irish whiskey and chain-smoke cigarettes, but Odell was in better shape than he appeared to be! Marlin grabbed Doodlesticks, lifted him up by his underbelly, and handed him to Odell on the other side of the fence and Odell grabbed him and set him on the ground and gently patted his back as the pig rubbed into Odell and snorted in friendliness.

Crump offered his hand, which Marlin promptly ignored, and she too, in one graceful movement, jumped over the fence and landed on her feet. Crump leaned into the fence, swung his legs over, and landed on the other side in an awkward plop.

"Better hit the gym and training there, Crump," Odell commented with a smirk, "you are lookin' a little stiff in the ole ass."

Marlin quickly renewed the tracking efforts with a very anxious, Doodlesticks. Off they went and after some circling for scents, the team ended up on a weed-covered stretch of what used to be a parking area on the side of the factory, next to the loading dock for the building.

Doodlesticks snorted and sat down, and Marlin watched him carefully before proclaiming, "He is done. He lost the scent here. Perhaps this is where the killer parked." Marlin looked all around and after a careful scan of the areas, added, "This is an excellent location to park. It is concealed from the street and the nearest house." Marlin reached into her bag, produced the water spray bottle and began drenching her companion, who snorted and welcomed the water. Marlin also rewarded the grateful and accomplished tracker with a drink from another water bottle and with a handful of snacks produced from within the depths of her bag.

"Maybe the neighbors spotted something, or a car, or someone last night or in the early morning? Obviously, the killer picked a strategic spot to park a vehicle and since this complex is long since abandoned, there is no camera surveillance or even a watchman on duty," Marlin said as Odell carefully studied the asphalt surfaces for any clues or something disturbed.

Odell did not answer her, unless a mumbled grunt or two or three counted as an answer. His eyes remained focused on the surface of the parking areas, as he kept his head down; he slowly walked around and studied the area where Doodlesticks sat down. Odell ran his head through his hair; he tapped at his pockets, realized that the cigarette was still in his mouth and he plucked it from his mouth and jammed it into his shirt pocket while mumbling where he placed the cigarette and other ideas and thoughts. He was mumbling the entire time in a low and an inaudible string of chatter.

The detective suddenly stopped his study and wandering. He looked up and focused his attention upon Marlin, and finally answered her.

His eyes wandered from here to there and all around that area, while saying, "Yes. The evil bastard has now made three mistakes. Four to go. Maybe a neighbor spotted something. Perhaps the older man, who walked out on his porch a minute or two ago. You can just see into here, from a certain angle. He looks as if he has insomnia. Sucking on a cup of coffee now, at this time of day, might not be a good idea. He is still in his pajamas and slippers. Obviously, he has been awake all day and night, too.

Officer Oliver Crump and Marlin moved all around and peered into the distance, angled and adjusted their heads, but after some study, they both shrugged their shoulders, unable to see the older man, the porch, or any elements of what Odell just described. It was uncanny, because he did not seem to lift his eyes from the asphalt surfaces.

Odell spoke again, while remaining oblivious to everyone's collective confusion. "As far as the asphalt or the parking area, there is nothing here. Tomorrow, I will enlist the aid of the faithful Sergeant Grundy to recruit some uniforms to interview the insomnia-ridden man and the rest of the neighbors, and we might get lucky with a lead or two. I am afraid, though, if we do, unfortunately, it will only be something we already know." While turning to Crump, Odell added, "Please, Crump, don't take my word for it. Please do have your team perform extra diligence here and on the trail that Doodlesticks and Marlin detected. At least we have something a little more encouraging and solid now. Thanks to Doodlesticks and Marlin."

Odell patted Officer Crump on the back and said, "And Crump, thanks to you and your team, too. Thanks, Oliver, for a fantastic job. Please do me a favor and call old man Travers and ask him the questions that we outlined. You know what to ask. Now, it is just a confirmation of what we know. Thanks again. For everything. Please call Grundy with the results because the chances are very high that my cellphone's battery is gonna be dead."

"Will do, Odell. Take care and try to rest." Crump lowered his voice, "With that hottie around . . . it might be difficult to do so. Then again, rest is overrated."

Odell nodded wearily and after deftly hopping the fence again, and assisting with the handover of Doodlesticks, Odell slowly ambled to the front of the house along with Marlin and Doodlesticks, to where the crowds of the zealous media shouted at him for comments.

"Detective Odell! Detective Odell! What is going on? You have a pig and a woman helping you! Are they tracking scents? Did you find something? Please! Is she a pig whisperer?"

Doodlesticks stopped walking. He pawed at the ground and grunted, squealed, and snorted in protest.

Odell reached down and patted him on the back.

"Easy big guy. What the hell do they know?" He reached out his hand, Marlin took it, and the three of them walked to the crime scene tape and ducked underneath it as the reporters and cameraperson surrounded him.

"That is not a pig," Odell growled. "His name is Doodlesticks. Really? A whisperer? Other than asking stupid questions, don't you guys and gals have anything better to do on this hot-ass day than stand out here . . . I have no comment."

They lifted Doodlesticks up into the bed of the pickup truck. Marlin sprayed him down with the water, gave him another drink, patted him on the back and whispered something in his ear. Marlin walked him into his cage and with the reporters still shouting questions and filming every movement, the two investigators climbed into the cab of the truck. Marlin started the engine, turned the air conditioning on, reached into her leather bag, and handed Odell the flask as they pulled away. Odell took a long sip and handed it off to Marlin, who did the same.

"Technically, drinking alcohol from an open flask or container while driving is illegal," Odell said, while Marlin handed the flask back to Odell.

"So, call the police, Detective Odell. Call the police."

"I might do that. Say, let's head back to the house, finish up the rest of those bottles of Irish, and crash our thoughts. I also want to tune in the news and see what frenzy the media is whipping up. I better call Cap Moore too, or chances are he is ringing my cellphone right now. Oh, by the way, do I?"

Marlin tried to keep her eyes on the road and the front of the truck, where the reporters and camera persons still flooded the road and clamored to capture a few last shots.

"Do you what?"

"Do I smell?"

Marlin laughed and waved for Odell to lean in closer. She lowered her voice and said in a seductive whisper, "Odell . . . I live on an onion farm with a p-i-g. What the hell would I know about smells?"

Odell turned and snuck a quick glance outside the rear cab window of the truck, and checked on Doodlesticks riding happily in his cage in the rear bed.

He smiled and asked, "Can Doodlesticks spell?"

"He might be able to. Yes. I suggest we not test him. His abilities seem unlimited."

Odell nodded, as he tilted the flask back and took a long sip. He looked out the window of the truck as it rolled down the street and mumbled, "Yupper. Unlimited. We ought to drink some water with this whiskey. It sure is hot."

CHAPTER FOUR

"Is Captain Moore pissed?" Marlin asked as she glanced first at the television screen and then she alternated quick glances at Detective Lyle Odell as he pushed at the buttons on his cellphone and then gently set it aside on the end table next to his easy chair.

Odell looked like a train wreck. His hair stuck up in all directions, his necktie sat askew on his chest, his shirt wrinkled beyond repair from a normal pressing, and despite the rather rambling and fruitless attempts of the air-conditioning to offset the ungodly heat of the now fading day, his face remained flush from the heat and the whiskey.

Odell rubbed at his forehead, picked up the glass of Irish whiskey, took another sip and finally answered, "Yupper. He is not happy, but he will get over it. I did what I had to do. I told him that I used all my available resources. So, fate determined that those resources included a beautiful woman and a super-intelligent and ultra-cool Yucatan pig. Grundy called and left a message too. He wanted to give me a heads up on Captain Moore's displeasure, but he added, how even for me, this one was a bit off the chain. I gotta do what I gotta do. If you are always worrying about what everyone else thinks of you, then you never live your own life or do your job."

Marlin shrugged her shoulders and said, "Oh well. That was cool of Sarge Grundy to try to give you a warning. I mean, the captain has to be pleased that you have a few leads. Right?" Marlin blinked a few times as she studied the face of Odell and she asked as she sat cross-legged on the hardwood floor in front of the television set, perched upon a plastic storage container turned upright in the corner of the living room of Detective Lyle Odell's living room.

"Commanding officers are never pleased at anything other than arrests, convictions, positive news reports, and happy chains of commands. Whatever. Perhaps I have been doing this for too long. It is now down to blood and whiskey. Is Doodlesticks settled down and happy?"

"He is. Your backyard is fenced in. He has his favorite food, his water, his mud and thankfully, the heat of the day wanes. I just checked on him while you spoke with your captain and he is in his glory. Simple things make him happy. We all could learn some lessons from him."

After speaking, Marlin studied his face for a reaction to her words. There was none. She searched for a glint of happiness. It was difficult to find. Marlin thought how the pain of his career became such a burden to his soul, and there suddenly was a profound ache to assist him within her heart. Marlin thought how his disarray and his on and off drunkenness were a rather brilliant disguise to hide his quest for the truth and his never relenting mission to destroy evil.

After a long pause, Odell waved his hand in the air, he picked up the glass of Irish whiskey, downed the remaining swill in one shot and after smacking his lips and plunking the glass down upon the end table, Odell managed to push out the words, "Please, Marlin, shut that damn television off. As nice as your ass looks in that screen shot, and I am sure Doodlesticks and Marlin Santini are now local and maybe even national television stars, the entire episode and the lunacy of all of this is weighing heavily upon me now. The media is out of control. How I wish there was something else for them to report upon tonight, except for how Homicide Detective Lyle Odell is off on the deep end once more."

He pointed at the bottle of Irish whiskey sitting on the floor next to Marlin.

Odell quickly added, "Is there anything left in that bottle?"

Marlin carefully studied Odell as she aimed the remote

control at the television and pushed the off button.

"A little. I will split it with you."

"Fair enough."

Marlin poured some of the remaining whiskey into her glass. She held the bottle up to the light to see through the bottle in order to check the contents and then nodded to Odell to hand her his glass. Odell leaned in and held his glass out as Marlin poured the rest of the bottle into Odell's glass.

"One down and one more to go," Marlin said as she tilted and twisted the bottle and worked the last drop of whiskey out of the bottle. Odell leaned into his whiskey and peered at Marlin over the rim of his glass.

He asked, "Are you sure that Doodlesticks is all set? Does he need anything? I have plenty of apples if he wants more of them."

"He is as happy as a . . .." Marlin took a sip, and she laughed a little at Odell's reaction to her words. The detective narrowed his eyes, pretended to ponder the answer, and then he set his whiskey glass on the rickety end table and set his hand upon his chin and rubbed at the black stubble of an aspiring beard in a display of exaggerated pensive pondering.

Odell smiled.

He tugged at his necktie, pulled it off, and tossed it on the end table, and then he opened the first few buttons of his shirt.

Finally, Odell answered and filled in the blanks, "As a detective deep into Irish whiskey."

Marlin smiled, laughed, and dismissively waved her hand at Odell. She then set her eyes on him, narrowed them, and blinked a little before folding her hands in her lap. Marlin moved her legs a little and adjusted her position, but she remained tightly cross-legged upon the floor.

Beneath her eyeglasses, her eyes flashed with quiet contentment as the words rolled from her lovely mouth, "Odell, you should smile more. You have a magnificent smile. You should pull that tie off more often and open a few buttons on your shirt too. I think that you would clean up rather nicely."

Odell did not react with any words; instead, he picked the whiskey glass up and took a sip.

He kept the glass in his hand as he waved back to the television and said, "He will not kill tomorrow. The evil bastard is going to break his pattern and he will not kill. We managed to shake him up a little. Cap Moore is ticked, but he should be thankful that we caused such a stir. As much as they are off the chain and they grind at my soul, we actually should thank the media. I confess that part was something that I did not plan, but it bought us a day or two."

Marlin's face showed her fascination with Odell's statement. She stood up, picked her glass up from the floor and the empty whiskey bottle, she looked all around the living room, and then her eyes glanced at the dining room. There was not much in the way of furniture or furnishings in the home. Odell's easy chair, the old television sitting upon an upturned, plastic storage container, Odell's end table next to his chair had an old table radio on the lower shelf, his whiskey glass, an ashtray of tarnished silver, a tilted lamp with a sad lampshade perched upon it, Odell's pack of cigarettes, his discarded necktie and that was about it. The dining room had one table and two folding chairs. There were no pictures on the walls, no knick-knacks, no decorations. Yet, despite the bareness of the home, Odell was correct when he said that it was clean. It was spotless.

Odell watched as Marlin looked around the home and he pointed at the dining room table and said, "Please, set the bottle on the table and you can bring one of those folding chairs in here. My apologies. I don't have too much in the way of luxuries around here."

Marlin nodded and said, "Chairs are not luxuries, Odell. They are ordinary household items of usefulness in ordinary homes across the world."

"Well, you just nailed it then, Marlin. The word ordinary categorized it," Odell answered.

Marlin laughed and said, "Sure did, Odell. You are certainly not ordinary in any way."

Marlin turned and walked into the dining room and as she did so, Odell tried hard not to study her rather perfect female figure, her tanned and toned, long legs, her shapely backside and how the shorts clung to her hips and curves. Odell never missed any details. It was his job.

He failed miserably in his quest not to stare.

As a diversion to avert his eyes, Odell reached down and flipped the old table radio on and as some waves of gentle classical music flowed out of the bronze-colored woven speaker cloth, Odell fiddled with the volume control to maintain the volume as background noise.

"Hmm . . . somehow, I knew you were a classical music guy," Marlin said as she carried the folding chair and set it a few feet in front of Odell's easy chair, but off to the side.

"It helps to relax me. Irish whiskey and classical music, they both have no melodies. Melodies are distractions."

Marlin sat in the chair. She crossed her long legs and Odell withstood the urge to stare.

She took a sip of the whiskey and finally asked, "How do you know that he will not kill tomorrow? That will be huge for him to break up his pattern and change his usual killing mode up after so many kills and nary a whisper of a trail or a clue to track him down."

"It will, but he is on full alert now. He is not afraid, but he is on alert. The killer watched the same news that we did and he saw Doodlesticks and you, and the team working the side of the porch where he knows and now, we know that he jumped over the railing and landed in the ivy bed. That fact, and the fact that he is most likely combing the internet for facts on how good a pig's scent is, has him going into a bit of an alert mode. Before this, the bastard was flawless . . . never made a mistake. No clues, no trails. Murder after murder and no one had anything on 'em. Now," Odell ran his hand through his hair and then smoothed it down, "for the first time—he screwed up."

"Gotcha. Well, that is significant news. What next, then? What is our next move? I guess that we wait for the results from

Officer Crump and his crime scene boys. And autopsy results, too."

Odell nodded and added, "Correct. Now, I need to think. We all need to think. We have some parts and pieces. We know that the killer wore sneakers, where he parked, his entrance and escape route, and we know that old man Travers is innocent. We have the matchbook. We have a weak imprint and a strong sneaker imprint. That allows us to establish the killer's proportions, his foot size, his height and weight, and so forth. He will ditch those sneakers. We will never find them because he burns evidence. Military man. Military training. Burn shit up. The matchbook, well, that is good, but it might be a needle in the haystack type of thing. The killer still wore his gloves, so chances are there are no prints on the matchbook. I am not the expert here on lifting prints, but I am not sure if you can even find fingerprints on a cardboard match book. That is Crump's expertise, not mine. I think it depends on the surface. Whether it is porous or smooth. However, Crump and his team are the best there is, so I know they will do their best. If there are no prints, then perhaps there is a scent on the matchbook from being in the killer's pockets and next to his body. A scent that Doodlesticks can assist us with detecting. I don't expect the autopsy's results will be much of an eye opener for anything significant."

Marlin studied Odell for a few seconds, then as her eyes went up and down and across his face, Marlin said, "I understand. I am sure we can get Doodlesticks to try to detect a scent and attempt a match. I know that Crump and his team are on their game. You said to me at the crime scene that the killer has now made three mistakes and there are four to go. What does that mean, Odell?"

"Yupper. I have made an in-depth study of this madness and the killer's previous actions and patterns, and it will take seven mistakes to end his reign of terror.

"Seven, Odell? That is random," Marlin commented while leaning in closer to Odell, displaying her obvious intrigue at his statement.

Odell explained while using the same explanation that he

provided to Captain Moore for the ultimate capture of the killer via his mistakes.

"The killer is so good, so brilliantly smart and cunning that I need a precise number of mistakes to solve the case. In my study of the case so far, I determined that exactly seven mistakes will do the trick. The first three mistakes that he makes will give me the background and direction that I need to get on his trail. The next two mistakes will identify the actual killer to me. The sixth mistake will confirm the killer's final intentions and victim for murder and the last mistake will be his final mistake. He will be dead or in handcuffs."

Marlin nodded and smiled and said, "You truly are brilliant beyond words or descriptions. So, the mistakes so far are. . . what?'

Odell studied Marlin and leaned back in his chair. He ran his hand through his hair and shook his head a little before speaking. Marlin studied him and Odell spoke. "No disrespect meant . . . in fact, total respect to you, Marlin, but the first mistake is something that I am going to hold on revealing to you or anyone else for now. Just because I do not want to throw you off course with my thinking and influence you. And because you just stated that you think that I am brilliant, please, let me pose the question to you. Mistake two is what? Mistake three is what? Because I think you are beyond brilliant."

Marlin's eyes opened wide under her eyeglasses with the challenge and with a wide smile, displaying her joy at Odell's confidence in her.

Once Marlin Captured her emotions, she answered without any further hesitation.

Her voice was strong and confident as she said, "Dropping the matchbook by jumping over the railing was mistake number two. Mistake number three was the escape route and parking his vehicle where he parked. You feel as if that will lead to further clues and some further revelation of evidence."

Odell blinked a few times, his face reflected his pleasure as a smile slowly broke out on it and he said, "I can see that this is the beginning of a beautiful relationship, Marlin."

"I agree and hope so, Odell."

Odell tapped his shirt pocket. He mumbled, "Front shirt pocket," and after finding his pocket empty, his eyes darted around as Marlin pointed at the pack of cigarettes sitting on the end table. He picked the pack up, tapped out a cigarette, and stuck it in his mouth. Odell offered Marlin one, and she reached over and took it, stuck it in her mouth, leaned back, while reaching into her shorts to pull out the lighter. Without speaking, Odell waved for her to give the lighter to him, and Marlin smiled at his etiquette. As Odell flicked the lighter to a flame, Marlin leaned in and Odell's eyes traveled to her open shirt blouse as the gentle silk slipped away and revealed her stunning cleavage captured in a tan brassiere. When she did so, Odell glimpsed the necklace that she wore around her neck. A necklace with a gold metal insignia hanging from the end of a heavy chain. The insignia nestled nicely between her generous breasts and as Marlin drew in the flame, the insignia danced and fell alongside her breasts. Marlin looked up as she leaned back and caught Odell's eyes and while blowing out the smoke from the drag on the cigarette, Marlin adjusted her shirt and brassiere a little, to fit around her breasts and then she unbuttoned one more button of the blouse. Odell lit his cigarette and took a long drag, and while blowing the smoke out, he spoke out of the side of his mouth.

"Nice . . . necklace, Marlin. So, your dad, he was a United States Army Airborne Ranger, huh?"

The cigarette now hung on Odell's lower lip, as a million other predecessors have done so. Like glue.

Marlin reached into her blouse, pulled out the necklace, and dropped it on her chest. "I am a little disappointed. You actually were staring at my necklace and the insignia on the end of the chain. I thought you were admiring my boobies, Odell."

"Don't be disappointed. I was, and I was. You said that your dad is gone now. Is he a casualty of combat?"

"He was. Some bullshit Middle East mission. Not sure exactly what went wrong, but he is a k-i-a. Yupper. That makes me a potential target for this nutcase, huh? Am I incorrect? Doesn't it?"

"It does. He needs to perform some research. Find out your name and your background. Your total identity. He will. He is good . . . too good. So, yes, you and your mother and sister all make the hit list. I am very sorry, but you are correct. Your father is gone, so whatever is wrong with this evil bastard is a rage that he willingly invokes on the combat vets, and if he cannot access them, he kills their loved ones. Over the killing patterns over these years, sometimes he alternates in his choice of victims from the vet to the loved ones. Who knows why? Availability? Rage? A pattern? Sicko stuff. These are revenge homicides and I am not sure why. Just a guess at this point. He must have a perception of combat vets as killers, so he needs to kill them to even the score. He seems to alternate to loved ones of the vets if they are beautiful or young or successful. Such as this young woman was here in Mohawk City. There was an identical homicide in Westchester County. When he first began this killing madness. He killed a beautiful young woman—the daughter of the vet. She was a law student. Just passed the bar exam. It is all part of untangling the tangled web woven. Getting into the mind of a lunatic. A sick, raging lunatic hiding in and amongst the population. There are many of them. Too many, in fact. It's a tainted and screwed up world."

"Do you ever tire of this madness, Odell? I mean, it has to take a toll."

"I don't and as to taking a toll—it does, but I don't care. The madness lodges in my soul and, by solving cases, I cough the madness out of it. Someone has to do this bullshit. I think my role is to neutralize evil. Chase the phantoms away that haunt me. You have the same desire, Marlin. I can feel it. You sought me out to help, but you have a bond with the previous victims. When your sister's friend became a victim . . . it hit home. I understand. You were safe out in Greenfield, but still, you came here to Sin City to help. Put yourself in danger."

Marlin mumbled, "I ain't afraid, Odell. It's in my blood. Dad was a Ranger. I have weapons. Shoot damn well too."

Odell pulled a long drag on the cigarette and while he spoke, the smoke slowly escaped his mouth, "I bet you do. I have contacts in the d-o-d and Veterans Affairs running a list of combat vets living or dead in the surrounding counties. All the way down to Albany. Just in case, evil returns there because of us poking around here. All branches of the military. The evil bastard will be on that list. Navy. I am sure of it."

Odell took a last drag on the cigarette, reached for the ashtray on the end table, and ground out the butt. He handed the ashtray to Marlin, who did the same. Odell returned the ashtray to the end table and Odell picked up his whiskey glass. Odell finished his whiskey; Marlin did the same, and she stood up.

"I am a little wasted here, Odell. I will need to crash here. I can't drive back to the farm. I have an overnight bag in my truck."

Odell thumbed at the stairs to show upstairs. "You can take the bedroom upstairs. I usually sleep right here. Let's order a pizza. The number of the pizza joint is on the fridge. Landline on the wall. Frank's West. They know me quite well. I think that I paid for Frank's house. Matty is the delivery guy tonight. Nice guy. Give 'em a five for a tip. Cash is on the table there. I am gonna take a shower and wash away the sweat and the blood, but not the whiskey. Please call the pie in and we can open the next bottle of Irish and brainstorm some more. I can feel it now. Something is going to stick out to us. Something will pop. Soon."

Marlin nodded and picked up the empty glasses and made her way to the kitchen. She turned and said, "I knew that you would still have a landline. It fits you. Is a just cheese pizza, okay, Odell?"

"Whatever you want. It is pizza. Ain't nothing bad about pizza. Except no anchovies. Fish are our friends."

"Reminder . . . and so are pigs, Odell."

Marlin smiled and stared at Odell while he had one foot on the first stair of the staircase, and one foot on the floor and his hand on the railing.

"Hell, yeah, they are. Hell, yeah. So, no pepperoni or ham either. Just cheese. There is beer in the fridge. Mugs in the cupboard above the toaster oven. Gotta have sum beers with the pizza. Irish later. Beer now," Odell said as he ascended the staircase.

'Damn,' Marlin thought, 'Odell cleans up nicely.'

She gazed at him as he ate a slice of pizza. His head was down; he was chewing a bite of the pizza. He seemed as if he was deeply in thought and had not said too much. Perhaps he was just hungry. They had not eaten anything all day long. Just drinking the Irish and a few glasses of water. The classical music still floated in the air just above the drone of the air conditioning system. The music stopped and the radio announcer droned on in a monotone voice to begin to announce the name of the piece and the performers of the same. Odell walked over the top of the voice of the announcer and beat him to the punch.

With a nod in the radio's direction, Odell said, "Requiem Mass in D Minor. Mozart. He wrote it while on his deathbed. Actually, Franz Sussmayr finished the piece. Remarkable work. Sussmayr only had fragments dictated by Mozart. Sounded like the Chicago Classical Symphony. Maybe. Very sad music. Fitting for the tone of today."

The announcer confirmed the piece and the performer. Odell was correct. Marlin studied him as he lifted the slice of pizza from his plate and took another bite. No, he might not be the most handsome man in the world, but she found him sexier and more captivating than any man that she ever laid her lovely eyes upon in her entire life. He was handsome in an unorthodox manner. No movie star looks; real man looks. He had to be at least ten years or so older than she was, but it was difficult to tell with a man like Lyle Odell. The weight of the world and his career either aged him or kept him younger than he actually was—it was impossible to determine which it was. His gray eyes captivated her. His intellect was remarkable. Her professor was wrong. Odell was a super-genius. Yet, he was so sad. So, tortured. As he told her, "Flawed." He was fresh from the shower, the stubble from his face was gone, his gray eyes popped with the color of the deep blue of the tee shirt that he wore. A tee shirt emblazoned with the logo of the Mohawk City Police Department. His hair was still wet and for once, Odell combed it. He combed it back, and it was thick and black as coal, but one or two strands hung loose and crossed his forehead. Odell looked over at Marlin, and she blinked and swallowed. For some reason, she did not want him to catch her staring at him. Marlin was not sure why. His eyes watched her throat move as she swallowed.

Odell reached for the cold beer and took a swallow.

He asked, "So, I am guessing Iowa or Nebraska? You sound like that radio announcer over there. No accent. Is that where your family is from? One of those states. I am positive as hell that ain't no New York accent there."

Her eyes flashed as she smiled at his observation skills.

"Iowa. I grew up on a farm. That is where I learned as that reporter said, to be a pig whisperer. We left when I was around twelve. My sister was only five. Mom was from upstate New York. She is from Schenectady. We came here after Dad died. Mom wanted her family nearby. She works as an administrative clerk in a law firm down in Albany. My sister is back in school at SUNY Albany. She is a perpetual student. Now, it is a real estate career."

"Is that where you applied for police jobs? I mean, back in Iowa."

"It is. Des Moines. I like Iowa. It feels like home. They were not interested. Just a few credits short of finishing my college degree and no experience. Just a farm girl."

"Their mistake, Marlin. Does Doodlesticks want that last slice?"

"Yes, of course. He loves pizza. In fact, he loves all kinds of food."

"Can you please write down your cellphone number on the pad on the kitchen counter? There is a pencil in there somewhere."

Marlin posed with her hand on her hip and she playfully flipped at her hair as if she was teasing Odell.

"Oh my, Detective Lyle Odell, are you asking for my number for romantic intentions?"

Odell waved at her as he gathered up the slice of pizza for Doodlesticks. "Yes, I am. I want to give it to Crump and to Grundy so they can contact us when the crime lab results come in and Grundy finishes up some fieldwork. Chances are my phone will not work or be dead cuz, I forgot to charge it."

"Odell, that is hardly romantic."

"Best I got for now, baby. I put fresh towels in the bathroom for you. I will clean up here, give Doodlesticks the slice, and change his water while you shower. I need to crack open the other bottle of Irish and sip and think."

"Okay, Odell. Thanks."

Odell could hear the shower shut off as he tucked the corner of the fresh linens into the corner of the bed. He walked over to the closet, pulled a light blanket out of the closet, and turned to set the blanket on the bed. The bedroom light was dim, just a night light, and the glow of an old table lamp broadcasted some light into the darkness. Odell furnished the bedroom just as sparsely as the rest of the house. A bedside end table, the bed, a small dresser, one old chair, with a worn leather pad on the seat and that is it. Odell's shoulder harness, with his service weapon, hung over the top edge of the chair. His police badge was on the top of the dresser. The gold captured just a hint of the light in the room, and its engravings were faintly visible. Odell tossed the blanket in the air and it floated down on the bed. He smoothed it out when he heard the door to the bathroom open and heard the soft pad of bare feet upon the hardwood floor of the hallway.

He looked up as Marlin entered the room. Her hair was wet, and it hung down in luscious strands of glory. She only wore a towel around her body and just the top edges of her breasts were visible above the towel wrap. Beads of water ran down the front of her chest and rolled down between her twin mounds of allure.

"Sorry, I was just changing the linens and the blanket. Almost done. I seldom sleep in the bed. I wanted the linens and blanket to be fresh."

Odell swallowed as he looked up at her. In the dim light of the room, her face glowed in an angelic haze. The towel hugged her glorious body and Odell felt parts and pieces of his soul awakened as they slumbered from years of neglect. Parts of his body reacted too. Parts that he forgot about a long time ago.

He thought, 'My goodness, this woman is a goddess.'

Odell spoke before he lost his words and his soul in her beauty.

"You are not wearing your eyeglasses . . . or any clothes. You do have beautiful . . . eyes. Anyway, this is a light blanket. Too damn hot for anything else."

'Damn, you can still see the gray in his eyes,' Marlin thought and then she said, "Thank you, Odell. It's okay. In the summer, I sleep naked so the light blanket will be fine," Marlin said as she took a few steps closer to Odell and she studied his eyes for a reaction to her proclamation in the dim light.

"Well, thank you for that vision, Marlin."

"You are welcome. It is hot. Very hot and getting hotter," she commented with a flash of a smile at the double meaning.

Odell nodded, and he headed for the door of the bedroom. Disappointment weighed on his every step, and Marlin's shoulders dipped a little as she watched him move away and head for the door.

"Sleep, well, Marlin," Odell said as he placed his hand on the doorknob of the bedroom. "I will check in on Doodlesticks throughout the night."

"Thank you. You too, Odell. You too."

He nodded and gently swung the door closed and it hit the strike latch with a click. A few seconds later, there was a quick knock at the door and the door slowly opened. Marlin stood watching.

Odell stuck his hand around the edge of the door and spoke in a voice just above a whisper, "One half of me, the weaker half, hopes that you are decent. The stronger half wishes that you aren't."

"I am decent, Odell." The door opened more. He stood on the threshold of the doorway, and he ran his hand through his hair. His hair was back to the normal mess.

"Ah, as a pig in the mud. Happy as a pig in the mud. Good night, Marlin."

Her smile lit up the darkness and as Odell slowly began to close the door and just before he disappeared, Marlin blurted out a question and asked, "Did it really look great?"

Odell stopped, and he turned and smiled at Marlin. "Touché. Using my own techniques. It is mostly because my mind wanders. I always come back with thoughts or questions. Sometimes, it trips the bad guys up. Impressive that you catch on every word. However, you made an error. I said nice, not great. Generally, I choose my words carefully. Yes, your ass looked nice, but you know sumthin'?"

Marlin shook her head.

"That time, I picked the incorrect word. I should'a said great."

"Sometimes, your tricky technique trips the bad guys up and sometimes it melts a woman's heart," Marlin said. Her voice lowered to a gentle whisper, "Good night, Odell. Go find all the answers."

With no further words, he turned and closed the door again and he disappeared.

Marlin listened for his footsteps on the staircase and she dropped the towel and stood naked in the dim light of the room. Her large breasts heaved as she took in a deep breath. Her eyes went to the door, then to the bed, and she took a few steps to the door, then stopped and took another deep breath. Marlin turned to the bed, pulled back the blanket and the sheets, and she very gently and very reluctantly slipped under them.

Despite the fresh linens and blanket, the bed smelled like Odell.

Just a hint of Irish here and there.

Just a hint.

CHAPTER FIVE

"Hey, Odell, wake up. Are you in there? It is almost ten in the morning and I know you had plans for today. I need to get back to the farm. Hello, Odell," Marlin leaned over the easy chair in the living room and she gingerly grabbed Odell's shoulder and shook him while speaking gently to the sleeping detective.

Odell did not move a muscle.

His body lay prone across the easy chair. The back of the chair tilted back slightly, his hands remained carefully folded in his lap, and his eyes remained clamped tightly shut. He still wore his Mohawk City Police Department tee shirt, his hair stuck out in all directions, and his police issued work boots still were on his feet. The last bottle of Irish whiskey sat next to the chair. It was empty. The whiskey glass sat on the end table next to him and stacks and stacks of paper and bundled reports were on the floor in and near his chair. His cellphone sat on the table—as predicted, he forgot to plug it into the charger and the battery was most likely dead as a doornail. A flattened pack of cigarettes and a book of matches sat on the end table next to an overflowing ashtray of spent butts. Marlin picked up the cigarettes. She marveled at how Odell always flattened the pack, and even more so, how he smoked crushed cigarettes. He was not snoring; in fact, Marlin leaned in close to check to see if he was breathing. His chest barely moved. She smiled, because it looked as if, for the first time in the brief time that they met, that Detective Lyle Odell was at peace. With a careful study, Marlin took mental notes of the lines on his face. His furrowed brow was not as furrowed and she felt a powerful attraction to what she felt were his handsome looks. He was physically stronger and more muscular than you first perceive him to be under his rumbled up and messy suits. While he sprawled in the easy chair, with his boots hanging off the footrest, Marlin realized that he was taller too, primarily, because he was not hunched or slumped over studying things. Most of all, Marlin admired how his courage was immense, and his brain non-stop with thoughts.

Marlin took a deep breath, because she felt a tingle in her lady parts too. 'Damn, Odell is a sexy beast,' Marlin thought. 'How I wished he stayed with me last night.'

Odell was at peace. He was not running his hand through his hair, or tipping a whiskey glass, or chain-smoking or dangling cigarettes from his lips, or mumbling as to the location of his cigarettes or his magnifying lens or his other assorted gizmos and gadgets that he hid away within the caverns of his suits and attire.

Out of the old speaker grill cloth of the radio, classical music softly floated in the air. Marlin leaned over and turned the old radio off, and when she did so, Odell's eyes immediately opened wide.

He stared directly at Marlin and asked, "Why did you turn that off? What time did you say that it was?"

Marlin stood up in shock at his response and the fact that apparently was awake the entire time that she stood admiring him and speaking to him.

"Ah, well, sorry, Odell. I thought you were sound asleep. It is around ten or so. I know you wanted to get rolling and I have to get to the farm and get Doodlesticks back in his home mud. I will turn the radio back on for you."

Marlin bent down. She turned the radio's power switch back to the on position. The music returned, and she set the volume in its former location.

Odell nodded and waved a little, as he pushed in the footrest on the chair and it closed and snapped shut.

"Is Doodlesticks okay? Is he fed and watered?"

"He is fine, Odell. He is thrilled to have contributed to the case."

Odell nodded again and his gray eyes traveled all around the room and settled upon Marlin as she stood in front of him.

"Good morning, Marlin. You look and smell fresh. Showered and fresh. Quite lovely, too. I think it is supposed to be even hotter today than it was yesterday."

Marlin was dressed in a fresh pair of shorts, a similar summer blouse to what she wore the day before, and the same work boots with the laces wrapped around and a hint of black dirt of the onion fields on them.

"Thank you. I was up early, and yes, I took an early shower. It is hot out there. I am running out of clothes to wear. I fished through your tee shirts for something, but you are a much larger man than what you appear, so I grabbed this blouse. This is my last outfit; after this, all that is left in my overnight bag is a bathing suit."

"I bet you look awful in that," Odell said with a half-of-a smirk on his face. "And, I look like Hell."

"That's the thing, Odell, considering this empty bottle of Irish and the pain of yesterday—you don't," Marlin quickly spoke.

"Okay, well, I doubt that, but let me get my creaky old ass up and let me get cleaned up," Odell said while he stood up. He stretched a little, and he pointed at the papers on the floor.

"You might want to read through those. Not all. Of course. Too much stuff there. I already read it all last night and this morning. Please, just read the reports on the previous homicides. They are labeled, accordingly. We need to go to Albany. Today. We need to view the murder scene of one of the victims. It is very important. Can you clear your schedule and come with me?"

Marlin nodded and held back a smile at the prospect of continuing to work with Odell.

"Of course, I can. Thank you for the invitation. What about Captain Moore and the fact that you are working with a civilian? A chick civilian with Doodlesticks for an assistant."

"He is gonna be just fine. This case has kicked many detectives' asses before and the bodies are piling up. We gotta stop 'em. Moore will not argue. The guy is a class act. He is gonna be a good one. Just like Cap Tucker was and is. He will plow the road for me. For us. You are gonna be a consultant. Lookie here, Marlin, that is your new title and role. An official consultant now. Open the business now, Marlin. Open up a private detective business with the scenting services of Doodlesticks as your flagship promotional item and while you do so, continually reapply to police departments. If that is where your heart lies, then force the departments in Des Moines to revisit your applications. Don't give up. Never give up. Police work and detective work are what I always wanted to do. I read crime novels and comics when other kids read superhero stuff. I could have stayed in the Coast Guard, and comparatively, had a rather easy go of it. I earned rank rather easily and was an officer. Honestly, I would be retired by now and my liver might stand a chance." Odell paused as he studied Marlin's eyes and face for a reaction. Satisfied that she was hanging on his every word, Odell continued. Seldom, if ever, did he give career advice or life advice, but there was something about Marlin that caused Odell to open up more than he generally did for any other person. "Life is too short, so never settle for second best. Follow your dreams, abide by the truth within your heart, work hard, apply everything you can in the pursuit of those dreams and it will surprise you at how the world feels differently, how it opens your soul up, how it lifts your eyes to focus on what is really important. You have got so much to contribute to the world, to settle for second best, deprives the world of your spirit. You do not measure success with the accumulation of money or possessions. You measure it by accumulating joy in your soul." Odell stopped speaking as Marlin's heart melted at the words and his advice. The detective waved his hands in the air a little. He seemed surprised at his own words. Rather hastily after a short, yet pensive pause, Odell said, "Anyway, this is great. I can feel we are going to have a productive investigation today."

"Thank you for your advice, Odell. I just locked those words away forever in my heart," Marlin said while tapping her chest. "Did you find what you needed to find last night?" Marlin asked.

"Some." Odell kept his answer short and sweet until he added, "Please read the reports. Particularly, the case summary sheet. Can you make coffee, Marlin? A can is in the cupboard and the machine is. . . ."

"I gotcha, Odell. Coffee is life. I gotcha."

Odell turned and walked to the staircase. He stopped and spoke again. His thoughts were running from a stream of consciousness now.

Odell explained, "Sadly, we do not require the services of Doodlesticks today. The case is too old for even his immense powers to detect anything. Can we drop him off at the farm? You can grab some clothes and such for overnights and we can get back here by Monday. Does that work? Is there someone else on the farm to care for Doodlesticks? I know he is fussy about human friends. Rightly so. I agree with 'em. I try not to mingle with them, too. They are a pain-in-the-ass."

Marlin reached down for the papers and instead, she grabbed the empty whiskey bottle.

Odell, embarrassed at the mess, intervened and said, "Please leave that mess. I will clean up. Sorry. I am not used to visitors."

"I don't mind, Odell. I gotcha. You go ahead and get cleaned up. Yes, Doodlesticks will be fine. There are many workers on the farm and he enjoys most of the company there. He misses his swine friends and a certain female gal, too. And a chicken or two and a rooster."

"Well, now he is quite the lover, huh?"

"Something like that. I see you are out of whiskey and cigarettes, too. I will take a walk down to the corner liquor store and restock. My treat."

Odell mumbled a quiet, "Thank you," before he took a few steps and stopped. He put his hand to his hair to run it through it, but he did not do so. Instead, Lyle Odell stood straight up, his hand perched on top of his head, and he wobbled a little and then closed his eyes. Marlin watched him carefully. However, by now, she was used to his unusual behavior and moments of deep contemplation. At first, Marlin thought he was listening to the music to determine the artists, composer and the name of the piece, but Marlin thought there might be more to his deep thought.

Odell opened his eyes and said in a whisper, "Say hey to Danny for me and please pick up some matchbooks for me. They are in a dish on the counter."

"Okay," Marlin said and then she added, "Danny, is the clerk there?"

"He is. He will hit on you. Big time. He likes his women. He is a good-looking guy. Big guy. Lots of muscles."

Odell finished speaking; he leaned in as the musical piece ended on the radio.

Before the radio announcer could jump in on the broadcast, Odell lifted a finger in the air and said, "Rachmaninov, Piano Concerto Number Two. A very romantic piece. Incredible piece." Marlin smiled and paused in her clean up duties as the radio announcer spoke and confirmed that Odell was correct in his identification of the musical piece.

"Right on, Odell. Right on. You are a damn walking musical encyclopedia."

Odell took one more step, leaned over the staircase and added, "Oh, by the way . . . I was."

Marlin narrowed her eyebrows in puzzlement, as she now usually did when Odell pulled one of his delayed reactions to words or questions. She now surmised that he did not do this on purpose. His mind was always too busy with other thoughts, so he files the questions and words for a response later on when his mind clears out the backlog.

"You were what, Odell?" Marlin asked, as she played along.

"Sleeping, Marlin. I was sleeping. Sound asleep."

With those words, Detective Lyle Odell disappeared up the creaky staircase and she listened as she heard his steps upon the wooden stair treads and the door to the bathroom close.

Marlin picked up the empty bottles and the overflowing

ashtray and she shook her head while walking past the dining room table, where she dropped the papers and then continued into the kitchen. Her mind whirled with how to decipher the mysterious Lyle Odell and all of his complexities and interpret how he used his flaws and his genius for the good of this weary world.

Right now, it thrilled Marlin to do so.

"Nice joint here," Odell said as he waved his hand in the air to encompass the setting of the farm from the interior of the pickup truck. Marlin stopped walking, and she smiled, turned a shoulder and a glance to the farm and seemed to absorb it all in.

"Home mud, you know. Occasionally, you have to roll around in some home mud, Odell. It gives me peace."

"No arguments from me. My joint ain't much, but it has what I need. My old radio, my easy chair, a few sticks of other furniture and coffee and Irish whiskey."

Marlin laughed as she lifted a large suitcase over the bed of the truck and dropped it into the bed and then walked around the pickup truck, opened the door and climbed in. Odell was studying the landscape from out of the open window of the pickup truck. As usual, his eyes scanned every detail. Marlin watched him with fascination at how the man took in every detail of life and the entire world around him. Marlin watched as he glued his eyes upon the gravel driveway, then he moved his eyes to the farmhouse, in its enveloped glory of white starkness with happy blue shutters. Then the grayness of his eyes settled upon a tree on the right side of the driveway. He studied it for a long time, tilting his head at various angles and then leaning out of the window a little more.

"Did you see it happen?" Odell asked while turning to Marlin for her answer.

"Excuse me?"

Odell captured Marlin's question and then he pointed at a

willow oak tree about twenty-five feet away from the truck, on that same right side.

"The lightning strike on that willow oak tree there. Did you see it? From your bedroom window there, I thought that you might have had a good look at it happen. The bark wounds are deep, but healing now. So, was the lightning strike last summer, or maybe the summer before that one?"

"Last July. I did not see it directly. Heard the damn thing. The ground shook, I saw the flash over the house from the barnyard, but I was busy tending to Doodlesticks and his friends to make them safe. It was a horrific storm. One of those summer days, very much like today, where you could sense that eventually, the sky would explode. It exploded. I know this is most likely a stupid question and simply my curiosity poking around, but how did you know where my bedroom is in the house?"

Odell pointed at the house and said, "I saw you pull the blinds down in that front room there, over the porch. I knew it was your room. Regardless, it is a good idea to pull the blinds down to keep the heat out of your room. I knew you would do that. I studied the layout of the house from here and figured it was typical of a farmhouse of this era. Especially since the chimney stack is right in line with the living room." Odell displayed an outline in the air of the layout of the home, while Marlin watched in fascination. "Living room here, with an open dining room, on the left side, a sitting room, behind, on the right side, with a center staircase. The kitchen and powder room, with a half bath, are off the sitting room in the rear because the vent stack on the roof is there for the waste lines. There is a small porch off the kitchen. Upstairs is a center hallway, bathroom in the rear, four bedrooms, here, here, here, and finally, your bedroom is in the front of the home. I would take the same room because you can see everyone and everything that is coming and going."

"Fascinating. You are right on. That is the exact layout of the home. No errors at all. I thought that you were studying papers and making phone calls instead of studying trees and lightning strikes."

"I was, and I did. Grundy has uniforms working that side street behind the house, in and around the factories. Sarge said he would interview the insomnia-ridden guy himself. I briefed him. Still waiting on Crump's reports and lab and autopsy reports. It is Sunday, but in my world, that is not an excuse. I dropped a dime on Detective David Palmer, at the Albany Police Department, and luckily, he is working today on some paperwork for a follow-up to a case from last week, and he agreed to meet us."

"You are like a damn modern-day Sherlock Holmes. So, does that make me Watson?" Marlin asked as she spun the key in the ignition switch and the engine of the pickup truck jumped to life.

"Nah. You are much too beautiful to be, Watson. From the description in the books, Watson was an ugly mug, and he had a limp from an old war injury."

"Fair enough. I will take the compliment from such an observant man as you are. I guess you have made a careful study of me."

"No use in proclaiming the obvious. Sometimes, the smart move is to defer rather than dig yourself in deeper."

Marlin laughed at Odell's dry and subtle sense of humor.

"You don't miss a trick, Odell. You have the eye of a photographer. You take it all in. Never miss a shot that you can capture in your film, or on your digital card, or in your mind's eyes."

Odell shrugged at her words, but he did not comment.

"Get your head and arm outta the window, push that window, switch up and let's get some a-c pumping in here."

Odell did as Marlin instructed and he leaned back as Marlin spun the truck around in a turnaround on the side of the driveway.

"Front shirt pocket," Odell said as he tapped at the pocket of his shirt and he mumbled, "I won't light it in your truck. Just need a taste."

The taps came up empty. There were no cigarettes there. Marlin was concentrating on the road ahead as she pulled the pickup truck out onto the main road, but she could see Odell struggling out of the corner of her eye.

"You can light it in my truck, as long as we share drags," Marlin thumbed a thumb in the direction of the storage area behind the front seats of the pickup truck, "in the bag from the corner liquor store, behind your seat, Odell. I picked us up three packs along with three bottles of your favorite Irish whiskey. That makes it my favorite Irish, too."

Odell reached behind the seat, grabbed the bag, and fished deeply inside of it until he found the pack of cigarettes. He plucked the pack out of the depths of the bag and opened it by slowly unwinding the plastic zip line from the wrapper. Ever respectful and careful, Odell gathered the debris and tucked it back into the bag. After tapping out a cigarette from the pack, he tucked the pack into his front shirt pocket while mumbling the location, and then he leaned into the lighter from Marlin and took a few drags on the smoke. Odell cracked the window open and exhaled most of the smoke outside the cab of the truck. He handed the cigarette to Marlin, who did the same.

After a long exhale, Marlin handed the smoke back to Odell and said, "That store clerk at the liquor store, ah, I think his name is Danny. Yes, Danny Clark, he had high praise for you. He seems to be a big fan."

"He did, huh?" Odell said while puffing on the cigarette.

"Yeah, he did. While you cleaned up, I took a hike down there to buy the smokes and some Irish. He recognized me from the television news reports from yesterday. He said to me, 'You are the gal with the sniffing pig.' I laughed and said yes."

"Yeah, Danny has been there on and off for a few years. I guess that I am a regular. Bought a few million packs of smokes there, a few million gallons of Irish whiskey, too."

Marlin said, "Yes. He told me that. Not in such specific terms, but, yes, he told me that. He asked me for my name and my phone number. No doubt that he was a flirty one. He is a big, powerful guy. Tall, lots of muscles. I gave him my name but passed on the phone number. I did not give it to him. He also asked me where I lived."

Odell's eyes wandered around the cab of the truck, but he did not speak any words. He took a longer drag on the cigarette and, after doing so, he handed it off to Marlin.

While he exhaled the smoke, mostly out of the truck window, Odell spoke, and then, uncharacteristically, he stopped. "So," Odell ran his hand through his hair and then looked over to Marlin, while he paused in his comment, then continued with his words, ". . . ah, you know, Officer Crump has the hots for you too. So why did you not give Danny your number? He is tall and muscular, huh? Crump is 'bout your age. Danny is too."

Marlin took a drag and handed the cigarette back to Odell while answering his questions.

"I am not interested. They are not my type. Although Danny is a photographer. I like photography. Danny pointed his photographic work out to me and explained about his photography. He has his photographs posted in and around the store above the counter and thereabouts. Mostly black and white. I think photography is sexy."

Odell looked over at Marlin, and the good detective carefully studied her. "Photography, huh? Sexy, huh? Interesting. Tall and muscular. I noticed the photographs, but until now, I did not know that Danny took them. Thank you for those keen observations. So," Odell took a final drag, he checked the amount of the cigarette that remained, then handed it off to Marlin for a last hit, before continuing speaking his thoughts, "why are they not your type? What exactly is your type?"

With no hesitation, Marlin answered the question, "Sexy and intellectual. I am not looking for an everlasting kiss. On my pretty little ass or otherwise." She finished the cigarette, pulled out the ashtray from the dashboard and ground out the butt, then snapped the tray shut while commenting, "One of the few pickup trucks left with ashtrays. I bought this as a used truck. Old. Reliable. A most worthwhile purchase."

"I gotta agree with you on that and on your other statement, too. Generally, newer is not always better. Excellent research and even better observation skills. I got it. Lookie here, Marlin, you are young and beautiful. Never settle or underestimate yourself."

"Odell, thank you, but I know what I want outta this life. Career wise, spiritual wise, and partner wise. Neither Danny nor Crump fit the bill. Did you know that you photograph everything with your eyes and your mind? You do not always need a camera to capture life. You do it with your eyes and your mind. I imagine that is how and why you are such an incredible detective. No detail is ever missed."

Odell nodded, but initially, he did not comment. Instead, he tapped his shirt pocket, mumbled as to the location, pulled out the pack of cigarettes, and said, "Maybe. Part of the job. I guess. Time for another smoke." Odell tapped some papers now sitting in his lap and asked, "Did you have time to check out the reports and the summary sheets?"

Marlin checked the traffic on an on-ramp for the New York State Thruway and after seeing that the lane was clear of traffic, she pushed down on the gas pedal and the truck sped into the havoc of the merge.

"I did. The murder in the park. In Albany. What was it . . .Melrose Park . . . a Mr. Rollins . . . combat vet from World War Two? He was the murderer's first victim in the serial string of homicides and his body only had a single gunshot wound. A lethal shot to his chest. Right through his heart. Instant death. I guess it was a single shot because the homicide occurred on a Monday. If he began his madness spree of killing there, then it appears as if he kept the same pattern right up until now with the homicide in Mohawk City. Number of gunshots in the body equals the day of the week of the murder. Monday is day one in the killer's book, even though some people consider it the second day of the week. That was the most interesting thing that jumped out at me. If I push aside the murder aspect of things and focus on the details of the cases, then it is the most interesting of the all the homicides. I found it fascinating that he is the only victim murdered while outside and not inside a dwelling or in the victim's own home. Moreover, not a single witness. Despite it being a popular park in Albany. In a city. In a public park."

Odell did not try to hide his smile. He took a long drag on the cigarette, leaned over to the cracked window, and blew the smoke out into the rushing air of the passing landscape and the world going by at sixty-five miles per hour.

"A public park. Yes. Very scenic, too. Scenic might be the key. I am very eager to stand there—in the exact place of the murder and take it all in. Other aspects of that murder are most interesting too, other than being outside and such. Anyway, I think that I am in love," he said, while he passed the cigarette over to Marlin, who lifted her eyebrows in response to his words, took it in one fluid motion, stuck in her mouth and pulled on the smoke until the end of the butt turned from orange to a deep red.

"Is that a promise, Odell?" Marlin asked as she blew the smoke out of her window. "Or is it a threat?"

Odell did not answer; instead, he picked up the papers containing the details of the past cases and thumbed through them. His eyebrows narrowed and his mind was somewhere else. Somewhere where only he knew the answer to, or the location of, or where it all would end. Some minor detail or thought had caused a derailment of his mind and her question would go unanswered until many hours or even days later. It was how his mind worked. Odell became trance-like whenever something captured him.

Despite her frustration at not cracking the mysterious shell of Detective Lyle Odell, Marlin recognized the situation. She paid careful attention to the traffic and took a little drag on the cigarette while keeping her eyes glued up the roadway. After a few drags, she plucked the cigarette out of her mouth and handed it off to Odell. She offered up the cigarette in the air to Odell. Without lifting his eyes from the papers, Odell glanced out of the peripheries of his eyesight. He took the cigarette out of Marlin's hand and he stuck it into the usual position of his dangling lip.

There it remained. Odell simply let it burn, only taking an occasional drag on it. His mind was now deep into the clues, into the wanderings and conversation from now on, would be limited. Marlin understood. This is how he operated. He required the quiet time.

After a long silence passed, Odell mumbled, "I just need a puff. Or two. You need to call your mother and sister. Are they in Albany?"

Marlin's eyebrows went up a little at his words and question, but she knew and understood the direction of the conversation.

"They are. My sister is with her. Classes are out for the summer."

"Good. Tell 'em it is a good time to visit your dad's side of the family back in Iowa. As in as soon as they can buy a plane ticket home." Odell looked over at Marlin, and the cigarette dangled from his lip as he spoke. "As in tomorrow. If they need dough for a ticket, just let me know. I can get them protection, too. Please, Marlin, you gotta make the call."

Marlin nodded, and she understood. There was a hard swallow at her throat as Odell dug back into the papers. He lifted the cigarette off his lips and then replaced it.

Once more, he mumbled, "Just a taste or two." Odell then turned his head to Marlin and studied her out of the corner of his eyes. "You can go too, Marlin. You and Doodlesticks have assisted more than I can ever thank you. You don't have to do this."

Marlin shook her head and tightened her grip on the steering wheel while grinding the words out from between her teeth, "Ain't going anywhere, Odell." She turned her head and smiled at Odell and added, "Not without you."

Odell nodded and went back to his papers.

Detective David Palmer was overweight, greasy, sweaty, and a little grimy. He was middle-aged, worn out, heavily weighted, and incredibly tainted by the world of crime that surrounded him. His office was dark, sweaty, grimy, and hot. Not warm. It was hot. The Albany Police Department Headquarters building was old, and the air-conditioning was old and the walls were old, and the roof was old too. The water stains on the ceiling of the office proved the age of the roof and its vulnerabilities, too. On a normal summer day, the air-conditioning system most likely struggled to maintain a comfortable temperature within the old relic of a building, but this day was not a normal summer day. It was another disgustingly hot day in upstate New York. They are rare, but when they come along, they are no joke. The office was sparsely furnished, his desk was an old wooden oak desk, that his desktop computer and large monitor seemed to overwhelm and the few scattered papers upon the top of the desk, competed for enough space to remain there without flying off the edge of the desk and falling upon the floor. A file cabinet stood in the corner of the office with a fan sitting on top of the cabinet that was desperately trying to move air around the office as it oscillated back and forth in the air's thickness. The window behind Palmer's head looked as if it had opened once; perhaps, in and around the turn of the last century—the sad glass squeezed between the wooden frames was murky, the glass streaked with city road grime.

Even the paint on the walls of the office gasped for air.

Detective Palmer wiped the sweat away from his brow with his handkerchief, and he removed his suit jacket and placed it over the back of his chair. As he loosened his necktie, and lifted his arms, the pools of sweat under his armpits stained his shirt and seemed to reach halfway to his waist. He tugged at his belt and it was a vain effort to pull his pants over a rather immense belly.

"Hotter than twenty-seven Hells in here and out there too, Odell. You are looking as you usually do . . . a mess."

"Nice to see you too, Palmer," Odell said, as he mumbled, "Top shirt pocket" and tapped his shirt for his cigarettes.

"No smoking in here, Odell. I have breathing issues and

besides, according to the rules and regulations for this building and in fact, all of New York State, it is not allowed."

"Don't worry, Palmer. I just taste it. Won't light it. May we?" Odell asked as he stuck a loose cigarette into the usual resting place on his lower lip and pointed at the guest chairs in front of the desk. Detective Palmer nodded and then directed his attention to Marlin, who stood next to Detective Lyle Odell. Marlin listened and watched the meet and greet unfold between the two rather hard-boiled detectives.

"Sure, sit down. I would prefer the beautiful woman . . . alone. Without you here, Odell." Palmer continued his lustful study of Marlin and said, "What did the news call you? Consultant. Yes, a consultant. Ha! The great loner, Lyle Odell, takes a consultant with a sniffing pig. Who would-have-thunk-it? Anyway, please, feel free to turn around before you sit so I can see if the rear view on the television did you justice. Ha! I guess my words might be rude and slightly sexual in nature. Just kiddin'."

Detective Palmer's greasy eyes continually walked all over the body and face of Marlin Santini.

Marlin looked at Odell, and Odell shook his head in disgust at Detective Palmer's words and action. He then waved his hand at her as a sign for Marlin to take the lead. That was just another reason she enjoyed this man so much, perhaps even more with each passing hour. He allowed a woman to stand her own ground, to promote independence, to defend her honor, but she knew in her heart that if he needed to, Odell would defend her with his life.

"Slightly?" Marlin growled. "So, I see you are not only a sweaty mess, but you are a slimeball idiot, too. Go ahead, keep it up, because you are about to earn a swift kick in that big ass of yours, Detective Palmer. I couldn't miss it either."

"So noted," Palmer said with a chuckle while he waved at the chairs. "I deserved that one. My apologies. It is just police talk amongst old friends."

Odell pulled the chair out and sat down in it while he tugged at his necktie, but he left his suit jacket on for now.

"Kinda bullshit too, Dave. Marlin can handle herself for sure. You had better watch out. Anyway, please meet Ms. Marlin Santini. Although, it seems as if you already know her. Or pretend to do so. Looks as if qualifying for p-t might be an issue with you. Are you feeling okay these days? You said that I was a mess, and that might or might not be accurate, but you are not looking too swift yourself."

Palmer settled into the chair and wiped once more at his brow.

"I feel like shit, Odell. This heatwave is kicking my big ass. I have a dispensation for physical training. I have asthma and other stuff going on here. Look, let's go over the files and give you what you need and let me be on my way. I have to check something out on South Pearl Street and you have your things that you want to sniff out, so let's get it done. I want to get rid of you. My captain called me at the last minute when he got the call from your new captain there. Moore. I think that is his name? Honestly, this is a bit of a pain-in-the-ass for you and beautiful here to show up on a Sunday, but whatever. I dunno why you are wasting your time here, consultant or not. It's a dead end. This crazy killer dude is the best I've ever seen. No clues, no trail, no evidence. Nothing. I long since gave up on it. But you are Lyle Odell, the legend, the man, and I am not." Detective Palmer poked the pointy finger of his right hand into the paper files on his desk, thumbed through them, and then picked them up and handed them to Odell.

"Here. Good luck. Those are copies, but they are complete files. I held nuthin' back. My chain of command ordered me to release everything to you. Your, new captain, had your back, Odell. I am truly sorry that I cannot offer anything more to you and I am sorry that this sick bastard is now killing in your city. I have nuthin' to add. Sorry. Anyway, the files are what they are. I am sure you have seen most of this before because you are Lyle Odell and you are always poking around into crime scenes, even if they are not exactly in your jurisdiction. I guess that in looking back on all of this, we should've called you in back then to poke around and, ah, you know, consult on the case."

Odell ignored the comment; instead, he focused his eyes upon the files just handed to him. You could see the eagerness in his eyes to tear into the files and study them.

"Thank you. I have seen some of this, yes, but not all of it. Of intense interest is the photographic evidence of the crime scene in Melrose Park."

Palmer nodded and offered, "I am not sure why, but once again, you are Detective Lyle Odell. I am not. Photos are in there. The crime scene photographer who originally took the pictures retired last year, but he still lives in the area. In Colonie. He is available for questions if you got any. I go drinking with him here and there. He is a good old guy. I am sure that he will be thrilled to help. It will give him something to do."

Odell ran his hand over the top of the stack of files, then took the cigarette out of his mouth and carefully laid it on the desk. He took a deep breath, closed his eyes, and then opened them. Marlin knew that look now. In only a few short days, she understood when Lyle Odell was far away thinking of some aspect of the case that no one else even considered or thought of before now. His gray eyes glazed over now that they were wide open and his eyes remained glued now upon Detective Palmer as he ran his hand over the top of the paper files. It was as if he was absorbing some evidence from attrition through the paper files. Once again, Odell was somewhere else now; she had lost him and Detective Palmer had lost him too. Something triggered a thought.

After the pondering, Odell spoke, "Yes, the homicide of Mr. Rollins. We are most interested in that one. The first murder by this maniac and the only murder outside of the victim's home, or for that matter—outside at all. A military veteran in the park. Relaxing. It was where this lunatic got a taste of blood."

Palmer nodded his head and said, "Yeah. Just a poor old guy hanging out and feeding the birds, the ducks and the geese. In the wrong place at the wrong time."

Immediately, Marlin jumped into the conversation. Her voice was powerful and emotional. Palmer nearly jumped out of his chair at the sound of her voice.

"Wrong!" Marlin shouted and pointed her finger in the air toward Detective Palmer. She then turned and spoke directly to Odell, "I just thought of something else. I know you mentioned other aspects of this murder are interesting, but your supposed proclamation of love diverted me." Odell did not react, not even to the proclamation of love statement; Marlin jumped right back into the conversation with the same enthusiasm as she now addressed both detectives and sat sideways on the chair.

"Mr. Rollins was feeding crows. Not birds, ducks, or geese. Crows. The details of the case investigation, signed by you, Detective Palmer, stated that there were unshelled peanuts on the ground and a bag of peanuts next to the body on the bench at the crime scene. He was feeding crows. Cows love unshelled peanuts. Mr. Rollins befriended crows and fed them. That takes a long time to do. Therefore, Mr. Rollins did not just show up at the wrong place at the wrong time. He went there for a very long time. Same bench. Same place. Same public park. Same crows. Crows are suspicious by nature. It takes a very long time for them to trust you. They are pretty damn smart."

Palmer lifted an eyebrow toward Marlin, and Odell smiled. Marlin blinked and crossed her legs and smiled.

Her voice remained strong and confident. "I don't just have a beautiful face, a great ass, and an amazing chest. I have a great mind, too."

Palmer swallowed hard, tilted his head, and waved his hand toward his two visitors.

He confessed, "Since it got me in trouble before I will hold my thoughts. Feeding crows, it is. I missed that one. I am not up to speed on crow food. Or preferred food, that is. I will also pass on the supposed proclamation of love by Odell. None of my beeswax."

Odell said in a low voice just above a whisper, "Might have missed more than that, Palmer. Marlin is brilliant. Simply brilliant. Anyway, South Pearl Street, huh? Kinda rough neck-o-the-woods. Homicide?"

"Might have missed sum stuff, Odell. I am human. Not like you are. I see that the legend remains intact. You even know where the trouble lies in my damn city. Yup. Not a nice hood over there on South Pearl. Druggie overdosed. Happens all day long here," Detective Palmer said as he felt the burn of Odell's eyes.

"I understand. More than you know. Speaking about our mutual cities . . . how long were you in Mohawk City?" Odell asked, and then he plucked the cigarette off the edge of the desk and stuck it in his mouth. Marlin's eyes went from Detective Palmer to Odell and then back to David Palmer. She was not sure how Detective Lyle Odell knew that the Albany police detective had visited Mohawk City. She scooted her backside to the edge of the chair. This was more than intriguing; it was captivating. Odell had barely lifted his eyes from the papers tucked in his lap, yet he detected something obvious, yet hidden.

Obvious only to Lyle Odell. The rest of the world would miss it.

Detective Palmer seemed surprised at the statement, yet controlled. From the police detective circles of nearby cities, Palmer obviously had known Lyle Odell for a very long time, and Odell's uncanny abilities to perceive and detect things did not seem to shock Palmer as much as they did Marlin.

"I got in town on Thursday and left out early this morning. When my captain called me and asked me to meet you and get these files together. I have an old friend there. A military buddy," Palmer said while his eyes scanned Odell's face for any reaction to his testimony.

To Marlin, this was all fascinating. Seeing no outward reaction from Odell caused Palmer to react first.

He quickly added, "How did you know?"

Odell pointed at a small paper on the desk in front of them. A sales receipt. No normal eyes would have even noticed it. Lyle Odell did not have a normal pair of eyes. Marlin was now convinced that he was superhuman.

"The sales slip there. On your desk. It is from Millie's Diner. On First Avenue and Main Street. Just off-center from downtown.

A very strange location for a successful diner, but it has been there forever. They serve excellent coffee. The coffee brewing machines are top-notch and cleaned and descaled regularly every Friday night by Millie's son-in-law, Jake. They have distinctive receipts. The little flower on the top of it . . . caught my eye. Millie is retired now. Her daughter runs the joint. Millie loves flowers, so she always had flowers on the receipts. Her daughter maintained the tradition."

Palmer's eyes went to the receipt. He quickly grabbed the receipt and picked it up and crumbled it in his hands and in one smooth motion, he tossed it into the wastebasket next to his desk.

Palmer's voice displayed his agitation, "It's good coffee, but I have had better. By the way, Odell. Your city is a dump."

"Yeah, it is. Nevertheless, it is home. Navy, right? You were a corpsman. Right?" Odell asked, as he waved toward Marlin and pushed his chair out from the desk. Palmer's face looked like he wanted to break Odell into pieces.

It was full of disdain because Detective David Palmer knew why Odell was asking the questions.

"Yes. Navy. Yes, I was a corpsman. I wasn't always a fat-ass. At one time I could run. You are such a smart-ass bastard. C'mon, man! You already knew all of that. Why did you have to ask?"

"Because, I did. To file it all away in my mind. It's what we detectives do. You should know and understand. Hey, thanks for everything. See you around," Odell said as he nodded. He stood up, and Marlin did too. He gathered all the files up under his arm, waved a little as Palmer took the same handkerchief out and wiped the seemingly never-ending streams of sweat from his face.

"See you around, Odell. See you, nice ass. Yup, it is really nice. Say there, honey. Call me if you get bored with Odell and his chasing clues and bullshit."

"Not even in your best dreams, jackass. You don't even deserve the time of day. And I would not give it to you," Marlin said as she waved dismissively at the sweaty detective.

Odell smiled and then as Marlin walked in front of him and entered into the main hallway of the headquarters building, Odell stopped, turned and said to Detective David Palmer, "Yeah, you should have."

"Should've?"

"You should have called me into the case, Palmer. You should have. The question that sticks in my mind is why you didn't? Have a nice day."

Odell and Marlin walked into the hallway, and Marlin smiled and looked at Odell as they walked to the front entrance of the building. "Geez, what a slime ball he is. Especially for a detective. Really? Is he really a police detective? Is he a suspect?"

"My dear Marlin, first and second and third lesson . . . always consider all the options for identifying a suspect. Wordplay can trip them up and reveal hidden clues. Most everyone is a potential suspect."

Marlin heard Odell's words; she abruptly stopped walking, and she tugged at Odell's shoulder to stop him at his quick pace.

She stared into his eyes and asked, "Most everyone, Odell?"

"Yupper. Most everyone. Not you, of course. Please do not even think that I consider you a suspect. This is a teaching lesson. Marlin, I trust you like I trust Sarge Grundy, Officer Crump, Captain Tucker, and Captain Moore. More than any other people in my life. I was simply probing Palmer for potential clues and issues. Palmer is a clown, and he is a lousy detective. Can't even see the plain and the obvious."

Marlin smiled and asked, "Okay, good. That is a relief. Thanks for the detective lesson. I think. The plain and the obvious. What are the plain and the obvious factors?"

Odell answered within a second, "Your ass isn't nice. It is fantastic. Incorrect description. Flawed investigation. Don't even need to be a detective to determine that. The guy is a clown."

Marlin laughed aloud, and she playfully bumped into Odell and fished for his hand at his side. She needed to feel his warmth. Despite the heat.

"I thought you meant the facts about the crow food."

"Nope. I meant what I said. Fantastic is the correct description."

Odell grabbed Marlin's hand, and they walked out the front door and into the hiss of summer. Into the heat of the day.

Into a world of chasing clues and bullshit.

CHAPTER SIX

"Right here, Marlin. This is the bench here. Right here," Detective Lyle Odell said as he pointed to a park bench and then he placed his hands on his hips and he stood in front of the park bench where Mr. Rollins sat about two years before this very date.

A bench where a cold-blooded murderer crept upon him and killed the defenseless man with a single gunshot to his head and then, when he was dead, had w-w-two crudely carved into his neck with a jagged edge knife. All to signify in some sick and demented way the victim's gallant service in the Second World War. Marlin glanced at the photograph from the folder and files that Detective Palmer provided, and she held the photograph up to the scene in front of her and agreed with Odell.

"Yes, I think you are correct. Yes. I think."

Odell did not need to use the photograph for a reference. He already knew exactly where he was. His mind was like a vault. Once something was inside, it remained locked there until Odell opened it or required it. Marlin had to keep glancing at the live scene and then to the photograph as she held it up in the air and continually compared the two.

Once more, she agreed, "Yes, yes, you are correct, Odell. That is the bench. For a moment, they all looked the same to me."

Odell did not answer; instead, he gazed at the scene in front of him. It was an asphalt-walking path, lined by a small patch of turf area, between lines of park benches that ran the length of the walking path. A small brick wall was on the other side of the patch of grass, with a storage shed for storing tools and equipment for the park maintenance workers, and then a stretch of open land, and finally a pond sat in the middle of the park. It was a shallow pond, with an aerator fountain in the center spraying water in the air, for not only beauty, but for aeration of the water to prevent algae and stagnation in the summer's heat. A small arched pedestrian bridge ran over the pond, linking the other side of the walking path to each other. The benches were identical except for different color paint. Odell turned around and scanned the other side of the path, away from the benches. The turf areas expanded along a long stretch, with beautiful trees and flowerbeds filled with flowers drooping in the heat and gasping for water and relief. A bucolic scene, and Odell scanned everything with his eyes, capturing every detail. Beyond the turf areas, there was a large parking area, where Marlin and Lyle Odell had parked Marlin's pickup truck. Odell waved in the air as if to dismiss the scene behind him. He turned to face the bench, ran his hand through his hair and messed it up entirely. Marlin stood rather awkwardly, a few feet away from the park bench where the horrific event occurred, and she stood in silence and watched Odell as he studied and worked the scene through his eyes and his mind. She knew that he was getting into his zone and although it was awkward and Marlin wanted to offer help, words, and advice, she knew not to speak and break his concentration. There was no way that Marlin Santini knew what Odell was studying, but she knew enough not to interrupt his thoughts.

Odell bent down. He supported himself as if he was a baseball catcher behind home plate, and his eyes thoroughly scanned the scene in front of him. He took his hands as if he was a photographer and framed the scene with his hands and fingers in a square and he focused between his hands at the view while squinting tightly with his eyes to capture whatever detail he was searching for in the world in front of him. Satisfied, Odell nodded. He stood up and then looked around and studied the trees in the area's vicinity. His eyes went from the ground to the trunks to the tops of the leaders of the trees, and Odell blinked a few times as he studied the trees. After a careful study, the words came out in a low rumble of his throat and chest.

"Fantastic oak tree. Such a majestic tree. Trees are amazing. They sustain life on Earth. We do not give them enough credit for all that they do for us. That one there," Odell pointed, and he spun on his heels, turned, and pointed to one enormous oak tree looming over to the right side of the park bench, "is amazing. That must be where the crows sit and watch. I bet they miss Mr. Rollins. What a shame. A brave and courageous man, a hero who faced Hell in combat only to die in an ambush by a crazed and vindictive madman. Damn, it is hot. The hiss of summer is so powerful. Top shirt pocket."

While he searched for his pack of cigarettes, between taps and probing, Odell ran his hand over his forehead and wiped away the sweat. The sun was bearing down now, yet Odell refused to lose his usual attire. His necktie, his jacket, remained intact. Loose, but intact.

Odell mumbled, "I think they are here," as he tapped his shirt and Marlin instantly reached into her ever-present leather bag and produced a lighter. Odell found his cigarettes, tapped out a smoke, and stuck it into his mouth. Marlin walked over, flicked the lighter to life, and Odell leaned into the flame and puffed hard and generously. He needed the smoke. After exhaling a long smoke into the air, Odell plucked the cigarette out of his mouth. He offered it to Marlin, who took it, and she too took a long drag on it and exhaled slowly. Now Marlin seemed to think that it was time to see what her partner was thinking.

"Okay, Odell, the suspense is killing me here. What do you see that I don't?"

Odell studied Marlin carefully, his eyes went from her work boots, to her leather messenger bag, to her tight shorts gripping her lovely hips, then they scanned her tanned and toned legs, and then they lingered on her perfect breasts tucked in her summer blouse. It was as if he had forgotten that she was even there until now. Just a hint of a smile appeared on Odell's face. He was happy that she was here. He admired her beauty and needed her brilliance.

"Marlin, yes, thank you. I see a horrific and wretched murder scene. Right here." Odell handed off the smoke and Marlin took it. Odell suddenly jumped into action. He went from zero to full-bore within seconds. Odell ran over to the bench and his hands displayed his thoughts as he waved in the air to enact the scene.

"Rollins never even knew the killer was there. His hearing was not the best. He wore hearing aids. It was in the autopsy report. I am sure you read that and recall that fact. The killer snuck up from the pond side. A silent ambush while Rollins called for his crow friends and lured them with the unshelled peanuts. As you correctly noted . . . they are a favorite food of crows. It was very early in the morning. Crows rise early. So do lonely old men. No one around . . . maybe some joggers, but the reports have no witnesses, no one around. The killer scouted this out for a long time . . . it does not matter because no one would hear the low pop from the silencer-equipped twenty-two . . . anyway . . . I mean . . . what was the time of death in the reports?" Odell asked, but he already knew the answer. From her studies, so did Marlin.

"Around five in the morning," Marlin answered.

"Yes, five in the morning. On a Monday when everyone wants to hide and not wake up. Incredibly bold of the killer to perform this hideous murder in a public park. But that is part of his madness. He got extra joy out of this homicide," Odell repeated some of the facts of the homicide of Mr. Rollins as if he wanted to file away the information in his vault forever.

"Days or even weeks earlier, the killer befriended Mr. Rollins. They met arbitrarily. By chance. I am now convinced more than ever that my assessment is correct. It came to me when I saw how he posed the beautiful young woman on her bed. It was a pose. The killer is a photographer. Maybe not a professional, but a hobbyist. What constitutes the difference?"

Odell ran his hand through his hair again as he asked the question. He did not even allow enough time for Marlin to answer before he continued speaking in a stream of consciousness of his thoughts. Odell answered his own question and Marlin remained fascinated as he rambled with his thoughts and words and, by doing so, Odell worked deeper into his investigation.

"Marlin, please hold your answer. I can answer that. Please forgive me for framing that as a question. The answer is . . . nothing. I have seen photographs by so-called amateur photographers that were much better than the professional photographer's shots. Critique of photography, like so many of the arts, can be so subjective. This scene is right over here. . .." Odell ran over to his previous position and he stood in front of the bench and once more framed the scene with his hands before continuing his thoughts, "this scene and setting is fantastic. It is idyllic, exquisite, and perfect for taking peaceful landscape photographs. The killer came here very often. He admired and used the setting for his work. He is demented but appreciative of the world and of beauty. An artist per se. He took some photographs, and he saw Mr. Rollins sitting and relaxing and feeding his crow friends. . .."

Odell's voice and his thoughts trailed off, he walked back over to Marlin, he motioned for the cigarette, Marlin took one last drag, handed it off to Odell, and while the detective finished the smoke, Marlin jumped in and completed his thoughts.

"The killer was curious as to the feeding of the crows. He walked over, took some pictures of the crows. The two men struck up a casual conversation. Mr. Rollins was happy to have some conversation. As you mentioned, he was very lonely. A relationship ensued over a few days. The killer is very engaging. A nut job but a good conversationalist. The killer takes his pictures and Mr. Rollins is relaxing and enjoying his pastime of feeding his crow friends. Within the exchange of conversation, Rollins told the killer that he was a combat vet in World War Two, the killer ticked that detail off on his sick-o-checklist, it triggered his madness, his sickness whatever it is, and he planned the murder. He crept back a few days later after their initial meeting. Whenever . . . a few days later . . . who knows? Then he ruthlessly killed the elderly man. As you said, Odell, Mr. Rollins was a hero."

Odell finished the cigarette, and he eloquently savored the last drag.

"Exactly, Marlin. Superior analysis. Excellent."

Odell exhaled the last of the smoke. He tossed the spent cigarette onto the asphalt walkway and he ground it out somewhat forcibly underneath his foot.

Then Odell reached down, picked the cigarette butt up, and stuck it in his suit jacket pocket while mumbling, "Right side suit jacket pocket." Odell looked up at the sky; he checked the direction of the sun and then checked his watch. "Left side suit jacket pocket," Odell mumbled, and then his hand dove into that pocket and he fished around until he found his folding magnifying lens. He opened the glass up, dropped to his knees while Marlin circled in, and observed Odell silently, while she remained in awe at his methods.

While studying the wooden surfaces of the bench from every angle, Odell mumbled aloud, "Carvings. Many carvings. An unusually exorbitant amount, in my opinion. Some are old. Some are new. It looks as if the park maintenance workers painted this bench since the time of the homicide. Most likely a rotational maintenance duty for every few years to paint and repair the benches. Just a guess. Woodcarvings. Of course. An American pastime. Everyone's done it at one time in their lives. I have. Maybe you have, Marlin. Carving initials and lover's hearts with the initials of the lovers carved into wooden park benches."

Marlin was positive that Odell did not want or need her to comment on his thoughts, which he just mumbled aloud for her to take mental notes of his observations. Odell peered into his magnifying glass, oblivious to the hard stares of some pedestrians and the runners trotting and sweating as they jogged by the scene. One male jogger slowed at his jogging pace, stared over at Odell, and the jogger stopped in his tracks.

He watched Odell as he covered every inch of the bench, and Marlin turned and said to the curious onlooker, "It's okay. Really. He is a police detective. A modern day, sort of Sherlock Holmes type of detective. An official investigation. Sort of."

The man raised his eyebrows and waved his hand as if to dismiss Marlin's explanation in favor of Odell being off his rocker. After all, Lyle Odell really did not look like he was a police detective. Odell's hair was longish, and it stuck up in all directions now, from his constant running of his hand through it. He mumbled to the world as he peered through his glass. And of course, Odell displayed no official police badge. Marlin knew that the chances were very good he did not even have his service weapon on him. It was still in the bedroom, slung over the back of the chair in the room where Marlin slept. Odell stopped his intense scanning of the bench areas and ran his hands and then his fingers over one location on the back of the bench. One slat near the top on the left-hand side seemed as if it caught his attention. He peered in, and then shifted his angle, pulled back with his glass, and then he crept in slowly and held that position while studying that area for a long time.

"Marlin, are there photographs in the bench's file, without the dead body on it? In the files?" Odell asked as he peered in through the glass.

Marlin, already familiar with the photographs from her previous studies, quickly answered, "Yes. Two."

Odell mumbled, "Thank you," and then he studied that area one more time. Odell leaned back on his folded legs while still on his knees, and he folded up his lens.

Marlin marveled at how limber Odell was. He climbed all over the ground and onto the bench as if he was a contortionist. She thought in her own mind, 'How that surprising flexibility might come in handy very soon.' Then she withheld a laugh at her slightly sensual thought and brought her mind back to the duty at hand.

Odell stood up; he did not even take the time to smooth out his wrinkled suit, or his necktie, or his hair. He tugged at his waistline and pulled his pants up a little, folded his lens back up and dropped it in the suit jacket pocket.

"Left side suit jacket pocket. Good. We need to contact that photographer that Palmer mentioned and get the originals on those pictures. I need Crump and his crew to work some magic on them. This bench has been painted and some of the carvings are filled in, but it is most interesting."

Marlin nodded and said, "I could tell. You scanned every inch of it. What did you see?"

"Lots of initials. Not much more than lots of initials. Some love hearts. One vulgar obscenity. It will take time to decipher it all."

"Okay, well, what next?"

While looking at Marlin, Odell spoke quietly but with a purpose, "It is late in the afternoon now. The heat is on and the day is waning. I would have hoped that some crows would be around, but they are smarter than we are, Marlin. They hide in the shade of the trees at the peak of this God-awful heat. However, we can try. Here. Please sit on the bench with me. Place your bag on the ground next to where we sit." Lyle Odell walked over to the bench. He sat, and Marlin sat next to him, removed her messenger bag and placed it down next to the bench.

Odell's eyes scanned the nearby trees, and he spoke, "Did you know a murder of crows, if they find a dead crow, they study the death scene? They gather in a group, chatter in their secret language, and try to figure out what caused their fellow crow's demise. Many people think they are conducting a funeral, but they are not. They are simply trying to discover why the crow died. They are very social, keenly intelligent and curious, but wary. Brilliant."

Marlin nodded her head, and as she did so, she was studying Odell's gray eyes in the bright light. She fell into his eyes in the light, in the dark, everywhere. His eyes to her . . . were magnetic.

"I did not know that, Odell. I never spent much time studying crows. We have a few crows that hang around the farm, but onions are not what crows usually eat. We don't grow corn or other crops that crows might get into. There are no crows around today. I guess because of the heat, as you said. They were here in one picture that I saw," Marlin said as she leaned over the edge of the bench and reached into her bag. She fumbled around inside of the depths of the bag and then pulled out the file folder of pictures. She placed the folder in her lap and thumbed through them. After a few seconds, Marlin found the picture that she wanted, picked it up, and studied it as Odell lurched forward and leaned in to study it, too.

"This one. Here," Marlin pointed. "They were in the lower branches of that tree right there." Marlin turned and pointed at a tree on the left side of the park bench. "Watching the scene?" Marlin asked as she handed Odell the picture and Odell intently studied it, and then he too turned and studied the tree.

"Crows are brilliant and you are too, Marlin. Thank you for this. Yes, they were watching. Studying why their friend was dead. Trying to figure out who were the good guys and who were the bad guys." Odell slid his backside to the edge of the bench and mumbled, "Front pants, right side pocket."

"No, your smokes are in your shirt, Odell. Top pocket." Marlin thought Odell was searching for his cigarettes, but he shook his head and he dug around in his pocket and produced a bag and a small device. A metal device shaped somewhat like a cigar shape, with a whistle-like tip on one end.

"Nah, we can't smoke right now. We might scare them. Mr. Rollins did not smoke."

Marlin pointed at the device in Odell's hands and said, "Okay, I understand. Ah, Odell, I know that is a crow call. I know that much. I bet the bag has peanuts inside. Are you really going to call the crows?"

"It is. Yes, and yes. Crows live around seven to ten years or so. You can bet your beautiful ass that there are still some crows living around here that were friends with Mr. Rollins. It might be hot today, but they are around. Watching."

Odell stopped speaking; he raised the device to his lips and gave it a blow. A "Caw" sound echoed out of the device, and Odell gave it a few more quick blows with brief pauses in between the calls. A few path walkers, some joggers and other park dwellers gave a glance at Odell and Marlin, but they went on their way. It seemed as if in a park in Albany, New York, a person might encounter many things. They might even hear a person call out to some crows. Odell opened the bag, pulled out a few peanuts, and tossed them on the ground in front of the bench. He gave a few more calls, and they sat, watched, and waited. Odell sat in silence and Marlin sat in silence, too. Her mind whirled with many thoughts, but above all, she marveled at the eccentric brilliance of Detective Lyle Odell. Here they were about two years later, trying to piece together parts of what other detectives and police officers deemed an unsolvable crime. No clues. No trail. Nothing. Yet Odell was keenly onto something. Marlin knew that he had some ideas and in time, he would share them with her. Odell already knew about feeding the crows. Marlin revealed nothing new to his brilliant mind. Odell came here prepared with the calling whistle, the peanuts, and a plan. He had made a big deal about Marlin's observations of the crows; however, it was obvious that Odell already knew the facts that Marlin presented.

Odell looked at Marlin, and he studied her eyes and face. He read her mind.

"Because crows recognize humans. For years. They study human faces, bodies, and everything human. The crows know who murdered Mr. Rollins." Marlin smiled and nodded. Her magnificent eyes lit up underneath her eyeglasses, and she gently touched Odell's arm.

"You sensed my puzzlement. Initially, I did not want to ask. But my next question is. . . ." Odell reached over and gently placed his fingertips on Marlin's lips. She wanted to kiss them. Sweaty, peanut dust, or whatever else was on his fingers. She wanted to kiss his fingers and embrace his hand. Marlin resisted.

"Please don't say that crows cannot talk because they can. Humans just don't know their language. Yet, when a human harms crows, or a single crow, or they see something they perceive to be dangerous, they recognize that person and the danger. Forever." Odell's eyes flashed and Marlin smiled. He rather abruptly removed his fingers, as if he sensed the effect they had on Marlin. Odell ran his hand through his hair, tugged at his necktie and mumbled a little under his breath, "Damn this heat, man, you have gorgeous eyes, Marlin."

He made a few quick calls, and they sat in silence for a few minutes while alternating their staring at the peanuts on the pathway and glances at trees for any signs of the arrival of crows. So far, there was nary a crow in sight.

A male jogger ran past them and after a quick glance at the peanuts on the ground, a quick shuffle of his feet, the jogger waltzed past the peanuts on the ground and side-stepped them and continued on his way.

"You must think that I am nuts. Do you, Marlin?" Odell asked as he made another call.

Marlin smiled and shook her head a little while saying, "A little, yes. All geniuses are crazy. You have an idea of where this investigation is heading toward, hell, knowing you as I do, and it is only a few days, but I think you might even already have a suspect in mind at this point. Not Detective Palmer. I can't see Palmer, in the physical condition that he is in, jumping that railing or the fence in Mohawk City. Plus, with his weight . . . that imprint would be very deep. As in that he would sink down to Australia. Someone else. I am not sure why you are not choosing to share ideas, or thoughts, or what you are thinking with me, but I respect that."

Odell nodded and turned to study the trees. Marlin followed his eyes while the detective scanned the sky.

"I am a little crazy, yupper. But lookie here, Marlin, not as crazy as that guy jogging in this damn heat." Odell pointed down the pathway and added, "Now he is crazy."

Marlin laughed and she once more gently touched Odell on his arm and said, "No doubt."

Suddenly, Odell's keen eyes caught a flutter in the sky and he grabbed Marlin's hand and gently said, "Pay dirt, baby. A crow. Forward recon." Odell took her hand, and he lifted it and gently pointed at the tree next to them. The same tree that the photograph captured the crows hanging out in during the investigation. The crow landed in a lower branch and the corvid hopped and danced on the branch, looked toward Odell and Marlin, and then he leaned into a few loud calls. Odell lifted his crow call and answered the crow, which hopped and danced even more when he saw and heard the answer from Odell.

"Let him study us, Marlin. He is checking out the scene. If you study the notes on the homicide of Mr. Rollins, they found a crow call in his vehicle. Mr. Rollins parked his vehicle in the upper lot there. He no longer had to use the caller to summon his crow friends. Chances are the routine was firmly in place by the time of his murder. The crows waited for him, saw his vehicle, and moved into position to enjoy the peanuts. We will sit here for a minute or two, then please gather up your bag and let's head out of here. The crow will never bring his friends with us sitting here. That call was to make his buds aware of something, but not to join him. Yet. He will never come down here for the peanuts until we leave. He is not sure of who we are. We have to leave. Yet, we laid the groundwork. We will be back tomorrow before we leave Albany."

Marlin nodded, but she was well aware of the fact that during the entire conversation, Odell continued to hold her hand. He used his free hand to operate the crow call. Odell studied the crow, and the crow studied Odell.

Detective Lyle Odell dropped Marlin's hand, patted her leg, and said, "Grab your stuff and let's go. We can watch from the truck." Marlin reached over and grabbed her bag. She stood up and quickly hit her full stride to catch up with Lyle Odell, who was hustling across the open areas of the park as he made a beeline for the truck.

"Whoa, Odell. What's the hurry?"

Odell turned around, faced Marlin, and answered her as he stopped walking and waited for her to catch up. "You left your cellphone in the truck and mine is in my pocket here, but the battery is dead. I am sure Grundy and Crump are calling them both. I gave both of them your phone number. Romance, right? I want to see what the latest news is."

Marlin caught up with Odell. She brushed her hair away from

her face and wiped some sweat away from it, too.

"Okay, Odell. Gotcha. Why didn't you tell me to bring my phone?"

"I didn't want any noises, you know, disturbances."

They made it to the truck, Marlin unlocked it, they climbed into the cab, and Marlin immediately started the engine and flipped the air-conditioning controls on.

"Gotta get some air in here. It is so hot."

Odell was carefully studying the area around the bench, and he did not acknowledge the air rushing from the truck vents or the words of Marlin. She had lost him again.

"I will check the phone," Marlin said, as she opened the center console and plucked her phone out of the confines of it.

Her eyes narrowed as she peered into the screen and then held it up to Odell and said, "Two missed calls. Two voicemails."

"Uh? Huh? Yupper. Grundy and Crump. Can you listen to them? Please. Thank you. Lookie there, Marlin, Mr. Crow has flown in for a snack." Odell pointed through the windshield and Marlin turned and watched as the two of them studied the crow as it hopped and jumped in and around the peanuts, carefully checking them, before finally picking one up and then flying back to the safe confines of the lower branch on that same tree. Marlin operated the phone as they watched the crow eat one peanut, and then the crow made the calls for snack time for his friends.

Marlin operated the cellphone, and she listened to the voice mails and smiled as she ended the call. "Grundy, mad as hell that he can't get a hold of you and Crump about the same, but Crump was gentler. He said, 'at least he now has my number.'"

"Yupper. Crump will ask you for a date the next time you speak with him. Can I please use your phone? I will call them both. Lookie there . . . five crows now."

Marlin handed the phone off to Odell and while he stared at the phone and studied it, Marlin watched as the crows gathered up and enjoyed the remainder of the peanuts.

"Odell, how do you know the recon crow is a male? Are the

males of a different size or something?"

"I dunno. They seem kinda sexless like I am. I just called the crow a him. Say, Marlin, how the hell do you work this phone?"

Odell said as he handed the phone off to Marlin, who smiled and took it while Odell tapped pockets, mumbled and found his cigarettes after some fumbling; he shook one loose and stuck one in his mouth. He placed the cigarette pack on the console of the truck.

Marlin waved the phone in the air and said, "I know, I know, you just need to taste it, but I need to puff on it, so here is my lighter and light that sucker up, Odell. Who do you want to call first?" Marlin reached in her bag, grabbed the lighter, and handed it off to Odell.

"Grundy. Sarge Grundy," Odell said out of the corner of his mouth as he lit the cigarette, took a few puffs and pushed the window switch down to let the smoke roll out of the truck and into the air.

"Here . . . it is ringing," Marlin said as she handed the phone off to Odell, who took it, and handed the cigarette off to Marlin who took a long drag on the cigarette and she studied Odell as he awkwardly held the phone up to his ear. She thought he was so adorable when he fumbled with technology or anything that he wanted no part of. Cellphones seemed to be rather high on his annoyance list.

"Nah, it is not Marlin. Odell here."

Marlin could hear Sergeant George Grundy cursing, even with the phone in Odell's ear. She laughed a little, took a drag on the cigarette and handed it off to Odell, who patiently listened to Grundy ranting and raving.

"Nah, we are in Albany. Took a lookie at the homicide scene of the Rollins murder, met with that ding-dong Detective Palmer, and picked up some ideas. Ok, ok, great."

Odell handed the cigarette back to Marlin, and she tried to piece the conversation together from one side. She took a long drag and smiled when she heard Odell say, "Okay. Great work. Yupper he is an insomniac, huh? Too bad he could not catch a license plate number or even a few parts and pieces of it, but whatcha got is wonderful. We now have sum good stuff, George. I appreciate it. Gonna be back by midday tomorrow. Huh? Nah. Well, maybe. I have no plans. We are now at four mistakes, George. Three to go. Thanks. See you tomorrow. Just leave the d-o-d list on my desk. Say, George, it is hotter than hell here. Bet it is there too. Did you get the grass cut?"

Odell sat in silence as the conversation went one way for a long explanation from George Grundy on the other end of the phone. Marlin enjoyed when Odell ventured outside of just conducting work conversations. It seemed as if he had no friends other than George Grundy and now her. And Doodlesticks.

"Well, the hell with it, George. Drink beer, watch the Clippers game and stay inside. Yupper. Bye."

Odell stared at the phone as if he could not figure out how to end the call. Marlin held the cigarette out in the air and she said, "Here, switch. I will work on the phone. Finish the smoke, Odell."

They switched items and Marlin hung up the call and looked at Odell, who savored the last puff on the smoke and blew the smoke out of the window of the truck.

"Four mistakes, baby. Four. Three to go. The guy on the porch. He can't ever sleep. He saw a compact car. Small. Two doors. Japanese manufacturer, but he did not know the exact make or model. Silver, kinda generic description, but the time works and get this . . . the old guy is fairly observant. Despite his lack of sleep. He spotted that the car has a bumper sticker stuck on its ass. The sticker is torn up, but the sleepless guy was in the Navy and he swears that the bumper sticker is one of those that says, Go Navy. He has one on his own car. Go Navy with the Navy logo and all those Navy guys and gals love to stick 'em on cars and stuff as a badge of honor. Unfortunately, he focused on the sticker and missed anything to do with the license plate on the car, but we have the torn sticker, a rough idea of a make and model and a color of car. That, in my opinion, is fantastic."

Marlin smiled widely and her happiness at the news was

radiant, along with her beauty.

"Three mistakes to go, Odell. Of course, you were correct. Twice. Maybe more. An insomniac and a Navy man. You want to talk to Crump?"

"Yes, the killer is a Navy man. We can use the d-o-d list and identify corpsmen and then narrow it down to any corpsman who served in combat. Then I am very sure that we will have our killer on that list. I am sure of it. Then we need to find the car with the remnants of a Go Navy sticker on it. Anyway, yes, please. Crump. Next. Thank you."

Odell finished the smoke; he pulled the ashtray out and ground the butt out in the tray and Marlin handed him the phone.

"Don't get your hopes and testosterone levels up too high, Crump, and get all sloppy and sexy on me. It is Odell, not Marlin. Don't ask me for a date. Sorry, but better luck next time, Officer Crump. Yeah, she is here. Huh? Nah, she doesn't wanna talk to you. Whadda mean how do I know if I did not ask her? Maybe I did."

Marlin laughed, and she stuck her hand over her mouth when she realized how loud her laugh was.

"Okay, get to it, Crump. It is hotter than thirty Hells. We have not eaten all day. I stink like an old mule and we need to get in some cool air."

Odell motioned at the pack of cigarettes on the console. Marlin nodded. She took them, plucked one cigarette out, and reached for her lighter. Marlin flicked the lighter, and it failed to light. Marlin tried again, and once again, but no flame arrived.

"Damn, it is out of fluid. No trouble," Marlin whispered, and she held up a finger in the air to show to Odell that she had a backup plan to light the cigarette up. Marlin opened the center console of the truck and she fished around a little inside the console and pulled out a book of matches. Marlin opened the matchbook, broke one off, struck it and held the lit match out for Odell, who nodded and leaned into it and smiled a "Thank you." Marlin noticed how Odell's eyes carefully moved and watched her as she tossed the matchbook into the center console of the truck and closed the lid. At first, she thought, or even hoped, that Odell was studying her open blouse to catch a glimpse of her breasts as she moved into the seat and leaned over. Then she realized that his eyes followed the matchbook.

'Who knows with this guy,' Marlin thought, 'Odell studies everything. He never misses a trick. I could dangle bare-ass in front of him and he would look for scars on my butt and ask for their origin instead of grabbing it and making love to me.'

Marlin sighed.

Odell leaned back into the passenger seat of the truck and he took a few drags while he continued to speak with Officer Oliver Crump. After some careful listening, some sharing of the cigarette with Marlin, and after a long period of silence. Odell finally spoke.

"Okay, well, it is more than I thought we would have. I appreciate it. Great job. Many thanks to you and your crew, too. Yeah, Grundy hit pay dirt. Yupper. Three mistakes to go, Crump. Huh? No, it is not a random count. I will explain some other time. But, Crump, I need your help with some photographs. Need 'em enhanced and that computer magic stuff used on 'em. Need details. We will send them your way. Okay, thank you. Be back by midday tomorrow. Sure, I will. Bye. See you around."

Odell did not even try to hang up the phone. He handed it to Marlin, who dangled the cigarette in her mouth and operated the phone to end the call. After enjoying a long drag, she handed off the cigarette to Odell and replaced the phone on the console.

"So, what did Crump find?"

"Not a whole helluva lot. No unusual fingerprints. They lifted a solid sneaker imprint from the bed of ivy. It matches the sneaker imprint under the bed at the edge. It is a generic sneaker, nothing special. Just a common, cheap sneaker. No high-end fancy-ass sneakers. Common. Available in any big-box store. At least we have an imprint. Estimates by the depth of the print, tell us we are dealing with a big man. Heavy, most likely tall. We have the chemical analysis of the lawn fertilizers . . . that residue should be on the pedals of the car . . . say can I finish this?" Odell held the cigarette out in the air.

"Sure. By the way, where are we going? I need to move this truck before we overheat here."

"Just drive out of the park. Make a left turn, then make the first right. I'll direct you from there. We are heading towards the airport. Wolf Road. A hotel there. We have an account. I think."

"A hotel, Odell. We are spending the night here?"

"Yupper. The matchbook is generic too. From most, any store in Mohawk City that would have matchbooks. Convenience stores, gas stations, liquor stores, anywhere they sell smokes. The printer says he ships 'em all over the city through a cigarette distributor. No fingerprints. No d-n-a, no stuff like that. But as we discussed before, since the matches were in his pocket, then maybe Doodlesticks can match a scent."

Marlin answered, "Maybe. We will try."

Odell said, "Good. We will arrange that when we return. But for what it is worth, we have the sneaker. It is nothing special, but we know his shoe size. Big foot. Size fourteen. Proportional to his height. Big guy."

"Which most likely, the killer ditched the sneakers when he saw the news," Marlin said while she put the truck in gear, checked behind her and slowly pulled out of the parking space. There were very few cars or people around in the park now. The heat drove them all for cover. It was near three in the afternoon now and the sun had turned up the knobs to full power.

"Yupper. You are right on, Marlin. That's okay though. We are okay." Odell finished the cigarette and ground it out in the ashtray. He pushed the window switch and rolled the window up and he leaned deeply back into the passenger seat.

"What is so much more than that, Odell? You said that to Grundy."

"Huh?"

"You said it is so much more than that. What is *that*?"

"Oh, yeah, Grundy asked if we are gonna share a bed and hookup tonight. If we will . . . make love all night."

Marlin smiled and laughed and said as she winked her left eye at Odell, "Okay, well, are we?"

"Marlin, I have no plans."

"Hence your answer. I get it. Tell me where to drive to Odell. The best plans are no plans."

"Make a right at the light. Get yourself onto the main drag there."

"Okay."

Odell leaned back deeper into the passenger seat of the truck. He wiped at his brow, reached over and redirected the vent on the dashboard to blow directly on his face and he loosened his necktie even more. His eyes wandered to the window as they scanned the city while it passed by the truck. Marlin eased into the traffic on the main drag and picked up speed.

Suddenly, Odell spoke in a softer than usual voice while keeping his eyes on the scene outside the window, "The air feels good. Much colder now that we are moving. Air through the condenser. Works every time. I don't want to suppress your brilliance. Your thoughts. I need you to think all the time. On your own. No influence from me."

Marlin listened to his words, but she kept her eyes on the busy city traffic, but she allowed her mind to wander all around as she searched the indexes of recent Odell conversations for exactly what he was answering or saying. Their relationship was now a few days or so old and she already understood how his very complex mind worked. It was not because he did not pay any attention to questions or statements; in fact, it was just the opposite. He chose to answer them or address them later. Sometimes much later.

"I am so sorry, Odell. I lost you on that one. I tried to recall where we were and what was said to cause you to address something we discussed previously, but I am lost." Odell seemed surprised that Marlin did not follow him.

He pushed his body up into the seat and stood up taller before speaking, "You asked, why don't I include you in on all the details? Why I do not share ideas or my thoughts or what I am thinking with you. That is why."

"Oh. I see."

Marlin kept one eye on the traffic and one eye on the road, and she addressed Odell out of the corner of her mouth.

"Thank you for your answer. Better late than never. I guess. You think that I am brilliant?"

"Yes, of course, I do. That is Albany Medical Center on the right side there. Great place. I hope that you never have to go there. I really do think that you are brilliant. Very brilliant. Beyond brilliant. Keep going straight here, Marlin. I will tell you when to turn. I should've said human witnesses. Not that there were no witnesses at all."

Marlin smiled, and this time, she understood his reference. "Yes, you should've, Odell. Because we have Mr. Crow."

"Yes, we do. Now is that crow a male or a female Crow? I am not sure which it is. And I am positive that it does not really matter," Odell said as he flashed a quick smile at Marlin. After speaking those words, Odell sunk deeply into the seat and he went silent.

Marlin knew that he wanted his alone time. It was now Odell's deep thought time. His Odell thinking time. She understood him more and more each second, each minute, each hour that they spent with each other. She enjoyed all of him and absorbed him into her soul.

Odell flashed his police badge for the first time that Marlin had seen in their time together.

"Yes, okay, well, welcome back, Detective Odell," the front desk clerk said while the clerk smiled a quick, yet fake smile. Odell lifted his eyebrows at the desk clerk's reaction to studying his badge and his announcement of who he was and that they needed hotel rooms. Marlin understood that Odell reacted because he knew that the front desk clerk did not like police officers, especially detectives. Marlin stood next to Odell, and she noticed his reaction. She smiled at how Odell never stopped tracking crimes or criminals. He was already working the angles in his mind to determine what the desk clerk dabbled in, other than working at the front desk of a hotel. The desk clerk was short, dark-haired, with no unusual or outstanding facial features. Not handsome but not unattractive either—he blended rather well. Except that he was nervous in the presence of Detective Lyle Odell.

The desk clerk cleared his throat and spoke, "I know you have been with us before. I recognize your name. Here are the notes. No reservations, but walk-ins are certainly acceptable. We have an account for the Mohawk City Police Department and you are on the approved list here. Okay, let's see here." The desk clerk leaned into the computer screen of the computer to study the current room availability.

"Two rooms. I have some availability here on the sixth floor. One for you and one for the young woman here," the desk clerk said as he nodded in agreement with what the computer screen reported.

Marlin quickly moved into action. She had a plan.

Marlin stepped in front of Odell and leaned into the front desk. "How much is it for a room with two twin beds rather than one king bed or separate rooms? Taxpayer's money, you know."

The desk clerk stared at Marlin. He allowed his eyes to wander her face and then he caught a quick glance at her exposed cleavage in the open neckline of her blouse. Marlin was hot, sweaty, and worn out, but she was still stunning. Perhaps even more so than usual.

The desk clerk's eyes then went over to Lyle Odell and the clerk swallowed hard before speaking, "Yes, well, very . . . prudent. A single king bed hotel room is one hundred and twenty-nine dollars per night . . . the twin bed room is fifteen dollars less. One hundred and fourteen dollars per night." The desk clerk looked up and added, "Plus tax."

Marlin jumped in and said, "We will take the room with the twin beds. We not only saved fifteen bucks, we saved one hundred and twenty-nine dollars, too."

Marlin flashed a smile and the desk clerk frowned. It seemed as if waves of jealousy had arrived all over his body. Odell was sharing a room with a gorgeous young woman—the desk clerk was not.

"Please, I need to see your identification, Ma'am. Even though I saw you on television. With your sniffing pig."

Odell piped up now and asked, "It made the news here, too?"

"It did," the hotel clerk said as he leaned in and studied Marlin's identification. "Yes, it did. Thank you, Ms. Santini. Hot on the trail, huh? Detective Odell, I saw your badge. You are good to go. Here are the room keys. Our bar and restaurant are open in an hour or so. Full menu, cocktails, beer and wine. The elevators . . . are that way."

The desk clerk handed the room keys to Marlin. He pointed to the elevators, and she thanked the clerk and reached down to pick up her bags, stopped, and then said, "We will stay in the room. Not in the mood to leave. It has been a long and very hot day. Can you recommend a great pizza shop that will deliver here? Can we buy beer over the bar?"

"Yes, of course. Luigi's Pizza Shop. Great pies. The information and number are on the information list inside the hotel booklet in the room. Yes, you can purchase beer at the bar to bring to your rooms. Correction . . . room," the desk clerk said as he rolled cautiously into his words.

Marlin nodded, smiled, and picked up her bags as Odell did the same and he followed her to the lobby elevators.

"In the mood for pizza, huh? We just had it last night."

"Something like that. Odell, damn, it is pizza. Better known as cheesy Heaven. We have three bottles of Irish packed. We can buy some six-packs of cold beer over the bar and we are good to go."

Odell leaned in, pushed the button for the elevator, and said, "Or something like that."

The table was so typical of a hotel table. It was round, brown, and odd and tucked itself into the corner of the hotel room next to the heating and air conditioning unit like a cat sleeping in a corner using the walls behind as protection. The two chairs at the table were orange with brown stripes, and it looked as if whomever the hotel chain hired to choose the décor had made a gross error in judgment. On the other hand, perhaps, they just were looking to do it on the cheap. The matching hotel artwork on the walls matched the oddness. Flowers and street scenes are generally not brown and orange too. The table held an open pizza box, a few glasses of Irish whiskey, and plastic hotel cups filled with beer. Two bottles of Irish sat on the credenza in the hotel room, next to the television, and two six packs of beer were on the floor next to the table. One six-pack of beer was open and the other one was intact. Marlin and Detective Lyle Odell sat at the table with the pizza box open. They used the cardboard lid of the pizza box as a mutual plate.

"You know sumthin', Odell?" Marlin asked while waving a pizza crust in the air; a crust with just a hint of burned and bubbled cheese and sauce riming along the edges. Another bite and it was just crust left, "I am gonna weigh a whole helluva lot more by the time we solve this case, but this food mixture, of yours, a warm-up with the Irish whiskey and then ice-cold beer with the piping hot pizza is amazing. I am so glad we ordered the pie and ate here rather than eat at the bar in the lobby.

"Your weight is fantastic. You have a perfect figure. Besides, anything you eat these days and nights, this hiss of summer will melt it off of you in a day, and you will need more pizza. We probably lost five pounds out there today. Ben Franklin only had it one-quarter correct," Odell said between swallows, "when he said that beer is proof that God loves us and wants us to be happy, but he should've added pizza and Irish whiskey too. I will be dead with this menu. Dead eating it—dead with not. Might as well enjoy it."

Marlin finished the last bites of the slice and she checked the crust, and then she tossed it into the lid with the other spent crusts. "Ben was a genius. Like you, Odell. So, you did not argue with the God part of Ben's proclamation. You only take issue because Ben omitted pizza and whiskey. Huh? So, does that mean that Detective Lyle Odell believes in God?"

Marlin asked and lifted her plastic cup to wash down the bites of pizza with the ice-cold beer.

"I do. I pray every day."

Upon hearing the words and proclamation of Odell, Marlin's eyes lifted over the rim of the glass and her head bounced in surprise at his statement. While taking a gentle sip, Marlin studied Odell, and then she smiled and placed the glass on the table. Odell was studying the pizza for his next slice selection when he felt her eyes studying him.

He looked up at her, then to the pizza and while pointing a finger at a slice, Odell asked, "You seem as if you are worried about a few ounces on your beautiful ass, but can I have that small slice over there? I need to leave room for the Irish."

"It's yours. Here. Because I too think that my ass looks great. Please, let me have that giant slice over on your side."

They nodded, plucked the slices out of the pie and exchanged them.

Odell took a bite, chewed, and swallowed, and then he looked at Marlin and said, "I think by your reaction to my statement that I surprised you."

"You did. I mean, what religion are you, Odell? You are Irish, so you are Catholic?"

Odell shook his head and answered, "I said that I believed in God, not in religion. They are very different things. There is no way that I could deal with the evil bullshit of this sad-ass world without God. Some people might consider me to be a Catholic... I am more inclined to classify Odell as simply a believer in God. It seems stupid, rude, and profoundly arrogant of a person to proclaim that whatever religion you believe in is the last word. To point your finger at others who do not practice your brand of religion is wrong and those who do not share your love of your particular flavor of God practicing are condemned to a fiery Hell . . . seems like a ton of bullshit to me. Just who in Hell do you think you are to judge me and tell me that I am wrong in my beliefs? It seems contrary to what all religions preach. Cuz, some scholar took sum words and made sum stuff up? I can find another scholar to pull a bullshit card on your religion. It is endless bickering between humans who are arrogant enough to think they understand God. Lookie, here, Marlin, I take parts and pieces of all religions, all the words of the various wise prophets, all the teachings and that is what I believe in. I think that Buddha was a rather cool guy and so was Moses. So were Jesus and Mohammad. All of 'em can teach us sumthin.' God does not only come out on Sundays, or for morning or evening Mass, or for special prayer times, or on a holiday. Humankind made that bullshit up. I kinda lean to Jesus. The ground at the foot of the cross is even. Jesus Christ endured the pain and the mockery of a Crown of Thorns. Imagine thorns to be your crown. Piercing, bloody, biting, and intense. It is maddening. The way that I see it is that . . . Christ, because of his courage and his holiness, gave every person a fair shake. Because of his sacrifice, well, everyone can choose their own direction."

Marlin smiled and between swallows said, "Powerful words, Detective Lyle Odell. Maybe you should have been a prosecutor or an attorney general, rather than a detective. Or maybe a pastor or preacher in some hell-fire and brimstone church."

Odell smiled, and Marlin admired the way his worn face crinkled up when he smiled. How she wished that he smiled more often. She placed her elbows on the table, folded her hands together and supported her chin on top of her folded hands. She was admiring Odell and relishing the simple yet profound time they shared together.

"Nah, I love what I do. Judges generally don't like drunks in their courtrooms. Neither do congregations."

"Odell, you would be a success at whatever you do, or did, or decide to do in life. So, can I ask? Why do you believe in God?"

"Because I am a detective. I go by the facts. No God? So where did all this come from? I ain't buying that proton blast bullshit or whatever it is. The God particle stuff. That first particle came from something. Moreover, there is good in the world. Still."

Odell waved his hands in the air and he seemed to take in the entire world by a wave in the hotel room. When he needed to be, Odell was a powerful speaker and influence.

"I look at this weary-ass world, and deal with evil every single day. Only the greatness of God counters it. God gives me the strength to plod onward. My flaws are powerful. They are horrible and overwhelming. I do not ask God for forgiveness of them or to overcome them. I ask him to allow me to use them to accomplish the mission and to live my life with some elements of happiness. I ask God to help me contribute to good in this world and destroy evil. God wants us to face our inner truths, accept them, and be happy in them. Not to hide them away and allow them to burn away at our souls because they don't adhere to some perceived rule some humans made up. The truth is in us all. We need to feel it and use it and be happy. I don't only worship the bottom of empty Irish whiskey bottles or empty pizza boxes. I see the good and the beauty, too. I look at trees and flowers and pizza and . . . you . . . and I see beauty. Fantastic beauty. That means God is active in my life. In my eyes. Opening me up to the world. Telling me to be happy in simple things and people that are important and not toxic and are joyful in my life."

"You think that I am beautiful?"

Odell answered right away, without any hesitation.

"I do. You are absolutely stunning. Beyond beautiful. Of course. You have mirrors. Pay attention to your reflection. You take my breath away with your beauty. The evidence is overwhelming."

"What do you pray for, Odell?"

"For God to allow me to do my job. To guide me. To bring justice to those wronged, those ruthlessly murdered for some perverted sick-ass reason, to crush those evil bastards that continue to wage war in human's hearts. I pray that someday,

I can find peace. I would find a woman who thinks that I am actually fun to be with in her life. She will see a man who is worthwhile. She will see a man to partner with, and she will not see what everyone else seems to see that I am an eccentric nutcase, lost in a world of clues, tracking down the phantoms, and just an old washed-up drunkard. She can be younger than I am, or the same age as I am, or older—it does not matter except to the age in our hearts. She will make love to me every night and see me as I am or as I might be. We will share pizza, beer, Irish, and wine and laughs and joy. I will listen to music with her and she will play for me, her favorite music in her heart too. I will finally find some peace with her and she will find what she needs too."

Odell set the plastic cup full of beer aside. Now, he reached for the glass of Irish whiskey and downed the remaining whiskey in one shot.

He pushed the glass across the table and then lifted his eyes to Marlin and said, "That is what I pray for."

Marlin smiled widely. She took a long sip of the beer and remained silent. Their eyes remained locked on each other and they studied each other. Odell ran his fingers through his hair as he always did and then, realizing that he made it stick out in all directions, he smoothed it down into place. He seemed to be pondering whether he should have exposed so much of his soul to Marlin. Odell was usually so reserved, so alone, so compact. Something about this woman opened his soul up and made him become unhinged.

"You know what, Odell? I believe in God too. I pray too and tonight and maybe from here on, I will add something to my prayers."

"What is it that you are adding?"

"Maybe I am that woman."

Odell stared at Marlin, and he blinked a few times. He smiled and Marlin smiled too. His smile was amazing. Perhaps no other person on the face of the earth felt that it was—but Marlin did.

Finally, Odell said, "It is a promise. Not a threat."

Marlin had waited a very long time for those words and remarkably, this time, she recalled the previous conversation and understood exactly what his words meant.

Odell showered first. Marlin heard the door to the bathroom open and his steps upon the small section of carpet on the floor outside the bathroom, and then his steps quieted as his feet hit the carpet on the floor of their hotel room. Odell mumbled something to Marlin as she sat on the end of the bed closest to the bathroom, one eye on the television that had the sound turned down and one eye on Odell as he walked past her. Her glass of whiskey was in her hand and the remote control in her other hand. He was dressed how she preferred to see Odell. In the Mohawk City Police Department logo tee shirt, a pair of black jeans and sneakers.

'Who wears sneakers when they come out of the bathroom?' Marlin thought. 'But damn, that slick-backed jet-black Irish-heritage hair, slightly wet, one or two strands hanging down on his forehead.' Marlin had to admit that he made her spine shiver.

"It is all yours. I need to check some of the shots taken by the Albany police photographer. Without too much stalling and bullshit hassle because we are poking around in their cold case, I wonder if we can find out the type of camera and the focal length used on some shots? I am sure that we can. Slime-ball Palmer said that he tipped a few with the photographer. We need to call him and find out that information and get those original photo files for Crump to check out and enhance. In the mornin'. Tomorrow will be a helluva busy day."

Marlin smiled, and she watched as he stopped by the table, poured about four fingers full of whiskey into a glass, walked over to the bed, grabbed some papers and sat on the edge of the bed intently thumbing through the papers to find the photo section of the homicide reports.

She thought, 'His mind never stops. Soon, she will give him a brief escape.'

"I'll be right out," Marlin said, but Odell did not answer.

He was lost to her for now, but she planned to regain him very shortly.

When Marlin walked out of the bathroom, Odell was thumbing through papers while sitting on the bed. The glass of Irish stood proudly while remaining half-full on the end table next to the bed. He looked up when Marlin exited the bathroom. Her glorious body remained wrapped and concealed in a bath towel. However, it was easy to tell of the glory underneath that towel. She did not wear her eyeglasses, and her eyes were wide and perfect. Odell noticed, perhaps for the first time, perhaps because he was a detective that missed no detail, or perhaps he always noticed—that her eyes were almond-shaped, and they were laced in a deep brown color with a little touch, or just a hint of a lighter brown color along the edges.

With a great deal of effort on his part, Odell's focus shifted to the papers on the bed and the area next to him on the bed. He set the papers aside, first onto the bed, then after thinking about it for a second or two, he picked them up, gathered them into a neat pile, and placed them on the end table. Next to the whiskey glass. There was no ashtray on the end table, only the whiskey glass. It appeared as if the string of chain smoking for Odell stopped a few hours earlier. His sneakers were no longer on his feet, nor his socks. They sat next to the bed, carefully tucked together in a tidy package of combined footwear. His feet were bare and Marlin flashed her eyes at them for a second.

She pointed at his feet and with a laugh combined with words, Marlin said, "It felt so good to wash away the sweat and work of this day. I gotta say, Odell, that you have cute feet."

Odell looked up again and this time, he intently studied her. Her hair was still slightly wet, and she shook her head to allow her hair to fall all around her as she reached behind her head and removed a hair tie that held her waves behind her head. Drips of water ran down her neck, channeled along her chest, and disappeared into the glory of her breasts.

"Ah, something tells me that you are not planning to use the bed over there," Odell said, while thumbing in the bed's direction next to where they stood.

"Correct, Detective Odell. Quite correct. As usual, expert detective work," Marlin answered in a seductive growl.

"Why did we rent a room with two twin beds then?" Odell asked as his eyes remained locked onto her eyes.

"To save the taxpayer's money and your new captain's budget a few bucks. It *was* fifteen bucks cheaper. Not to mention saving one hundred and twenty-nine dollars on a shared room rather than separate rooms. Odell, you are no longer sexless. Grundy might have been onto something. Something big, something grand and something glorious."

Marlin let the towel unravel. It dropped to the floor, and she paused for a few moments in the fading light of the hotel room and allowed Odell to study her. Then she gracefully moved to climb into the bed next to Odell. Detective Lyle Odell admired the evidence. Marlin Santini was a goddess. Her body was immaculate. The detective examined and concurred with the evidence. Perfect. Beyond perfect.

"You are stunning," Odell said as he marveled at her beauty. "That clown who let you go must've been nuts." He shifted his weight on the bed to make some room and looked up as Marlin climbed into the bed next to him.

"But, Marlin, I am so much older than you are."

"Exactly," she said as she finally ran her hands through his glorious hair and their lips met for the first time. "That is exactly what I am counting on tonight," she whispered into his mouth just before she buried her lips into his.

During the night and in the ensuing early morning light, Odell returned to some semblance of being a man. He returned to this world. He had been absent for a very long time.

After they made love for the first time and lay exhausted in each other's arms while counting the beats of their hearts, Marlin leaned in and whispered in Odell's ear, "You just rocked my entire world, Odell. Finally, Odell, you found some peace."

Speaking no words at all, Odell rolled her over in his powerful arms and then he made love to her again as a prelude to a magnificent evening and morning.

Marlin was not disappointed. They made love all night long. Until dawn and just past the crack thereof. Odell was in great physical condition. His stamina was beyond impressive. Marlin never had a lover like him. He hid his muscles well. Very well. In fact, he was perfect and so was Marlin.

For one night in the weary world of Detective Lyle Odell, he relaxed and left a world of evil, a world of clues and hidden facts that waited for the detective to uncover them, he left empty whiskey bottles, and squished cigarettes, and he escaped from the haunting of the phantoms that constantly chased him everywhere with nowhere for him to hide.

On this night, he hid, in the arms of her beauty, in the throes of growing love, in a world that Odell deserved to visit. He paid his dues and then some.

Moreover, Marlin realized that she loved him.

CHAPTER SEVEN

"Lookie here, they came right away, Marlin. Two calls."

"I would do the same thing, Odell. Whenever you called me," Marlin answered, as she gently nudged the side of Detective Lyle Odell. There was an implied innuendo to Marlin's statement, which produced the slightest of smiles from Detective Lyle Odell, but no further words or comments.

"I wonder if these crows know of our love, Odell?" Marlin asked as she studied the face of her lover for a reaction.

There was none, and Marlin understood. She had lost him once more. By now, Marlin understood how it happened. Odell now shifted to the alternate world in which the detective lived. Even her beauty and the memory of their lovemaking could not return him to her, or rather, to their world. Right now, Odell existed only in his world. A world filled with criminals, with mysteries, with clues, and riddled with unsolved crimes. Unsurprisingly, Marlin understood his lack of a reaction and his motives. It was time for business now. Odell's eyes locked on the crows gathering in the nearby tree. He reached into his bag and tossed the unshelled peanuts onto the ground in front of the park bench and he watched as they landed on the asphalt path in front of them and his eyes watched until they stopped rolling and settled upon a spot to stay in and to roll no more.

Odell returned to their world. His voice was soft and confident. It reminded Marlin of the whispers he made in her ear while they made love during the previous evening.

"We need one piece of the puzzle here before we allow our friends to have their morning snack. Do you have a camera on your phone there, Marlin?"

"I do. So does your phone, but let me guess, the battery is dead."

"It is. I was very busy last evening and into the early morning hours and forgot to plug it into the charger," Odell spoke as his eyes remained glued upon the branches of the tree where five or six crows now gathered. The crows landed on the branches, stared down at where Odell and Marlin sat upon the park bench and began their secret language of chatter and communications. Odell gently tapped Marlin on her leg, and he smiled at her. His smile could break her strongest defense. This smile did exactly that.

"Lookie here, Marlin, I had a glorious evening and morning. I returned to the world yesterday. The last thing on my mind was that stupid phone."

Marlin leaned into Odell and gently touched his arm and teased him with her touch and a gentle laugh at his words.

"It was beyond glorious, Odell. I love the taste of you . . . whiskey and cigarettes laced with the honor of your love and your heart. Who knew you have so much passion inside of you and such amazing equipment to back it all up? Damn, you are the perfect man. Passion carefully hidden by that unruly, disorganized, and gruff exterior? It is magical."

"Well, I dunno 'bout that, but I will take your word for it. We are in this case now. Deeply into it and now, it is time to make our move. I know you will follow along with me. Gonna need everything that you have."

"You already had that and have that, Odell. I did not and will hold nothing back."

Odell displayed a hint of a smile at the duality within her statement. He ran his hand through his hair and his hair sprung from its early morning captivity of a shower and, despite still being slightly damp, his hair stuck out in all directions.

"Marlin, Lookie here. It is about to get dicey. We need to take a picture or two. I wish we had a quality digital camera, but your phone will do." Odell finished speaking; he tapped her gently on her back and signaled for her to stand up as he rose from the bench. Marlin grabbed her leather shoulder bag; she stood up and followed to where Odell now stood in front of the bench, a few steps off the asphalt path.

The crows hollered and chattered and Odell looked up at them, waved a little in the air and spoke, "You guys need to wait one minute. I need one minute and then you can eat."

The leader of the crows tilted his head and listened as the crow watched Odell carefully. It seemed as if the leader understood exactly what Detective Lyle Odell had communicated. He quieted down, bobbed his head, and danced on the branch as the rest of the murder of crows stood on their own branches and watched and waited. Marlin watched as Odell carefully stood and looked over at the bench scene. He shifted his feet and framed a portion of the scene with his fingers and hands to capture something that only he knew what it was that he was looking for in the view. Odell stepped back. He duplicated the movements and positions. He stepped to the side, framed the shot, and then he bent down a little. He was searching the area of the bench, but he also was looking at the entire scene, with the pond and fountain in the background and the pedestrian bridge in the distance.

"Here, Marlin. Please stand here and take a picture. Right here," Odell said while he stomped on the ground a little with his right foot to signify the spot.

Marlin nodded. She reached into her bag and pulled out her phone. She fiddled with the settings and once she activated the camera, Marlin walked over to Odell. Odell blinked in the sunlight and the heat that was already gaining in intensity caused a drop of sweat to run down his forehead. He was hot, and by looking at the beauty of Marlin Santini, he only grew hotter. This morning, Marlin looked ravishingly beautiful. The long night and morning of lovemaking had left her enthralled and satisfied. Her eyes were wide and beautiful underneath her glasses. She wore another pair of those gloriously tight shorts that hugged her hips and body as only Marlin shorts could. Her blouse was open with a few buttons on her neckline, and it was light and airy and, in the heat, Odell could see tiny droplets of sweat on her chest, just above her cleavage, and Odell knew of the beauty that lies therein. Then there were the work boots, with the wrapped laces and her socks pulled up onto the toned, tanned, and perfect legs. Odell knew every inch of her body now, both naked and clothed, and he mapped it forever into his mind. He did not want to lose the thoughts of how she looked, how she felt, how she smelled. Ever.

Odell caught his thoughts, and he moved away as Marlin took the spot that Odell carefully identified. Until now, no single person could move Detective Lyle Odell's thoughts away from his intense focus on a case.

Marlin Santini could do just that. That fact amazed Odell and gave him some pause all at the same time.

Odell leaned into her and Marlin lifted the camera and held it up for Odell to see the screen and the view.

"Okay, here you go, Odell. Tell me when you see what you want."

Odell nodded, and he spoke in a low whisper, "Down a hairpin, Marlin. Just a smidge to the left and there. Can you adjust the zoom . . . you know, adjust the focal length?

"Odell, I don't know. It is a damn camera on my phone. I just point it at stuff and push the shutter button when I wanna take a picture of sumthin'."

Odell let out a chuckle at her honest and snarky response before replying, "Okay, gotcha. It is fine. Snap a few shots right there where you pointed. I will get Crump to do his magic with them."

Marlin pushed the shutter button; the camera on the phone made a few noises and captured the scene. After snapping a few shots, Marlin studied the shots, and she showed Odell. The good detective leaned into the pictures as Marlin scrolled through the shots, and Odell nodded to signify his satisfaction with them.

"Good, great, okay, perfect. Just what we needed," Odell growled as his eyes studied the shots. He then looked up, attempted to smooth his hair out, and then quickly gave up.

"Okay, let's roll back to Mohawk City, Marlin." Odell looked over at the tree, waved and shouted, "You guys can eat now!" Odell shouted at the crows as he tucked his arm into Marlin's arm and guided her back to the parking lot. They took two steps, and the crows flew off from their branches, landed on the path, and attacked the snacks. Odell watched for a second, and then he continued to walk back across the lawn area leading to the parking lot. Marlin was curious as to what Odell knew and where the direction of the case was now heading, but she did not want to interrupt Odell's thoughts. She now developed a sense of when he wanted to reveal information and when he did not want to do so. Yet Marlin knew that he wanted her to think on her own. To use her own thoughts on the case and to learn from Odell. It was as if Odell was now grooming her for something. A future mission, perhaps? A life together? Marlin was not exactly sure; it was just her intuition entering into the situation and feelings. While they walked, Marlin saw Odell begin his now familiar search routine of tapping various pockets and locations on his body, and Marlin jumped in to intercept his wandering.

"You sat on them. They are squished," Marlin said as she gently tapped him on his backside under his suit jacket. "They were in your right side back pocket."

Odell stopped walking. He shook his head and dug into the identified pocket and pulled out his pack of cigarettes.

"Damn. They are a mess. I blew that one. Could not recall where I stuffed 'em."

While Odell mumbled about his destroyed pack of cigarettes, Marlin reached in her leather bag and produced a pack, and within a few seconds, Odell leaned into the flame and took a drag of a cigarette before handing it off to Marlin to do the same.

"My coffee?" Odell asked.

Marlin thumbed in the truck's direction and answered, "Left it on the center console." Odell nodded and picked up the pace. "Odell, was this a worthwhile visit here? I mean, aside from last night, which was most definitely amazingly worthwhile . . .

I mean, you seem to have drawn some serious conclusions. Admittedly, I have some thoughts and understand if you don't want me to share them and you to share yours. Just give me a hint."

Odell waved for the cigarette and, after taking a puff on it, he answered with the words that Marlin was sure he would say even before he did so.

Odell said, "For now, let's hold our individual thoughts. I need Crump and the original photographer guy and . . . you, Marlin. Mostly you. We need to go to Mohawk City now, Marlin. Yes, this visit led us to the killer. I will comment on our love later. I am sure we have 'em now. Our work here, for now, is complete. For now, we have all of what we need. We will need to return here. Perhaps tomorrow, or at the very least, on Tuesday. When we do so, we will have the evil bastard cornered and ready to surrender to us. To justice. To give it all up. Hopefully."

Marlin was confused; she did not understand what it was that Odell referred to in his words, his guidance, and his direction. Yet, her faith in Lyle Odell was strong, and in response, she smiled back, nodded, and she continued to walk aside of him. The words arrived slowly, yet they arrived.

"Okay, let's go, Odell. I just have one more huge-ass question," Marlin asked as she extended her outstretched hand to Odell, who took it and when he did so, Marlin felt his warmth permeate her soul as he took her hand, "What the hell are you talkin' 'bout? What do you mean that you mostly need me?"

Odell turned Marlin around. His powerful arms pulled her as if she was a toy and he engulfed her body into his. He held the cigarette in one hand, but he still grabbed her with his free hand and spun her around and embraced her with his gentle but absolute power. Marlin let out an exhale of air in surprise at his reaction. She felt his hot breath on her neck as he buried his mouth in her throat. She felt his warmth, his heat, his sweat. Marlin knew that Odell felt the same. This day was just as hot, sticky, and nasty as was yesterday and all the days of the heatwave before this were. Marlin basked in his touch and grip.

After the hug, Odell leaned away and, with Marlin still in his arms, Odell asked, "Please, tell me. Push all your love aside. Are you ready to confront the evil, Marlin? We have him now. With our prodding and influence, he is about to make the last three mistakes. Unfortunately, you will be in his gun sights. We can divert and lure him. Together," Odell spoke the words, then Marlin pulled away and locked eyes with Detective Lyle Odell. A shiver went down Marlin's spine at the tone and the seriousness of Odell's words and his posture. Gone was the disarray, gone were the disorganization and the eccentric ways. Odell was focused and intense, and he was very serious.

"Odell . . . I am with you. Already . . . told you that."

"I will never let any harm come to you. I appreciate your bravery. Just know . . . I will never fail you. I will gladly die for you."

Marlin heard his words; and before she could ask him what he meant by that statement—she could not react quickly enough. She pulled Odell down to her level. With two hands, she gripped his face, reached up and ran her hands through his thick black hair, and then she stopped and smiled as she studied his gray eyes.

"I have no idea of who, or how, or why, or what you mean when you say that we have him cornered now, and he has me in his gun sights and such. If you say that we have this maniac, then I believe you. Time to lay it all on the line, Odell. I love you, Lyle Odell. I know that you will protect me. I will protect you, too. Let's go get this bastard."

Detective Lyle Odell reacted. He kissed Marlin. Long and deep and powerful.

She felt her toes curl inside her shoes.

Odell whispered between their passions, "Can you please call Grundy and ask him to contact Palmer and get what we need from the retired photographer? Please. Grundy will work with Crump on that mission."

Marlin nodded while studying his lips.

"I don't want to offend you, Marlin, but let's drive back to

Mohawk City in silence. Or in a state of relative silence. I need to think. A lot."

Marlin nodded, and she kissed him, long, deep, and powerful.

Odell felt his toes curl inside his shoes.

They reached the truck, finished the cigarette, and Odell snuffed it out and stuffed the spent butt in his suit jacket pocket. Marlin wondered what his dry cleaners thought of his environmentally conscious habit of disposing of cigarette butts in his jacket pockets rather than tossing them on the ground.

'Still,' Marlin thought, 'if you were Odell's dry cleaners, you were used to finding unusual things in his pockets.'

They both climbed into the truck. Marlin started the engine and Odell took a few sips of the coffee while the air-conditioner fought with captured heat.

"I know that you want to sit and think, and I will respect that because it is how you are. I thank you and love you for the honesty to convey that to me, but before you go silent, one thing is bugging me and I need to ask. I need to share in my own detective work. Please forgive me if I bounce around on subject matter. Just like another detective that I know and love. Why did you not simply access the internet to find out what you needed early this morning?" Marlin asked as she glanced over at Odell. Marlin answered her own question before Odell could respond, "Because your phone battery was deads-ville and you did not really know how to use it, anyway. And you would never use mine. I saw you when I headed off to the shower and walked by bare-ass naked. You hardly lifted your eyes to glance at me. That alone made me know you badly needed some answers. Even my naked body only captured a quick glance from Detective Lyle Odell. And now you know every inch of it, too. I heard the door close when I climbed into my shower and heard it open when I got out of the shower. I watched you study the matchbook when my lighter ran out of fluid the other day. At first, I thought you wanted to check out my boobies, but that came later in the day. Thank God for that. I was dying here in lust. Anyway, you made a hit on the matchbook and yes, that matchbook was one of five that I picked up from the dish on the counter at the corner liquor store. Just as you asked me to do. I think you did that on purpose. I mean, when I look back on all of this, everything seems so calculated that you do. You think out every word and action to the smallest degree. You asked me to grab matchbooks because something in your mind was already triggered and onto the suspect. I never clearly saw the matchbook you recovered at the crime scene, but once I knew that you were not studying my boobies, I knew that it had to be a clue that was more interesting. I put it together but said nothing then and waited until now. However, I now know your intent for me. Your mission. Your support and, hopefully, your love."

Odell smiled a little and said, "Not more interesting, Marlin. Just my detective eye is picking and choosing. Your breasts are beyond amazing. I think that I made up for it. Right?"

"You did. Fully redeemed. It was the power of our desire that overwhelmed us both. Indescribable. I am so sore, but so happy." Marlin took a deep breath and her eyes rolled a little back in her head and she recovered and returned to the mission at hand.

"Anyway, so how many Lucky Leo's liquor stores are there in the areas that you searched? Did the lobby have a telephone book? I heard you opening and closing the end table drawers, looking for telephone books. I figured you were looking for telephone books and not a Bible, since man-made religion does not exactly inspire you. As you found out, Odell, they don't use telephone books too much anymore. Yes, he has big muscles."

Odell smiled widely, and he nodded his head. "Wow, great detective work. Truly, I fall in love more and more with each passing minute. The front desk had telephone books. Four stores. Two in Albany, one in Guilderland, and one store over in Colonie."

Marlin smiled back and said, "I know that I am in love. I wish you had proclaimed that when we were sharing our love, Odell. However, I will take what I can take from you."

Odell studied Marlin when she spoke, but he did not comment or react. His lack of reaction did not bother Marlin in the least.

She knew that Odell displayed his love, rather than spoke of it. Marlin continued to smile; she nodded and stared off at the scene in the distance. The crows enjoyed their snack and now they all sat in the trees watching to see if Odell and Marlin returned with more treats.

Marlin turned and said, “Thank you for that, Odell. I know that you didn’t want to share too many thoughts of the state of your heart and of this case, but as far as the case goes, well, I feel the burn and the pain, too. I had to confirm my thoughts or my mind would wander and it would be a little disconcerting. The scene *is* bucolic. I have seen it before and you have too. You need Crump to turn my photos into black and white to confirm it. I will text the pictures to Crump right now and ask him to retouch them and zoom in on the scenes and such.”

“Thank you. Yes, please. Crump will get his hopes up that they are pictures of you.”

Marlin picked up her phone, worked the buttons and the keyboard and sent the pictures to Officer Crump, along with the explanations and requests. After sending the texts, Marlin pointed out the windshield, over at the bench, the pond and the bridge.

“Crump is out of luck. However, say the words,” Marlin jokingly raised her eyebrows and wiggled them several times, “and pictures of me, bare-ass naked, are yours, Odell.”

Odell laughed and waved in the air, and said, “I will keep that in mind. I'd rather have the real thing than pictures.”

“That works for me, Odell. So, Odell, how many stores does Lucky Leo operate in Westchester County?”

Odell blinked, yet he held his reaction at Marlin’s detective skills.

After a brief pause, Odell whispered, “Two. The hotel desk clerk helped me find those stores. Not the clerk from yesterday. It was a different clerk. A more cooperative clerk.”

“I am going to be the lure, right? That is what you were telling me?”

“Yes. Unless you say no. Until the killer met you, it was Cap

Moore. I mean, I think that he would be a primary target. I was going to alert him and protect him and his family, but now you are a more attractive target. He wants to pose you. I mean, your immense beauty sends him into a wackier state of mind than usual. You can lure him where we need. Moore cannot. Nevertheless, Marlin, you can just say no and get on the plane to Des Moines and ship Doodlesticks out to the farm and forget all this madness and bullshit. Just say no and it is over and done with forever. We will nail the bastard another way."

"Already told you what I will do. I am in. Odell, to you, I will never say no. Anything that you ask me is yours. I am in. All in. Willingly."

"You are a brilliant detective, Marlin. Beautiful mind, beautiful body, beautiful soul, beautiful woman—perfect. Inside and outside."

"If you say so, Odell, then I have to figure you examined the evidence and made a typical Detective Lyle Odell conclusion. Thank you."

Odell nodded and took a sip of his coffee. His eyes remained keenly locked on Marlin.

As Marlin worked the shift lever and she prepared to back the truck out of the space, Odell pulled his glance away from Marlin and now the detective looked out the passenger window at the scene passing by the window. The truck was leaving the parking lot and Odell knew that when they returned, it would be an entirely different scene and event. Anything but bucolic. An intense scene. Full of danger, full of anxiety, and unfortunately, it needed to be so to put an end to it all. Odell already worked out the parts and pieces of the plan. He would recruit Grundy and Crump, and of course, Marlin played the key role. Early this morning, while his lover slept peacefully in their bed in the hotel room, Odell worked out the final parts of the plan and anguished over if there was a better way to do this. There was not, and Odell knew that Marlin was now a primary target. Odell felt better with luring the killer into the open now rather than wait for an ambush by the madman.

Odell spoke to the scene outside the window and the glass as his mind wandered to the potential danger of it all.

He asked, "Are your mother and sister leaving for Des Moines today?

"They are. A one o'clock airplane flight out of Albany."

"Good. Marlin . . . remember . . . I did not use the word never. I choose my words carefully and I always use the word seldom."

Marlin understood exactly what he meant by referring to how often he carried his service weapon.

With a smile on her face, Marlin answered, "Sort of like how often you make love to a woman, Odell. Seldom, but thankfully for me and for us, not never."

She spoke the words, turned and coyly winked, but Odell never saw her attempt at humor and seduction. For now, he did not remove his gaze from the window. When he finally did so, Marlin watched out of the corner of her eyes as he deeply sunk into the passenger seat of the truck and his eyes glazed over as the phantoms returned to haunt him. He needed the quiet time, and Marlin left him to it. To his world. A sullen and tortured world in which Lyle Odell had allowed her to venture into for a brief time. Marlin Santini would never be the same now. Her love for this eccentric, quirky, but in her mind, entirely perfect and genius of a man overflowed. But she knew that in the world of Detective Lyle Odell, she probably was just a visitor rather than a permanent resident.

Marlin turned the pickup truck into the city traffic and the park and the crows and the bench and the bucolic scene was in the rear-view mirror.

Now, Marlin needed to search her heart and soul for acceptance of the fact that in Odell's world, things are different and opening his heart and soul was a rare and guarded event. Acceptance of her status would be elusive and fragile and as human emotions often are . . . painful.

"A professional consultant? A detective agency with a sniffing swine available for scent-tracking services. Okay. I think." Captain Connor Moore crossed his mighty arms and stared down at Detective Lyle Odell as Odell buried his face into a stack of papers.

"When did you open up this professional detective consulting business?" Captain Moore asked as he directed the question at Ms. Marlin Santini. Marlin sat in a chair next to the desk of Detective Lyle Odell in the open office area of the Mohawk City Police Headquarters building. Sergeant George Grundy sat nearby Marlin and Odell while remaining, perched on the edge of a desk with his mighty arms crossed in front of his chest in a display of determination. Officer Oliver Crump held a fat manila folder in his lap that he fiddled with while he sat in another chair close by the group. Crump rubbed the back of his neck with his hand so that he could tilt his eyes toward Marlin and, as he did so; his eyes did the foxtrot all over her face and body. Crump was beyond smitten with her, but he knew by the glow of her face that she was lost in the world of Homicide Detective Lyle Odell. He wondered how much they shared and a hint of jealousy rolled over him, as he knew that Odell most likely was a very lucky man.

They all sat and watched the scene unfold.

"The day before yesterday," Odell answered as he continued to study the papers in his hands. He flipped through the papers carefully, but with purpose and intent.

"I asked her, not you, Odell."

Odell answered without removing his eyes from the papers. "With all due respect, sir, to my chain of command, you shouldn't use pronouns so much in your conversations. Marlin is her name. Marlin."

Grundy snorted, Crump laughed aloud and Marlin smiled, but Captain Moore remained stoic.

"With all due respect, so noted Detective Odell. May I ask . . . Marlin, how much are your services?"

Marlin spoke and her voice was laced with sweetness and it had a light air to it, "Of course. Right now, nothing. Odell and I have not agreed to any price."

Odell dropped the stack of papers on his desk, leaned back into the chair, and said, "Marlin buys the coffee, the Irish whiskey and cigarettes. We have an agreement on mutual fuel intake. And some other stuff. We will figure the rest of it out later."

After speaking, Odell returned to his intense study of the papers.

Marlin smiled when she heard Odell's explanation and added, "He buys the pizza and gives me other . . . stuff."

"Okay, sounds like some type of fair-trade agreement that I rather not get into right now," Captain Moore said while reading between the lines of their conversation.

Odell was now very intently into the study of the papers. His eyes were a deep gray and the lines in his face were powerful and deep with his focus.

"Cap, might I ask, how is Officer McNally doin'?" Odell asked as he scanned the pages of the booklet.

"Not good. I granted him an indefinite leave of absence."

Odell shook his head and mumbled, "Damn. He will never return. Damn shame. We have to get this evil son-of-a-bitch. When is the funeral?"

"Monday."

Odell nodded and mumbled, "Damn. We will miss it. I hope we send an honor guard and pay our respects. That still tears me apart."

Captain Moore nodded and said, "We will. It is all arranged, Odell. Full burial honors."

Odell then directed his attention to a booklet in front of him. He flipped the pages of the booklet. He quickly scanned the contents, and then he flipped the papers to the next page. His eyes studied the page in front of him and he stopped flipping through the booklet. It seemed as if the good detective found the page that he was searching for with the booklet.

Detective Lyle Odell ran his fingers along the surface of the booklet and then he stopped and lifted his eyes and said, "Thank you for the representation of the department at the funeral, Captain Moore. It is beyond being a horrible tragedy. There are no words, except that we will nail this evil bastard. To bring you up to speed, as far as the details of the case go, we made significant progress. Wonderful progress," Odell finished speaking. He took a deep breath and then he looked up at Captain Moore and over to Grundy and Crump, and then finally to Marlin. The two lovers locked eyes in unison, and Odell lifted his finger and landed it forcibly on the page that remained open in front of him.

"Thump." His finger struck the name on a long list of names typed on the sheet. To emphasize his point, Odell lifted the booklet in the air while keeping his finger on the one name and he shook the booklet in the air. The staple precariously held onto the edge of the booklet of papers. It was about fifty papers bound together and Odell had the stack open about one-third of the way through them. He dropped the booklet back onto his desk. It was a listing of the names and the information and some small biographies of current, inactive, retired, and other status of military personnel that live in the area. In fact, those that live in New York, New Jersey, and Connecticut. Odell requested the records from the Veterans' Affairs and Defense Department. Odell looked down at the paper and then he looked up as Marlin slowly rose from her chair and she leaned in over the desk to study the papers, too.

"Here is our man. Here is the sick, deranged killer," Odell said as he swallowed hard, and his temples pounded in anger. Captain Moore rushed over to the desk and peered in at the name on the list where Odell's finger pointed. The captain was eager for details. Captain Moore forgot all about consultants, pronouns, charges and scent-tracking swine.

"Excellent work, Odell! You said you had a chance at nailing this maniac quickly before too many murders occurred. Are we ready to move in for an arrest? The media and my chain of command are all over me. The city is in fear."

Odell leaned back in his chair and he shook his head to show no. Captain Moore stood up straight and his face turned ashen, and he frowned at Odell's reaction. Odell looked over at Marlin and tapped at his suit jacket, and shrugged his shoulders. His partner, who was now his lover, knew what he needed. Marlin waved to show that his pack of cigarettes was hopelessly lost and she reached into her leather bag, produced a spare pack, shook the cigarette out and handed it off to Odell, who promptly stuck it on his lip.

"No smoking in here, Odell!" Captain Moore's frustration with his genius detective bubbled over. Before Odell could answer with his now familiar explanation, Crump, Grundy and Marlin all chimed in simultaneously,

"He ain't gonna light it. Just taste it!"

"Oh," Captain Moore mumbled as he slowly understood the eccentric ways and methods of Detective Lyle Odell.

With the now glued cigarette on his lower lip, Lyle Odell explained, "Nowhere near moving in on 'em yet. For an arrest or otherwise. We ain't got nothing concrete on this guy. The way this plan is shaking out, I think that he is going to have to confess on his own or make his last move and do something stupid. For a change. He only has to make three more mistakes and we can nail 'em."

Moore folded his arms across his chest once again and his disappointment was clear, but he was ready to listen with some patience while Odell explained, "I need his complete military records now. I need a full background check. Now. On Daniel Wadsworth Clark. This information is very basic."

Grundy jumped up. He recognized the name.

Odell watched his drinking buddy's reaction; he explained and expanded on the information on the paper, "Navy Corpsman, Petty Officer. First class. Served in combat, First Gulf War. Honorable discharge, wounded in action, Purple Heart, decorated with some other medals." Odell looked over at George Grundy and said, "Liquor store, Danny, George. He is the serial killer."

Grundy's eyes opened wide. He put his hand on Odell's shoulder; because he recognized the name. Sergeant Grundy could not hide his wonderment at the statement and it was obvious that the identity of the notorious serial killer visibly stunned Sergeant George Grundy.

"Liquor store Danny?" Captain Moore repeated the name in a haze of puzzlement that a liquor store clerk was the enraged and brilliant serial killer that terrorized two cities and a county and eluded capture for years.

"Yes, correct Cap. Danny is a store clerk at the liquor store down the street from where I live. The store is on the corner of Fourteenth Street and Broadway. Lucky Leo's liquor store. The Mohawk City store."

Grundy growled in amazement, "Geez, Odell. Damn. Danny? A clerk in the corner liquor store is a notorious and calculating serial killer? A killer that no one could even find any clues on until now cuz he is so smart? In an evil sort of way. I mean, okay, you are Odell and you are never wrong, but liquor store Danny? He seems like a straight-up kinda guy. Are you sure?"

"I am sure, and, we are sure."

Odell looked over at Marlin to hint at a verification of their collaboration.

Marlin nodded her head and added, "We are sure."

George stared at Marlin, but he did not comment on her statement and the bond and partnership formed between Marlin and Lyle Odell.

"But you just said that you have nuthin' on 'em?" Sergeant Grundy asked.

"That is correct, Sarge. Correct. That is exactly what I said," Odell answered matter-of-factually.

"What about a search warrant for his home? Maybe find the murder weapon, the sneakers, find the vehicle with the torn bumper sticker, some clothing with d-n-a, or the knife?" Sergeant Grundy asked.

"Nope. No good, George. Even if we received approval for a search warrant, we will find nothing. There is nothing concrete to show the attorney general's office or the district attorney's office or a judge to get it. Too circumstantial at this point. They will laugh Cap Moore out of their offices. Ah, say there, Crump," Odell turned to Officer Oliver Crump and asked, "I have not seen too many of your reports or the autopsy report on the young woman, but let me guess. Same caliber of bullets, different guns fired the shots. Same type of knife, but a slightly different knife from the previous cuts in the previous murder."

Crump nodded and said, "Correct, Lyle."

"And you spoke with Mr. Travers and obtained his testimony again and confirmed our points of the investigation. Where he walked, how he walked, the fertilizer and such?"

"I did, Odell and, of course, *your* points were spot on and exact. All confirmed by Mr. Travers," Officer Oliver Crump explained.

"Thank you, Crump. Your assistance and skills are invaluable."

Odell turned back to his desk and the paper with the name and he stared in at the listing while speaking his thoughts aloud to his companions, "He ditches everything and anything associated with his hideous crimes after each murder. It is always the same pattern. He earns some decent dough and can afford to buy weapons. Super-evil and super smart. All that clothing is gone too. Most likely burned in a steel barrel. Military man, used to being in the field in combat. Stuff gets burned. You know how it goes. Burn everything, including human waste and such. You military guys 'member the training we all had. Now, I would love to find that barrel. Anyway, one-step at a time. The guy most likely has two residences. We need to focus. Maybe an apartment or a house here in the city and a hunting camp with a cabin out somewhere in the rural parts. We have the vague but not exact description of the car, from the old insomniac, porch dwelling man, but many cars have that same 'Go Navy' bumper sticker. Unfortunately, no license plate information. It is what it is. Finding the car really does us nothing to tie the killer or the vehicle directly to the murder. So, what if he drove down the street at that time? Means nothing. We have the chemical residue on his sneakers, which by the way . . . thanks to the overzealous media hounds . . . those sneakers are long since gone now too. The chemical residue will be in his car, on the pedals and on the floor of his house, and where he works, but hell . . . he can just fertilize his own lawn and have the same stuff. He is so smart that he has already done that to cover his tracks. He watched the news too and put the pieces together. Perfect lawn in the hiss of summer, Crump and his boys pouring over the lawn. The killer knew what was up. It was all over the news."

Officer Oliver Crump was taking copious notes on a pad as Odell spoke. Crump was used to working with Odell and he knew that there were many leads and items that Odell required Crump and his team to follow up on now.

Captain Moore cleared his throat and said, "Okay, Odell, I read Crump's reports and the autopsy reports on both victims, and I just heard you ramble on with supposition and such . . . so other than nothing and hearsay, what do your consultant and you have on this guy to make you land your finger upon his name? A clerk in a local liquor store is an enraged serial killer. I echo Sergeant Grundy's words and share his surprise. I am beyond perplexed now."

Moore leaned in and looked at the paper, and Odell spun the paper around and pointed at the name so that Captain Moore could read it.

While trying to focus on the name and information, Captain Moore asked, "What is this guy's full name again? A liquor store clerk that George and you know from, I suppose, from frequenting his store."

"Daniel Wadsworth Clark," Odell answered and then explained, "What do we have? Just some words, some actions, and our gut instincts, along with aforementioned circumstantial evidence. Oh yes, we have a photograph and a match for the matchbook. Marlin visited the store for a restock run for booze, beer and smokes. She met Danny, and I asked her to pick up matches for us. One of them is the same kind of matchbook as we found in the ivy bed at the homicide scene for the murder of the young woman. We also confirmed that Danny's uncle, Leo Clark, also known as Lucky Leo, owns this chain of liquor stores, has stores in Albany, in the Capital area, stores in Westchester and Danny spent time there working in those stores. He only recently returned to this store here in Mohawk City. It all fits. The time frames in different areas fit, too."

Moore jumped, and he almost smiled upon hearing the news of some hard evidence instead of Odell's ongoing ramble of his thoughts aloud. Marlin stood up straighter, and she studied Captain Moore's reaction.

"A photograph and a matchbook. Well, now that does not sound like supposition or having nothing to go on, Odell!" Captain Moore shouted in excitement and anticipation at the prospect of an incriminating photograph. Hard evidence.

"Yes, we have a photograph, but relax Cap, it ain't that exciting. Not yet, at least. I need to explain a little. And the matchbook, as Crump noted, is the same kind of matchbook found all over town. Ain't nuthin' special. His car blends. Just a typical Japanese imported sedan. It blends well. Even with the remnants of the Go Navy sticker on its ass. He tried to peel the sticker off and thought that he had done so and that no one would recognize it. That was mistake number four because it allowed me to confirm his identity in my mind."

Once again, Detective Lyle Odell's perplexing mannerisms confounded Captain Moore. He was not used to Odell and his vague testimonies and his incessant wanderings. Captain Tucker prepared Moore for an uneven ride when dealing with Detective Odell, but not this uneven. Captain Moore took a deep breath and decided the best plan and approach right now was to stand by and allow the testimony to unfold before jumping in and questioning Odell. And before getting his hopes up too! Grundy understood how Odell operated, as did Officer Crump, and especially, Marlin Santini understood that this was how Odell worked through cases as he closed the loopholes in his mind. However, Captain Moore wanted facts, and he wanted an arrest.

He would have to wait and he folded his arms across his chest and sighed as he mumbled, "Oh. I see. I think. More vague facts."

Odell ran his hand through his hair and plucked the cigarette out of his mouth, and dropped it on the desk. He smacked his lips to taste the remnants of the cigarette.

Odell turned to Oliver Crump and asked, "Officer Crump, we need you to arrange to meet with Marlin with the matchbook and see if Doodlesticks can match any scents from it to some other items we have that Danny handled. Some store items, bags, liquor bottles, cash register receipts and such. We need you to shoot some photos of Danny leaving the store, and of his home and his vehicles and stuff like that. Find that hunting and fishing cabin. I think it is in, on, or near Piseco Lake. Check real estate records. No tails for now. Not yet. Too risky. Gotta be super covert. A shot of that car with the remnants of the bumper sticker would be awesome, but chances are that is parked at the cabin now. I bet he drives all the same models of cars, with the same color and the same years, same type. We can run vehicle registrations under his name now to confirm. Can you supervise the photographer? No slips-ups, Oliver, or we spook him down again for a few days. Do you have the photos that Marlin sent? Did you get the photos from the Albany police photographer?"

"Okay, yeah, just let me know the plan and what you need and we will line it up. I gotcha on the supervision. I will be involved. Here are the enhanced photographs. Some from the original Albany crime scene photographer and the ones that Marlin took on her cellphone," Officer Crump said while he handed the manila folder that he held to Odell. Odell thanked Crump. He eagerly spread the folder out on the desk, and then he looked up at Marlin and pleaded for direction with his eyes. His intensity and eagerness did not allow him to have enough time to search his pockets.

Marlin met Odell's eyes and instantly pointed at his suit jacket and said, "Right side suit jacket pocket."

Odell nodded, mumbled a "Thank you," as he dug into the

pocket and produced his magnifying lens. Odell was on fire and he jumped into the fray with a fervor and intensity that Marlin had not seen before this. Well, she had seen him in an intense mood and actions, but that was under completely different circumstances. After unfolding the lens, Odell eagerly flipped through the pictures until he found the picture of the park bench. Odell peered in over the lens and once more, he focused in on that same slat on the back portion of the park bench.

Odell mumbled, "Crump, so how much is this photo magnified?"

"About twenty power or so. Our photography guy spoke with the Albany photographer and got the settings and specifications on the original photos. We did our best to duplicate them in the lab and on the computer enhancements. As far as the initials go, yes, I saw it too. Now that I know the killer's full name, yes, you are correct. The initials d-w-c are carved in the wood there. They are painted over a few times with a glossy oil paint, but they are still readable. Can I ask how in the hell you saw that, Odell?"

Odell smiled as his lens focused in on the spot, and then he stopped his examination when he heard Officer Oliver Crump's question. Odell flipped to the next picture. His eyes scanned the contents, and then he moved onto the next photograph in the file. "It is my job, Crump. I saw it because it is my job. And because this is mistake number four point five. It matches a wood carving hanging up over the counter at Lucky Leo's liquor store. And this is mistake point five." Odell held up a picture to Marlin and asked, "Lookie here, Marlin. Familiar?"

Marlin studied the photograph and recognized it as the photo of the bench and the bridge and the pond and such. It was the photograph that Marlin took earlier today under the careful guidance of Lyle Odell. However, this particular version was in black and white.

"Very," Marlin said as she studied the photograph. "Its companion hangs over the cash register area at Lucky Leo's liquor store on the corner where Odell lives."

Odell nodded his head and said, "Bingo. Yupper. Mistake four point five plus point five equals five mistakes. Two to go."

Captain Moore cleared his throat and after studying the photograph, listening to the testimony and ideas bounce back and forth, the captain finally sought clarification of what it was that Odell and Marlin were talking about and thinking.

"This photograph is of a park scene and a bench and a pond with a bridge in the background. Marlin and you both saw the same scene captured in a photograph hanging up in the liquor store. The store where Danny Wadsworth Clark works. I surmise that this is a scene from the park in Albany, which I know was the scene of the first murder by the killer. This Danny guy was there and killed the old veteran and carved his initials into the bench and took a few photographs. Or so you think it is this Danny guy. This Danny guy is a photographer. Because he works in a liquor store, he is a hobbyist photographer or an amateur photographer."

Odell looked up, and he blinked a few times as if he was counting the questions from the captain. Odell then grabbed the cigarette from the desktop and stuck it back on his lip.

While the cigarette danced upon his lower lip and his hair stuck out in many directions, Odell answered, "Correct, correct, correct, correct and correct, correct and correct and correct and correct, we know Clark is the serial killer and correct and correct."

Captain Moore shook his head; he pulled out a nearby chair and flopped down in the chair. While the group studied their commanding officer, Captain Moore let out with a deep sigh and after a long exhale; Captain Moore seemed to gather his thoughts.

"Strangely, Odell, this is making sense to me. Just the fact that you could actually count the times that I was correct and accurately repeat it back to me is remarkable. Please go ahead and explain the rest and I will sit and wait until you finish and you tell me what you need from me and what the plan is."

Marlin smiled widely, Grundy snorted out a laugh again, and Crump stood up and wandered over to the desk and stood near

Marlin.

Odell removed the cigarette from his mouth and this time, he tossed it into the trashcan next to his desk before saying, "Good. I know it is a complex case, and I did my best to clarify my explanation. I am glad you could all follow along. Lookie here, we have little time. His next victim has flip-flopped and his focus has changed since he knows he had potentially made a few mistakes in the last murder. He changed targets."

"I have one enormous question, Lyle. Why? I mean he is a vet, like you, Cap here, Crump, and me," Sergeant Grundy looked over at Marlin and waved his hand and shrugged his shoulders for her input and he waited for a response.

"Not me. My father. Army Ranger. K-i-a in the Middle East."

Grundy nodded, wrung his hands together a little and shook his head, "Oh, oh, I sense a connection. Anyway, I am so sorry. Thank you for his service and commitment. That sucks, Marlin. I bet you were young."

"I was, but have vivid and happy memories of him. Part of me is here because of him, part of me is here because it is what he would want me to do, and a part of me is here because of who and what he made me. Fearless and to always fight for justice."

Suddenly, all the men in the room, besides Detective Lyle Odell, saw all the beauty of Marlin Santini. A great deal was on the outside, but even more was on her inside.

Odell swallowed hard and answered, George Grundy, "As to why? I don't really know. He is one of us. A combat veteran. Saw some stuff. Made him crazy because of it. PTSD, I presume. The military made him a monster. Sometimes, it does that, you know. Yupper, it does that. On the other hand, maybe he hates me, he hates you, George, or he hates the entire world. Who really knows, George? We are vets too. Combat vets."

George Grundy nodded. He walked back to his chair and sat in it, and waited for Odell to continue. It seemed as if his potential role in triggering a madman disturbed the grizzled old sergeant.

"We need to dive into the military records. Find out exactly what happened to Danny Clark to trigger his madness. I dunno.

Let's get on with it. One of his cars needs to have the remnants of the Go Navy sticker on it, and be a small compact. A Japanese import. Run photos of the types of cars that match the killer's registration records by the insomnia-ridden neighbor. We need to move fast now. Unless we intercept him, the next victim is tomorrow, or at the very least, the next day. There is no time for fiddling around now. We need our plan in the works or a victim will die that does not need to die. He needs blood, and he needs his plan to unfold. We spooked him for a time, now—we need to nail his ass."

Captain Moore was captivated now. However, his detective and his skills and his brilliant mind jumping from angle-to-angle of this case were confounding, and Captain Moore tried to backtrack and follow the testimony of Lyle Odell.

After rubbing his chin, Captain Moore leaned in and asked, "You said he changed targets. How do you know this? Then, to make me more confused, if that is even possible, you said that his focus has changed?"

Odell needed to taste a cigarette, and this time; Marlin was ahead of him as she watched the beginning of his routine and had a cigarette in his hand before he went too deep into the hunt and the usual pattern of confusion.

Odell mumbled, "Thanks" and looked at Captain Moore as he said, "Yes, until he met Marlin Santini this past Sunday, the next victim was . . . you . . . Cap. If not you, then one of your family members. If he can't kill the vet directly . . . he kills a family member. I hate to tell you this, Cap, but your takin' over for Cap Tucker must have triggered his killin' urges again. It brought up the memories and the thrill of it. He read your bio in the newspaper and off he went. Sorry."

Captain Moore's face went ashen and even though he sat in a chair, he steadied his body by gripping the edge of the desk next to where he sat. "Damn. Me? My family, Odell?"

"Yupper, sorry Cap. A high-profile kill would get him all excited and hot and bothered. Now he has Marlin. He loves her beauty, and he loves the thrill of her. He loves everything about her, knows her name, where she lives, and now, I remain positive that he knows that her father is a vet and is a k-i-a."

Odell displayed his ability to read a killer's mind. He was part psychologist and part detective now. Entering supposition into cases and the minds of murderers was a huge part of his success. Deep in his mind, Odell prayed that he was correct on this one.

While the now familiar cigarette hung onto Odell's lower lip, Odell swallowed as he showed some rare emotion and added, "He can kill her, carve her and then . . . pose her glorious body as if she is in one of his photographs. The young woman, Miss Allison McNally, was beautiful, and now, he found another perfect victim that is even more gorgeous. This guy is on the edge of his seat, planning, hoping, and he skipped his pattern, so he is even more on edge to kill. For some reason, photography and scenes and posing victims are part of his motivation. He must have posed victims somewhere in combat. That is what we need to dig into and discover. Maybe he did combat photography along with the medical work. We have to find out what set him off on this madness."

Odell looked at Marlin to check on her reaction as Grundy looked over at Crump, who shook his head in discomfort at the details of Odell's assessment and predictions. Although Odell jumped all over in his thoughts and details, everyone in the room knew he was correct. They had no doubts whatsoever about the skills of Detective Lyle Odell.

Grundy cleared his throat and asked, "How do you know Cap and his family were targets? I mean, there are many vets in the area. Not sure how many are combat vets, but there are many. Right? "

"Yupper, there are many, George, and that goes back to what Danny said to me the other day that turned my ears up a little toward him. He asked about Cap. He was deeply interested in my new boss. He also brought up Derek Cramer. He harped on Cap Moore and mentioned how he was my new boss and a war hero. He told me that Captain Moor looked stiff. All hidden innuendos in his small talk. Unfortunately, my frequenting the local liquor store with a store clerk, who is a deranged serial killer, also fed his rage. He took me on as the ultimate challenge. In fact, he took us all on."

George sat back in his chair and asked, "Geez, Odell. Wacky stuff. I get the small talk about Cap and that he is focused on local war heroes. But Cramer?"

Grundy was a New York Clippers fan, too.

"Yupper, he said that even Cramer struck out. Indirectly, the bastard taunted me, knowing my fondness for baseball and for Cramer. Implying that I would not catch him or solve the case. He also noticed how I rarely carry my service weapon. He used the word never. I use the word seldom. Might have been mistakes, but I am not counting them as some of his mistakes. Too broad. Could be honest small talk. Still listing the mistakes at five. However, mistake number one was his eyeglasses. He wears the phony eyeglasses around me only. They are a prop. Danny made small talk about how his eyesight was weak now that he was older. Yet, I caught him reading without them and that initially turned me into something going on with Danny Clark. Most likely to make me think that he has weak eyesight and could never be the killer because in my studies of the case, the killer has fabulous eyesight both in his eye for details in photography and art, but also in his marksmanship and killing methods. It is just another ploy in his deception book. Just to confirm, George, have you ever seen Danny wearing eyeglasses? You go in the store almost as much as I do." Odell asked Grundy as he turned and waited for an answer.

Sergeant George Grundy pondered the question and rubbed at his forehead while he thought about it.

After some thought, George answered Odell, "I don't think he ever wore glasses. Not that I can recall. I am not half as observant as you are, Odell. But, no. No glasses and I don't go in there . . . as much as you do." George paused as Odell studied his face and then he confessed, "Well, maybe I do. Most of the time, it is beer for us when I come over to listen to the Clippers or the hockey games on that ancient radio of yours or watch 'em on that old television."

Odell waved his hand in the air and displayed some enthusiasm when he heard George Grundy's testimony.

Odell turned to Marlin.

"I agree. Danny never wore eyeglasses when I went to the store."

Odell said, "Bingo. Thank you, George and Marlin, for the confirmation. Now, here is the mistake summary to date. One is the phony eyeglasses. Two is the dropping of the matchbook by leaping over the railing and taking that backyard rear escape route. Three was parking the car in the factory lot and allowing the neighbor to spot it. Four was the bumper sticker and five was the carved initial on the park bench along with the bucolic photograph. The sixth mistake will be a confirmation of his intention of committing another murder and the selection of his chosen victim and revealing both of those to us. Seven will result in his demise. Thank you."

Captain Moore stood up; he mumbled, "Amazing. Odell, you are amazing."

Captain Moore then adjusted his necktie and paced the floor in front of the group, with his hands deeply buried in his suit jacket pockets. After pacing, Captain Moore stopped and faced Lyle Odell and spoke with a hint of apprehension in his voice. Captain Moore was a very smart man. Captain Tucker picked a worthy successor, and Lyle Odell knew this. Odell leaned back. He grabbed the end of the cigarette perched in his mouth and rolled it inside his lips, and waited for the captain's thoughts.

"Odell, lemme guess. Marlin is the victim involved in the sixth mistake. Marlin is going to lure Danny Clark into the open and force some brutal action, a confession or a confrontation, because we have no other angle to nab him."

Odell listened carefully to his commanding officer's words. After pondering the words, Odell remained motionless. Marlin wiggled a little on the chair, and Officer Oliver Crump held his breath and Sergeant George Grundy swallowed.

Odell finally answered, "Yes. His lust for Marlin's beauty and selecting Marlin as his next victim will be his sixth mistake."

Captain Moore placed his hands on the front of Lyle Odell's desk, leaned in, and forcibly said, "No. I cannot allow a civilian to be put in that type of danger!"

"Technically, I am not a civilian, Captain Moore. I am a professional detective. Remember. New business and all. I have to do this. My father would not back down and neither will I. I carry a mean-ass handgun and I can shoot the eyes outta shit from one-hundred yards. I do not miss. I am not afraid," Marlin Santini stood up, and she folded her arms across her chest. Her breasts bulged out of the top of her blouse and she sent shivers down the walls of the police headquarters building and down the spines of every man within twenty miles of the same.

Marlin pushed her eyeglasses up her nose a little and she blinked underneath them.

Her voice was strong and forceful and reflected her confidence.

"It's the only way. Danny Clark is a calculating nut job, but he is brilliantly smart. Without me, he will not make any other mistakes. I can lure him into his ultimate mistake because I have what he wants."

Oliver Crump mumbled, "What every man wants," and Captain Moore lifted an eyebrow in Crump's direction as to signal a gentle warning to contain his admiration of the stunning Ms. Marlin Santini.

"I will not allow any harm to come Marlin's way, Cap. I assure you, all of you, that I would die first," Odell said. As he now stood up from his desk, he closed the booklet on his desk and tapped the top of the booklet with his fingers. He took the cigarette out of his mouth and gently placed it on his desk next to the booklet. "Yeah, Cap, I know that bringing Marlin into this is unorthodox and breaks all kinds of rules and shit like that and puts you in a rough spot. My apologies for that. Until now, no one can nail this bastard. So, you gotta think outta of the ordinary on how to do it. To win where others failed and to stop a lunatic. A lunatic that is targeting you and your family and a bunch of other fellow vets, fellow humans. Fellow police officers. Grundy will be there. Crump too. They will never let me down. Never have and never will. These guys and this gal here are the best there is. I stake my life on all of 'em. We will all be there. Together. Locked and loaded. Me too. I always use the word seldom, but I never use the word never when it comes to carrying a service weapon."

Captain Moore shook his head, scanned Lyle Odell, and asked, "Do you have your weapon on you now, Odell?"

"No, sir."

"Are you even wearing your police detective badge?"

"Not now, no, sir. It is somewhere here," Odell tapped various pockets while Marlin shook her head to show that it was not on his person.

"It is in your bag, Odell. In my truck," Marlin explained.

"Odell, you are an unadulterated mess. You drink too much. You are a hundred million times worse than what Captain Tucker told me. Now, under all of this stress and madness, you are putting me in a terrible spot only a few weeks into the job. I know why Captain Tucker retired and plays the violin now."

"Cap, I understand. I do have flaws. Major flaws. I assure you that right now, I am not drunk. That is the truth. Let me explain. A little. We will have a sniper or two in the trees. A team. We are going to lure him to Melrose Park in Albany. It is a careful plan. I have it worked out in my mind. I will need you to plow the road with Albany and, in particular, Detective Palmer. He is a slimy-crumb. I don't know the Westchester boys, but in Albany, I can easily see how Clark evaded capture. There, in the park, the witnesses will identify Clark and we nab his ass."

Upon hearing Odell mention witnesses, Grundy jumped up, followed by Crump, and Captain Moore's head spun around at the potential of the development of the presence of witnesses.

"Witnesses! You never mentioned witnesses, Odell!"

Odell threw his hands up in defense and quickly added, "Easy now. Let me explain. They are not human witnesses. Doodlesticks and a murder of crows that live in the park will identify Clark and he will confess. Well, sort of confess in uncertain terms and manners. Thinking that there were never any witnesses to his many crimes will be another mistake. We will see where we are with the mistake counts at that point, but I think that will be his final mistake."

Captain Moore threw his hands into the air in a demonstration of his frustration, and then he rubbed his face with his hands. He looked around for the chair, and after locating it, he gladly sunk into it.

"Doodlesticks is the sniffing pig and you have a bunch of crows that live in the park as the other witnesses?"

"Correct," Odell immediately answered.

Officer Oliver Crump cleared his throat, lifted a finger in the air, and said, "Sir, might I add a brief word of advice? When and if you meet Doodlesticks in person, please, don't call him a pig. He gets upset and bumps the hell outta your leg. Doodlesticks is kinda big and strong. It hurts when he bumps you."

Captain Moore stared for a long time at Officer Crump and then slowly nodded his head and said, "So noted, Officer Crump. Thank you for that. I think." Captain Moore sighed once again and then looked at his detective and said, "Odell, I will plow the road with the Albany Police Department for you. Also, with my chain of command here in Mohawk City. God help me. Please let me know what the plan is. Maybe I need to have a few shots of your beloved Irish whiskey before I go in and explain this to the chief. I usually steer away from whiskey. Except at Christmas and . . . right now. But what the hell else can I do now? On the other hand, I can always take violin lessons with Tucker and enjoy retirement. Maybe work in the diner pouring coffee for side money when they revoke my pension."

Odell, mussed with his hair, reached for the cigarette and stuck it on his lip.

It bobbed up and down as he spoke, "Can't take violin lessons, Cap. At least, not with Cap Tucker. You can't. Maybe on your own. Tucker is learnin' guitar. He has a crush on his instructor. I hear that she is really pretty. As a point of information, technically, it is called a murder. A group of crows are called a murder, not a bunch'a crows. A murder of crows. Ironic, right? Did you know that in England, a bloodhound's testimony in court can convict a criminal?"

Captain Moore sighed again. He sighed more in this past hour or so than he had in the last five years combined.

Captain Moore said, "No, I did not know that Odell. How about a . . . pi . . . a . . . a . . . Doodlesticks?"

"Nah. Not here or in England. Not yet, at least. Maybe after this case, it will receive some consideration. Thank you for the green light, Cap. We will nail 'em. Geez, I am dying here for this smoke. I need to smoke this. Anyone wanna join me outside?"

Marlin stood up; Crump waved to bum a smoke from her.

As Marlin handed Crump a cigarette, Officer Crump said, "Hey, Marlin, maybe after all this is over, we could go out on a date? A few drinks, maybe a movie or catching a local music act?"

"Sorry, Crump. I do not date. Besides, even if I did, you are not my type of guy."

"Can I ask what your type is?"

"Eccentric."

"I am eccentric," Officer Crump replied.

"No, you are not. You are normal."

Crump's face sank in disappointment as Marlin turned and offered George Grundy a cigarette.

"Cigarette, Sarge?"

Grundy mumbled, "Hell, yeah. Are we gonna eat soon? I am kind of hungry."

No one answered Grundy as he looked around at everyone, rubbed his stomach, tugged at his gun belt and shrugged his shoulders at the lack of a reply.

Captain Moore surprised everyone by saying, "Yeah, let's go. Marlin, can I bum a smoke too?"

"Sure, Cap. Here you go," Marlin said as she passed out the cigarettes.

"I did not know that you smoked, Cap?" Grundy asked.

"I just decided to begin right now. I hope that it is my only stupid decision that I make today."

Odell led the way, and he suddenly stopped short in his tracks and closed his eyes while everyone studied him. He opened his eyes and rubbed his head and then gave up when he realized that his hair was a mess.

"Damn, I need a haircut. I will get one the day after the day after tomorrow. After we nail Danny Clark. By-the-way, one-thousand-eight-hundred and forty."

Of course, no one knew what Odell meant.

"What is that, Odell? Forty what?" Crump asked.

"That is how many times that Derek Cramer struck out. I might add that those strikeouts were in eleven thousand-one-hundred and ninety-five at bats. Both numbers kinda stuck in my head. For some reason. I am not sure why they stuck in my mind. But . . . they did."

Odell began to walk toward the rear door to exit outside when Marlin gently grabbed him by his shoulder and turned her lover around until their eyes met.

"How many times have you struck out, Odell? How many cases did you not solve in your career?"

Odell smiled. He deeply studied her face for a very long time, and everyone in the room knew that they were deeply in love. It was obvious. Plainly.

Odell finally said, "None. Never struck out. Nowhere near as many cases as Cramer had at bats, but I never struck out. Don't intend to now, Marlin."

Marlin tapped Odell on his backside much in the same manner as a baseball manager would do to his star slugger and said playfully, "Then go and get your ass the hell in the batter's box and hit one into the upper deck."

"That is my intention, Marlin. I gotcha, baby. Oh yes, Cap. Slade. You wanna go with Slade. Very smooth. It is a damn fine Irish whiskey. It is a nice beginning to dabble in the world of Irish with. You might begin there and end there too. It is that good. Not pricey either. Kinda not known as one of the big boy players in the Irish circles, but it is fine. Not too harsh, and even if you get heavy with it and make love to it all night long, this whiskey will leave your head in fair shape for the next mornin'."

Captain Moore smiled as he realized that he was slowly beginning to understand Homicide Detective Lyle Odell and his eccentric ways. Thoughts popped out of his head from previous conversations and later on, when the rest of the business cleared from his mind, the words arrived. Odell did not miss a single thing. Conversations, questions, words and actions all went into a vast filing system in his complex mind for retrieval at any time.

"Gotcha, Odell. I will pick up a bottle. Or two, or even three. I have to tell you, though, that I will not buy 'em at Lucky Leo's liquor store. Anyway, in the meantime, let's go outside and smoke our brains out and nail down this plan."

"Sounds good, Cap," Odell said as he ran his hand over his head in a futile effort to smooth out his hair. His suit was a wrinkled mess from the long day that began in the early morning hours back in the hotel and the park in Albany. Odell's hair stuck out in many directions at once. His necktie was askew, the knot barely hung together, and his walk was slow and thoughtful as they made their way outside the building.

Odell spoke in a disturbed mumble as he walked, "It has been a long day already and we will need to continue working on the plan past the dinner hours and a little into the night gang. Buckle up and settle in. We need to go over the plan. I have the parts and pieces in my head, as if it is a musical composition. Now we need to put it all together and play the piece."

"I sure hope that we can at least order a pizza," Grundy mumbled after hearing Odell's testimony.

Odell stopped walking and turned to the rest of the team and he blinked a few times and with the now customary cigarette stuck on his lower lip, Odell added, "Nothing can be unplanned or out of place or unthought-of." Odell's eyes went over to Marlin. He took a deep breath before pushing open the exit door leading to the rear parking lot of the facility and as he did so Odell said, "Too many people are countin' on us. Let's not forget McNally and all the rest of the families too. Far too many lives are at stake, and I gotta say that all that is rare and precious to me in this weary-ass world hangs in the balance."

It was nearly eleven o'clock in the evening. Odell did not even have a clock on the wall in his house. You needed a wristwatch or to check your cellphone screen to determine the time. They did not finish working on the plan at police headquarters until almost nine o'clock. Upon returning to Odell's humble abode, Marlin and Odell had shared another pizza from Frank's West. Matty delivered it, and Odell gave him a five-dollar tip. They washed it down with ice-cold brews, and afterwards, Odell retreated to his chair, his smokes, his Irish, and his old radio.

Marlin Santini stood over Lyle Odell as the good detective lay sprawled across his easy chair. The ashtray upon the end table had the usual ground-out-half-smoked-cigarettes, the whiskey glass sat empty and the old radio joyfully played classical music.

Through the old brown and worn grille cloth.

She stood in front of him and she smiled her usual knockout smile. She knew that even with his eyes closed that he could see her smile. Never had she met such a man. A man that controlled her every move, he captured her soul and her senses. He looked so peaceful, his dark hair flopped in front of his eyes, still wet from a shower, much-too-much Irish whiskey floated through his veins and she knew better than to think that his mind was not whirling with thousands of assorted thoughts. Yes, indeed, Marlin knew so much better. If ever there was a person who walked this world that a person should not judge on their outward appearance, it was the man in front of her. Marlin recalled how he said that he was going to trim his hair the day after the day after tomorrow. His words. When the case was history. He was so calculating. She would miss his longish hair and the sexy manner that it flopped in front of his face.

In her heart, Marlin knew that she would miss him too.

Was he as good-looking as a Hollywood movie star was? Did his looks cause a woman to stop in her tracks and admire him as he walked by her? No, but Marlin Santini was not an ordinary woman, and Lyle Odell was anything but ordinary. For Marlin, Odell filled her soul and overflowed her heart with love. She knew the power, the passion and lust that lay deep in Odell's soul. Odell consumed her now. She was a witness to his power; she experienced it, and she knew that she could never love another man how she loved Lyle Odell. All his flaws only made him more attractive and added to his brilliance in her heart and in her eyes. There he lay. His mind captive with thoughts of the phantoms that continually haunted him, of criminals plotting their next evil plan, of Danny Clark, of the mission that loomed tomorrow and the day after, and above all, she hoped that somewhere in the deep dark recesses of his complex mind that a beautiful woman named, Marlin Santini had a small nook reserved in a corner of the enclave of his mind.

"I know that despite your outward appearance that you are not sleeping, Odell. Your handsome ass is not fooling me. Not one bit. You are not doing this to me. Not now. Not tonight. Not with what will lie ahead of us tomorrow and the day after that. You'll open your eyes, you will tell the name of the musical piece currently playing on the radio, the composer, the artist and then I will take you by the hand and we will go upstairs and make love all night long."

Odell's eyes opened wide.

He smiled.

"Hoedown, Aaron Copland is the composer. Perhaps, at least, in my opinion, the greatest American composer of classical music. Ever. It is slightly difficult for me to determine, but it sounds like the Philadelphia Orchestra. Did you know that Copland was born in Brooklyn, New York? He studied abroad in Europe."

Marlin held her hand out and said, "That's nice, Odell. No, I did not know that until now, and honestly, I don't really care. C'mon upstairs and make love to me. Every which way but loose."

"We also need to come up with a name for your new business."

"Later, Odell. We will work on that later. Much later."

Odell kicked in the footrest of the easy chair and it snapped shut with a loud crack that broke the magic of the glorious music that emitted from the radio just as the piece on the radio finished. The now familiar radio announcer's voice cut in, and, of course, confirmed Odell's proper identification of the musical piece, the composer, and the musical artist. Odell jumped out of the chair. He gently grasped Marlin's hand, and he followed Marlin along as she slowly ascended the staircase and dropped various layers of her clothes along the way.

"Every which way but loose, Marlin? Do you want a little sip of Irish? I can pour us some." Odell asked as he clenched her hand and he admired her waver, her wiggle, and the various stages of her unparalleled and glorious nakedness.

"As you say, yupper and nope and nope. . . ."

CHAPTER EIGHT

Luckily, the store was empty of other customers. They waited for the last customer to leave and prayed that the timing was right. It was perfect.

"Hiya, there, Danny. Three bottles of the Irish and a six-pack of the usual Red and White Label beers and three packs of the usual smokes," Marlin said in her most seductive voice as she leaned in over the glass counter of the store and gave Danny Clark the best view possible of her ample cleavage.

As Odell correctly assessed and noted, Danny did not wear any eyeglasses. They apparently were a prop for Lyle Odell only.

Her light summer blouse was open a button or two more than usual. It was a scorching day. The heatwave continued with no break in sight. Marlin provided Danny with the best view possible without being cold, stark naked, that is. Marlin dropped a wad of cash on the counter and smiled her best smile to Danny Wadsworth Clark.

"Please take what you need, Danny. Outta there. I swiped it from Odell. He keeps piles of cash hangin 'round here and there and everywhere."

It was time to light an irrevocable fire that would set an irrevocable trap. Marlin Santini was all in. Her tilted lean into the counter needed to be careful and calculated because she wore a wire that Odell strapped to her chest. Just underneath her breasts. Despite her boastful proclamation of being able to carry and to use a weapon, Marlin had none. She knew that right now; a carefully hidden sniper was directly across the street from the store, and he had this meeting centered in his scope. Right through the storefront window. Her instructions were to stay in front of the front sales counter. If they lost sight of her or the communications went offline, the team would rush in and the entire case might or it might not blow up. Marlin knew that Odell had his weapon drawn too, as did Grundy, Crump, and even Captain Moore had his weapon in hand. Captain Moore was in uniform and on duty for this assignment. He insisted on working on the stakeout detail. Odell, Crump, Captain Moore and Grundy listened in on their every word.

She never felt safer.

Marlin wore her now locally famous outfit of very tight shorts, gripping her hips as if they were glue and showing off her legs, topped with the light summer blouse that displayed her amazing breasts and then there were the work boots, with the wrap around laces tied across the top of them.

Danny Clark had not stopped grinning since the moment that she first walked into the store. An ear-to-ear grin that Marlin knew he laced with all his attributes of evil. Marlin studied him for a few seconds. He was built like a locomotive, he was tall, and his steel wool hair was jet black. Danny was trying his best to be charming. He failed in his efforts because Marlin could easily see now that he was disgustingly evil.

Danny set the bottles of Irish whiskey on the counter and gathered up the cash and quickly thumbed through it while saying, "I will take some of this and leave a little for you." He looked up, stared into Marlin's eyes, and said, "Marlin, if I took it all, you might not recover from it."

Marlin smiled and hid the shiver down her spine that the words created.

"Let me get the beer for you. The smokes are right here." Danny tossed three packs of cigarettes on the counter; he pointed and added, "Matches are there if you need 'em. So, how is the case going with Detective Lyle? Well, you know, mega-weird Odell?"

Marlin forced a fake laugh. "Well, it is a dead end, but, you know, I am learnin' . . . stuff from Odell. He sure is strange, but . . . you know . . . like . . . I need to learn . . . stuff."

Marlin played up the dumb language and laced it with excessive likes. Her eyes caught some dried-up blades of grass on the floor on the edge of the counter. Where the counter turns to the main floor of the stores. Dried blades of grass tracked off of shoes or sneakers. Danny wore sneakers. They looked brand new.

"I gotcha," Danny said as he grabbed a six-pack of the beer from the cooler case, "so you want to get into police work someday? Is that why you are hanging around with the doddering old guy? I mean, no offense, but a hot chick like you . . . can kinda pick who you wanna hang 'round with. I am not thinkin' that Detective Lyle Odell is much of a good time."

A large part of the game plan was for Marlin to play good cop and bad cop, and she was hitting on all cylinders now.

"He is strange. For sure. Maybe I wanna get into police work. I went to school for it. I dunno. But you know sumthin', Danny?" Marlin said as she leaned into the counter and once more allowed her blouse to fall open a little, as Danny set the beer upon the glass counter. Danny's eyes were a magnet to the top of Marlin's breasts. "Just between us," Marlin spoke out of the corner of her mouth while checking to make sure no other customer walked into the store, "I think he was so drunk the other day that he missed a few details on a key investigation. We went down to Albany, where the first murder by the serial killer occurred. To Melrose Park, and I swear he was so bombed that he missed the correct spot where the actual murder occurred. I kept trying to tell him that he was in the wrong spot, but he would not listen. He was . . . like . . . on the wrong side of the park entirely. I am not sure what he was even looking for, but the park was really cool and pretty. I wanna go back and check it out and just hang out and see what I can see. Even if I don't work on the case, I just wanna chill out in the park and kill some time before I go back to the farm. I don't think that Odell will solve this crime, so I am going back home the day after tomorrow. As I said, he has nothing to go on, and half the time, he is blasted and the other half of the time, he seems like he is lost," Marlin said as she gathered up the goods. She stuffed the cigarette packs in her pockets, reached for the dish of matches, grabbed a book or two, and stuffed them in her pockets too.

Danny licked the edges of his mouth as she forced the matches into the pockets of her skin-tight shorts. Her long, tanned and toned legs were on full display as she worked the goods into her pockets.

"I am goin' back to the park tomorrow morning without Odell to . . . like . . . poke around in the proper location. Not sure what I will see, but after . . ." Marlin thumbed a thumb at the whiskey, "Odell sucks down all of this tonight. He will not be in any shape to ride with me. Gonna go alone and check it out. See what I can see. Maybe I can make a name for myself."

Danny picked up the bottles of whiskey and his eyes went back and forth in his head, first from the few open buttons of her open blouse, to the tight shorts, to her lovely face.

Finally, he said as he wrapped the top of the paper bag holding the whiskey, "Sounds like you on the right track. As you said, even if you don't work on the case, it might be a fun day just chillin' in the park. Besides, I mean ditchin' the old drunk might be the right choice for your career. There is no question that you seem like you are very smart. You might do better on your own. Maybe his time has come and gone. The whiskey finally got to 'em. After all, even Derek Cramer struck out. Are you gonna bring your now-famous sniffing pig?"

Marlin forced a laugh while she expertly hid her shock at Danny Clark, using the same line that helped to first turn Odell onto the menacing evil within Danny Clark's mind and soul.

Marlin recovered, and she shook her head and said, "Oh no. Going by myself. Doodlesticks is back on the farm now. He is not of much use now. He really found nothing, anyway. This trail is so old now that he cannot detect anything."

It was time for a smoke screen and Marlin dialed one up.

"Hey, I made a good buck for bringing him out. The Mohawk City Police Department is gonna throw me a wad of dough for my services. I have my own business, you know."

Danny nodded and his hand lingered for a few seconds on top

of the six-pack of beer before he slid it over to Marlin, along with her change from the transaction.

"No kiddin'? So, you just in it for the dough. I gotcha. That is very cool. Say, Marlin, as I mentioned to you and showed you before," Danny turned and pointed to the pictures above the counter and above the cash register, "ah, yeah, as you can see, I do a little photography. I know Melrose Park. I have the day off from work tomorrow, and I am up for a brief ride to Albany. I would love to meet you there. Snap a few photos and hang with you . . . if you like. What time are you gonna go there?"

Marlin had sold the goods and Danny bought them all.

"Oh, yes, I love your pictures, Danny. I see them there," Marlin let her eyes wander across the photographic display and she was careful not to linger upon the now familiar Melrose Park photograph because as she studied the various photographs, Marlin could feel Danny's eyes carefully watching her. Marlin knew that she was almost home. Now she had to close the deal.

"Gonna be there by nine in the morning. Get there before it gets too hot. It has been some awful heatwave. Sure, call me when you get to the park, Danny. It will be cool to hang out a little. Please, hand me that pen and pad there and I will give you my phone number," Marlin pointed at a pad and pen on the counter and as she did so, she blinked a little underneath her eyeglasses and she turned on the shy charm button. All the actors aren't in Hollywood, and Marlin Santini was well on her way to an Academy Award for this performance. Off in the distance, hidden around the corner of the side street, Lyle Odell and Captain Moore smiled and fist-bumped each other as they listened to the conversation and admired Marlin's performance.

"I know that I didn't give you my number before, but Odell says that you are very cool . . . so," Marlin wrote the number down on the pad, tore off the paper and slid it over to Danny Clark, "here it is the number. After all, a gal needs to be careful here in Sin City. Please call me when you get to the park. I will direct you to where I will check stuff out. To the bench."

Danny picked up the paper, smiled, and said, "I will call as soon as I arrive. Best to be careful, Marlin. Yes indeed, very careful. Lots of crazy loons in the world these days, especially here in Sin City." He folded the paper and tucked it into his shirt pocket. "Yes, I am very cool. Odell is right about sumthin.' See you tomorrow. You got all that stuff?"

Marlin grabbed the paper bag and the six-pack and tucked it all away under her arms. "I am fine. It is a short walk, and the walking keeps me fit and tight. As you can see," Marlin winked and smiled at the meaning. She picked up the goods and headed for the door with an extra wiggle of her hips and backside.

Marlin backed into the door, it popped open, and as she did so, Marlin added, "Odell will be asleep by eight tonight. Get this . . . he listens to classical music!"

Marlin forced a laugh and Danny did, too.

He waved as he said, "See you tomorrow," and she walked out into the heat. As she walked down the sidewalk toward Odell's house, Danny ran to the window and admired her rear view as she wiggled down the sidewalk.

He licked his lips and said, "Yeah, see you tomorrow, baby doll. I am so looking forward to posing your beautiful lifeless body and snapping a few with my eyes to lock you away forever. Moore can wait his turn. Right now, you are too beautiful to exist any longer. Too gorgeous to glorify your father's sins. Such a shame to silence such a beautiful creature, but your father set your fate. Not me. Be sure to blame him when you meet 'em in wherever."

Danny turned away from the window just as another customer walked into the store and Danny spouted off his fake greeting, "Welcome to Lucky Leo's liquor store. It sure is hot today, huh? Every day, hot, hot and even hotter. The heatwave seems endless."

The customer grunted, nodded, and headed for the beer cooler. Cool refreshment was the priority order of the day.

"Tomorrow . . . it is gonna be the hottest day of 'em all," Danny mumbled in a whisper, with a hint of a grin on his face and clenched fists.

Detective Lyle Odell was waiting for her when Marlin opened the door to the house. He was in his easy chair and he glanced up at her and smiled.

The air conditioning was blasting full bore, and the house felt so refreshing. The heatwave proved to be relentless. Day-after-day it bore down on upstate New York with unyielding fury.

Marlin took a deep breath and relaxed at the rush of the cool air and the loving look on Odell's face. She realized how tense the situation was that she just pulled off. Her body felt as if an immense weight was now off of it.

"I am shaking, Odell. From my head to my toe. I hope that I did okay," Marlin spoke while her sweet voice reflected her anguish.

Odell jumped up from his chair and he grabbed the beer and paper bag full of whiskey from her and slowly walked it to the kitchen, while softly saying, "You did fantastic, Marlin. I am so proud of you. Thank you. Don't go far. I got this, baby."

Marlin nodded, and she recalled the cigarettes jammed into her pockets. She reached in and emptied the pockets of her shorts and placed the packs of smokes on the end table.

Marlin realized that her hands were shaking. Odell would steady her. Marlin needed him. She needed to hold him, to smell him, to love him. To run her hands through his thick, black hair.

The radio played softly with the usual classical music. Marlin knew that this time there would be no announcement of the song playing, no artist identified, and no identification of the composer. Not this time. Odell sensed and knew what she needed. All that she needed. After all, he was the brilliant detective. A modern-day Sherlock Holmes.

The cool air inside the home felt so good. She felt such relief. It was such a simple home with such simple things. The environment fit Odell so perfectly. Everything felt comforting here.

Odell returned with a glass of water stuffed with ice cubes. He handed it to Marlin, and he smiled as he did so. His pride in his lover shone through. Marlin needed the ice-cold water almost as much as she needed Lyle Odell. As she took the water, took a few sips, and allowed it to ease her thirst from the hiss of summer, Marlin thought about how she wished that Odell smiled more often.

He reached out his hand and motioned for the glass of water, which Marlin handed off to him. The glass was half-full. Odell did not say a single word. He reached out with his other hand. She took his hand as he led her upstairs. There, in his arms, amid their love, all would be well, perfect and as it should be.

Sometimes, words just get in the way.

CHAPTER NINE

The heat still relentlessly bore down. It was early in the day and right now; it seemed as if this was going to be the hottest day of the heatwave. Weather-wise and otherwise, too.

It might have been the weather or the circumstances, but Marlin Santini could feel the sweat running down between her breasts and she could also feel beads of sweat running down her legs, and into her socks inside her work boots. Marlin sat on the park bench in Melrose Park. She wore her usual attire. Along, with the same wire and transmitting equipment that she wore when she setup Danny Clark in the store. There was no doubt that this was a setup. Plain and simple and even though she wore the electronics, and a sniper hid in the distance in the park with the bench in the gun sights and Odell, Grundy, Crump, two Albany police officers and Captain Moore were also watching close by, Marlin knew that Danny Clark could potentially shoot her dead before they could react. Lyle Odell had a plan to eliminate that potential and to prevent that from happening. The entire team had meticulously gone over every detail of the plan. Marlin knew they missed nothing. Marlin trusted Odell. She loved him and respected him. She was not afraid . . . not in the least.

The team had been in the park since early in the morning. They arrived around four and set up in their positions and they hid so well that it would be nearly impossible to detect them. The conveniently located, nearby maintenance shed provided a perfect cover for the team.

Odell successfully argued his case with both Captain Moore

and Sergeant George Grundy not to put a police officer shadow tail on Danny Clark. Odell felt that any tail, covert or not, would be too risky. Clark was too smart, and any slight misstep would blow the entire case and spook him. They were in a perfect spot right now, and Odell felt that Danny Clark had left for Albany shortly after his shift ended yesterday at the liquor store and found a hotel room nearby the park and checked into it. He already checked the park out and his plan was not to kill Marlin there, but he would lead her at gunpoint back to his hotel room and kill her either there or in the vehicle that he used to ride to Albany.

The Detective Lyle Odell-led team had meticulously mapped out the plan at police headquarters the night they arrived back in Mohawk City. Odell planned every stage of the game plan. He said that start to finish; the last confrontation would take all of five minutes or thereabouts. Marlin did not doubt him for a single second.

"His cockiness will not allow him to call Marlin's cellphone. He will simply arrive at the bench because, of course, he knows which bench it was that he killed Mr. Rollins on and does not need Marlin to direct him to it," Odell predicted during their long game plan session.

As the time slowly ticked off slow and painful clicks in a slow march to nine o'clock, Marlin's eyes danced back and forth as she searched for the appearance of Danny Clark. Precisely at fifteen minutes to the nine o'clock hour, as Odell instructed her, Marlin fed the first wave of crows that arrived on scene after she made a few calls on the crow call. She tossed a handful of peanuts on the asphalt path in front of the bench. They enjoyed the peanuts. Marlin surmised that they missed them yesterday, so today the murder was ready for the treat when they saw Marlin arrive. Their comfort level increased, even without Odell sitting next to her as Marlin gently coaxed them to enjoy the snack with a soft voice. Eventually, the crows flew down out of the trees after their leader carefully scanned the area, bobbed and weaved, communicated in their secret language the safety of doing so and after picking the peanuts up, they hollered a few thank you calls to Marlin and flew back to the safety of their tree branches. Odell wanted the crows to enjoy the snack and hang around long enough, looking for another treat to sound the alarm at the arrival of Danny Clark. Then Odell would burst on the scene and the last confrontation would be at hand.

"Okay, team, the end game is here," Odell whispered into his radio microphone. "Any second now. When the crows spot him, the leader of the murder will go crazy, and warn the rest of the murder of the approaching danger. The leader's alarm call will give me the pause I need and then the second witness will make the final conviction of this son-of-a-bitch." Odell reached down, patted Doodlesticks on his back, and rubbed his neck and Doodlesticks rubbed up on Odell and showed him his love, and that he, too, was ready for action. Doodlesticks knew that his precious Marlin was nearby, and he knew about the mission.

Odell checked on the whereabouts of the matchbook and other evidence and then mumbled, "Left side suit jacket pocket." Odell added, "And that will be all she wrote for Danny Clark. Combat vets to combat vets. Intense. We have all been here before."

George Gundry nodded in affirmation of Odell's words as he stood next to Odell, along with Captain Moore and Officer Crump, their weapons drawn, cocked, locked, and loaded. Yes, Odell had his service weapon. Albany uniformed police officers would strategically cut off the jogging trail when Captain Moore ordered them to do so and protect any civilians in the area. Luckily, the heat was so intense today that very few people were outside and braving it.

Everything would all happen within seconds, and the reactions required perfect timing. The team would be right on time. The heat inside the shed was intense. Doodlesticks panted and snorted in protest to the heat, and Odell comforted him with a spray of water. The crows stood in the branches calling out a few loud calls to Marlin, asking her to toss a few more peanuts and Marlin sat at the bench ready, watching and waiting. The leader of the crows grew impatient with Marlin. The crows bobbed and weaved and danced on the branches and looked down at Marlin.

It was one minute after nine o'clock in the morning.

The air grew thicker and heavier and the sun, even at this early hour of the morning, turned up the burners. The silence was eerie and ominous. Sometimes it is like that in the hiss of summer. Thick and heavy and mean and nasty.

Autumn's cool air would be a great relief.

Suddenly, the leader of the crows went crazy. His head bobbed and weaved, and his calls echoed across the entire park. A large man appeared on the path and he was now walking within a few feet of Marlin Santini. Odell's feet shifted, and he tugged at Doodlesticks's leash to warn his companion that the end game was here.

Odell whispered, "Sixth mistake."

When the crows listened to their leader and flew off at the sounding of the alarm, Marlin's heart might have stopped beating for just a second and then she caught her breath and looked up, forced her best sweaty smile and said, "Hi Danny! I was waiting for your call. You found me on your own. Wow, those crazy crows startled me. I did not see or hear you walking. It sure is hot. Why are you wearing a jacket on such a hot day? Aren't you dying in that?"

Danny watched as the crows all flew off, screaming and hollering as they flew across the pond and picked trees in the distance to settle in. Danny's grin was pure evil. His eyes were intense and after watching the crows fly off, he focused on Marlin.

He wiped at the sweat beading upon his brows and said, "I knew where to go. It sure is hot today, Marlin. Gonna get hotter too. Nah, I ain't dying today. You know sumthin' Marlin? Crows are creepy."

"You know sumthin', Danny? You did not call because this is where you killed Mr. Rollins. You already knew where to go. You just said it yourself. Sort of a confession of sorts," Odell's voice echoed down the path. Danny never saw or heard him coming. The shed was in the perfect spot. Doodlesticks snorted and pawed at the grass as he dug a path towards Marlin and Danny as Odell held his leash tightly and had given him the secret "match the scent command" that Marlin taught Odell. "Funny thing 'bout crows. They are brilliantly intelligent. They recognize humans and never forget a face. If the humans are nice to the crows, the crows are cautious but friendly. If a human is mean or does harm to the crows or their friends, they never forget that either. Mr. Rollins was this murder of crow's friend, as is Marlin and I am too. And, well, Doodlesticks here. He can smell things twenty feet underground and he can detect odors and distinct smells from five to ten miles away. I just gave him the match scent command from the matchbook cover that we found in the ivy bed at the scene of the homicide of Miss Allison McNally. You know the homicide scene that you pointed out to me on the television in the store the other day? I also let Doodlesticks sniff around on the sales receipt that you handed me from the store and the paper bag from the store that the Irish whiskey was in. Funny thing," Odell stood up straight as Doodlesticks dug into the ground even more and charged toward Danny.

Danny's face turned dark and evil and menacing as he realized the setup and his final mistake was at hand.

"Doodlesticks is smarter than most humans are and he just matched all the scents to you. You are quite brilliant and, until now, infallible. When this madness began, I predicted that it would take seven mistakes to nail ya ass. This is your sixth mistake. Falling for the allure of a stunningly beautiful woman. You will not be the first guy to do so and you won't be the last. Ask Samson how that all worked out for him. Besides, Cramer did not strike out as much as you thought he did. Not for a twenty-year career and when you consider how many at bats he had."

"Damn, you to Hell, Odell! You just struck out! You should've brought your weapon this time, you old fool!"

With those words, Danny drew his handgun from underneath

his jacket and the shot rang out into the air. Danny Clark staggered backwards as the shot from Sergeant George Grundy's handgun hit him squarely in the chest, his eyes rolled back in his head from the pain. As his legs wobbled, he focused his eyes on Odell, then to Marlin and then to Doodlesticks. He tried to lift his gun and aim his gun as another shot rang out, this time, from Odell's handgun. That shot hit Danny Clark right between his eyes. Then he collapsed and sprawled onto the asphalt path.

Odell dropped his eyes and then his head, while Danny's dead body hit the ground with a terrible thud. Odell lowered his handgun to his side, and he sighed heavily.

With his head down and his eyes focused on the dead killer, Odell's voice came out as if it was a heavy whisper laced with pain, "I did. Just another clown who did not pay attention to my words. Seldom is the word that I use. Not the word, never. Seldom," Odell said as he placed his weapon back in his shoulder holster. "And neither do I. Strike out, that is. Mistake number seven. Dead. No handcuffs or trial required. Taxpayers just saved a bunch'a dough."

Marlin was in Odell's arms and loving onto him and Doodlesticks within seconds. Captain Moore and Grundy and Crump rushed in, as did the Albany city police officers. Police radios screamed with radio calls and chatter. They checked on Danny Clark, confirmed that it was over, and tended to the scene.

In the distance, the crows hollered and called. Under the guidance of their faithful leader, the murder of crows flew across the pond and landed in the tree nearby the bench. There, in the comfort of their branches, their leader bobbed and weaved to signal that the danger was gone. For now. Until some new evil rose out of the evil ranks. It always does. Odell and the crows were kindred souls. They both knew that evil never really rests.

Sergeant George Grundy walked over and placed his hand on Odell's shoulder as he looked into his friend's eyes and said, "Sorry, Odell. I might have been off by a second or two. I beat the sniper, though. I guess I was prophetic on my bullet prediction. Dropped 'em." The old patrol sergeant tugged at his gun belt and drew it up over his rather large belly. He wiped the beads of sweat off his forehead and looked over at Marlin, and then he reached down, patted Doodlesticks on his back, and rubbed some love on him. Grundy put his arm around Marlin's shoulders and pulled her in tightly while checking her eyes.

"How are you? Are you okay, Marlin?"

"I am. Yes. Thank you for you and the excellent aim," Marlin said as she nodded and appreciated the old sergeant's concern.

Grundy cleared his throat and said, "You know, Odell, I need to remind you that technically, I am a patrol sergeant. I am not sure how I always end up roped into your cases and bullshit, but anyway, I couldn't risk losing my drinking buddy, or the next brilliant detective, or her faithful assistant. Retirement and life would suck."

As Marlin buried her head into Odell's chest and Doodlesticks snorted and rubbed into the group, Odell reached out and shook Grundy's hand and said, "George, thank you. You are the best. No way that you are retiring. Yet. Too much evil out there, George. I need you. Besides, you still have all those horrible college student loans to pay off."

Grundy smiled and said, "I guess. Thank you for the reminder of those damn loans. Someday, Odell. Someday, I will pay those suckers off and we will be drunk for two weeks. It is painful as all hell to admit, but I would miss you, too. How the hell would I learn about random bullshit that no one else knows or cares 'bout? Say Thursday is my day off. You wanna all meet at Gulliver's and chow down on some grilled cheese sandwiches and suck down beer and Irish? Bring Captain Moore. Make 'em pay for the tab."

Odell looked at Grundy and then at Marlin and said, "Sure. What day is it today?"

"Tuesday."

"Okay, yeah, Thursday works unless sumthin' comes in. I sent you an email with the address of Clark's huntin' cabin and an attachment with all of his military records. I had some free time one night and could not sleep, so I did some research. Those should be a treasure trove of evidence and should wrap up the last details of why he went on a rampage. Maybe you can get Crump and his boys up there to the cabin and check it out? I was correct. It is in Piseco. Beautiful area. Great fishin.' Piseco Lake is deep. 'Bout one-hundred feet in spots. Cold water. Lake trout."

"Odell, I need to remind you again that I am a patrol sergeant."

"I gotcha, George, but Marlin and me and Doodlesticks, we are gonna take sum time off. Enjoy some pizza and Irish and other stuff. I need a haircut too."

Marlin smiled, and so did Grundy. He understood how they would pass the time.

"I gotcha. You really give me a pain-in my-ass, Odell. You really do. I was gonna cut my grass."

"Too hot, George. Wait until Thursday. The heatwave will break on Thursday. Watch the Clippers instead. Tampa is in town. They have good pitchin'."

"The weather guy said the heatwave won't break until Friday."

"Nah, he is wrong. As usual. Storms comin' in here on Wednesday night. Not downstate. The game will be fine. Only up here."

"Okay. I will handle it."

Odell tapped his pockets on a cigarette search, Marlin intercepted him, and she reached into his right-side suit jacket pocket and pulled out the cigarettes, emptied one out and stuck it in his mouth and magically produced her lighter and lit it.

After a few long drags, Odell said, "Oh, George, sorry, but I kinda told Captain Moore that you would pay when we went to Gulliver's."

George had started to walk away. He turned around and his face was red and flush. It was not just the heat.

"Odell! What? Damn pain-in-the-ass!"

"I love you too, George," Odell said.

Marlin laughed. She reached into her bag and tossed a large handful of peanuts onto the path. Odell watched and then he grabbed Marlin's hand and Doodlesticks's leash and together all

three of them walked to the parking lot.
    To Marlin's pickup truck.
    To the air-conditioning.
    Out of the hiss of summer.

CHAPTER TEN

On that following Thursday. . . .

The heatwave broke. The weather report said it would not break until Friday, but storms moved in on Wednesday night and the skies let loose as a cold front finally brought relief to upstate New York.

Since the heat did not bake the world, the ceremony was outside. A small group of Mohawk City police officers, the chain of command, the mayor and council members, along with some of the media and the local press. It was around eleven in the morning; the skies were a deep blue and some puffy clouds floated in the skies here and there. It was a perfect day for an awards ceremony in the park. The hiss of summer left and hints of autumn whispered in the air.

Marlin sat in a folding chair set up in the assembly area of the local park. Doodlesticks stood next to the chair. He snorted a little, but mostly; he was on his best behavior. From this position, he kept his eyes on his friend, Lyle Odell, as Odell moved along a small stage set up in front of the assembly area where family and friends and the media gathered to watch the ceremony. This park, amid downtown Mohawk City and the surrounding area, was where Mohawk City held various city celebrations. The local veterans, the police, the fire department, holidays and such. There were some plaques mounted on the stone walls in and amongst the walkways and display gardens, some memorial monuments for local war heroes and police and fire department members and officers and some flowerbeds, trees and shrubs. For Mohawk City, and its reputation as Sin City, it was a pleasant area.

Marlin sat in the audience within a small group of only about twenty people. Retired Mohawk City Police Captain Lawrence Tucker looked on as he sat with his wife and with some other retirees from the police force. Oliver Crump's family and some friends were in the audience, along with George Grundy's wife and his children and his family. Some crime scene technicians and their families and friends that worked with Crump on his team rounded out the rest of the onlookers.

Homicide Detective Lyle Odell had Marlin and Doodlesticks.

To Marlin's knowledge, Odell had no family, no living relatives, at least, that he mentioned or that anyone knew of.

George Grundy shook his head when Marlin asked him about that fact and George gently whispered, "Only us and his Irish, and that music on his old radio."

Marlin sat and patted Doodlesticks to keep him calm and quiet. She made careful note of how much smaller the media group was compared to the scenes of the homicides, when they surrounded the areas in hordes of madness.

Chaos and fear sell. Boring does not.

Earlier in the ceremony, the police chaplain led the group in a generic prayer and a thank you for safety and deliverance from the hands of evil types of words, followed by the police chief leading the Pledge of Allegiance. The chief spoke a few short words, and he did not linger. Then the crime scene technicians received some awards, as did Marlin, and even Doodlesticks received a ribbon for his "Civilian help and valor." He proudly wore his ribbon pinned around his collar. Despite her insistence that she technically was not a civilian, Marlin received the same award along with a contractor's cooperation certificate.

Marlin wore a pair of dress slacks that beautifully displayed her amazing curves and figure, a heavier blouse and dress shoes. No work boots. No shorts and no dress. Marlin Santini rarely wore dresses, although she thought that a wedding dress would not be such a bad thing to wear, especially if a certain homicide detective was the groom and she was the bride. As usual, she looked stunning and stopped a few hearts today.

Marlin watched the scene unfold as the police officers assembled on the stage and the three of them stood silently at attention. First, Captain Moore received a ribbon and some congratulations from the police chief, and now, Captain Moore honored his officers.

Homicide Detective Lyle Odell stood at attention on the end of line along with Officer Oliver Crump and Sergeant George Grundy. They all wore their dress blue uniforms, and it was difficult not to settle your eyes upon the many ribbons and decorations on the chest of Detective Lyle Odell. Today, Captain Moore would add two more.

Somewhere.

Odell needed a larger chest. He was the most highly decorated police officer in the Mohawk City Police Department. By far. Grundy had privately told Marlin that he was one of the most decorated active-duty police officers in not only New York State, but in the entire country. His reputation spread far and wide, but Marlin knew that Odell would take the ribbons off his uniform and toss them in a cardboard box in the top drawer of the dresser in his room. She knew where he kept them, along with a carefully folded piece of paper detailing how to pin them back onto the uniform. It was the way he was. He preferred his loneliness, his quiet time, his easy chair, his Irish, and his old radio to chase away the phantoms that haunted him. Marlin's heart ached to know that she could be a part of his closed-off world, but somehow, deep inside, she sensed what was coming.

Odell stood proudly, stiffly, and he looked amazing. It was in stark contrast to his usual unkempt and disarrayed appearance. Odell captured Marlin's heart even more if it was even possible to do so. As much as she loved when his longish hair flopped in front of his face, his new haircut displayed his rugged features. His fresh haircut was high and tight, he was clean-shaven, and his gray eyes were clear with no rims of redness or haziness from the whiskey or the bouts of all-night despair and struggles. Last night, they spent time in each other's arms, and Odell's face reflected the night of lovemaking and his peace.

Odell had peace in his mind and in his soul. The case was over. The evil subdued until the next wave rose from the ranks to challenge him again, as evil always does.

After awarding Officer Crump and Sergeant Grundy, Captain Moore moved to Homicide Detective Lyle Odell. The captain shook his hand, said a few words, and patted Odell on his shoulder, and Odell smiled as just a hint of a small smile gently worked along the edges of Odell's mouth. Marlin loved when he smiled.

Captain Moore carefully searched for an open location to pin the ribbons on Odell's chest, and as she watched the scene, Marlin's soul swelled with pride and joy and her eyes brimmed with tears. Even the media stood and clapped to honor the heroes, and they especially cheered when Odell received his awards. Generally, the press and media are not huge fans of police officers, but Detective Lyle Odell was an exception. On the other hand, as Marlin knew, he was exceptional. In so many ways.

Afterwards, there was a photo session, and the officers and the media even coaxed Marlin and Odell into sharing a kiss for the cameras.

It was a magical moment. One of many they shared. Life is full of glorious moments to file away in your mind and to pull them out and enjoy them and remember and cherish. This was one of them.

"Okay . . . Cap Moore, and Marlin, and Doodlesticks, don't keep us waiting here. If you got sumthin' to say about it . . . then spill your guts on it. I've been coming here for too long to endure any pussy-footing around," Sergeant George Grundy spoke rather harshly while the police sergeant leaned in and carefully studied Police Captain Conner Moore for his reaction and a response. Grundy's eyes then went to Marlin's beautiful face as she chewed and pushed her eyeglasses up her nose. Marlin held up one finger to show that she was still in the process of savoring the delicacy known as Gulliver's Magical Grilled Cheese Sandwich. Grundy looked down at Doodlesticks, and the crime-detecting machine snorted and pawed at the floor with his hoofs. Doodlesticks stared at his plate because it was already empty. It was apparent to Grundy that Doodlesticks loved it, and he was all in for another helping. On Grundy's tab, too!

Detective Lyle Odell nodded, and he watched while Captain Moore and Marlin slowly chewed and savored the food in their mouths. While Grundy tapped his fingers anxiously upon the bar counter, and Lyle carefully studied their faces for clues, Captain Moore finally swallowed and nodded his head. The captain picked up the pint glass of ice-cold beer, tilted the glass, and took a long sip of the brew. Connor Moore smacked his lips, leaned back on the bar stool and ran his fingers across his handsome face and then gave another nod of his head. Marlin swallowed, and she too smacked her lips together while she still held up the one finger. Then Marlin, too, reached for the glass of ice-cold beer and tilted the beer over in a long sip.

"Oh geezzzz, c'mon, Cap! C'mon, Marlin! What the hell? It ain't filet mignon! Damn! Doodlesticks loved it and he already woofed it down and is looking for a'nudder one! Tell us if we are right or not!" Sergeant Grundy grew impatient with the waiting for the opinion of Captain Moore and Marlin on the quality of the grilled cheese sandwich washed down with the daily special of beer. The group sat at the bar at Gulliver's Bar and Grille on Fifth Street and Main Street in downtown Mohawk City, New York, on Saturday afternoon around two in the afternoon. Doodlesticks stood on the floor next to Marlin and between Odell's barstool and Marlin's barstool, and he waited for another grilled cheese sandwich. Marlin with her ever-present leather bag slung over the back of the barstool, and Odell were sitting on barstools set in the middle of the bar with George Gundry on one side of Marlin and Captain Moore, and Officer Oliver Crump and retired Police Captain Lawrence Tucker sitting on the other side of Lyle Odell. Captain Moore, Grundy, and Crump were off duty, and

Odell, well, it was always difficult to determine when he was on duty or off duty.

"You are correct, George and Lyle. Best damn grilled cheese in the city. Perhaps, in the entire world," Captain Moore proudly pronounced as he picked the grilled cheese sandwich off the plate and took another bite. "The cheese melted perfectly and the crispy burnt edges are amazing."

Marlin finished her long sip of beer and she voiced her opinion.

Her seductive voice floated into the haze of the old bar and grille.

Marlin said, "I agree with Cap Moore. Simply amazing. And well, Doodlesticks, he thinks it is amazing too."

Doodlesticks snorted and pawed at the floor to show his vote and the fact that he wanted another sandwich.

George Grundy slapped his hand upon the bar counter and most of the nearby patrons jumped in his response. "Hot damn! Told you so. Now, I am having a'nudder brew and sandwich cuz, I was right. Annie, please, refills all around for us. A'nudder sandwich for Doodlesticks and for me, too! By the way, this is all on Captain Tucker's tab. He is retired."

Annie, the bartender, smiled, pulled pint glasses out of the cooler and filled the glass from the beer tap, pouring out the daily special. Annie looked as if she had poured a few million beers in her career. She was ancient, but effective.

"I think this is the first time that I ever had all these heroes here in one line at Gulliver's. And a," everyone lifted an eye towards Annie and Doodlesticks looked up and waited for her next words, "Doodlesticks."

Annie was right on and everyone relaxed. No one wanted an angry Doodlesticks on hand. In a crowded bar and grille where Doodlesticks was already a local celebrity and was keeping the bar patrons entertained with his presence.

Annie smiled at her tease and continued, "Usually, I am stuck with gloomy Odell pondering some case in his mind and sad sack Grundy complaining about the Clippers, or Big Blue, or the Rovers, or those damn parent college student loans, or the weather, or his captain. He always says what a pain-in-the-ass the captain is."

Captain Moore lifted an eye toward Grundy and then he looked over at Captain Tucker, who did the same.

In unison, the two captains joined in and said, "So, we are pains-in-the-ass, huh? Okay, George."

Grundy waved it off and said, "Thanks, Annie. There goes your tip. I will pay. Forget it. I got it all."

"Say, can Doodlesticks really smell that well?" Annie asked.

Marlin smiled and answered, "He can sure smell that grilled cheese on the grill over in the kitchen there. Yes, he can smell really well. As in, he can smell the money in Grundy's wallet and tell us how much is in there. If I commanded him to do so, he would smell it and then tap his hooves on the floor to tell me how much dough George had inside of his wallet."

"No kidding?" Annie said as she topped off the beers.

"No shit," George said as he reached back to his back pocket, touched the edges of his wallet tucked in the recesses of the pocket, and narrowed his eyes a little. George then lifted an eye to Marlin and Odell chuckled at the dupe by Marlin. "He can do that? That is amazin.'"

"Nah, just kidding you, George. However, he and his faithful friend and trainer can smell Irish whiskey," Marlin said, and she lifted an eye at Odell and gently leaned into him and playfully batted her eyes at her lover.

Annie set the beers in front of the group of men and Odell stared at the full glass of beer and mumbled, "I know where my bread is buttered and what my woman wants. Time to shift to Irish."

Marlin leaned over and whispered while grabbing Odell's arm, gently rubbing it up and down, and said, "Hell, yeah, you know what your woman needs and you sure do know what she wants too. Can't wait to get back to your house and finish this day how we started it."

Odell smiled widely, looked at Annie, and said, "Put the Irish on my tab, Annie. Make them doubles."

The old bartender smiled, nodded, and wobbled over to the rows of whiskey.

Annie's hearing was still sharp.

Annie paused at the whiskey bottles and asked, "The usual, Odell?"

"Please, Annie. Yes. The usual."

The food runner dropped the plates with the next round of grilled cheese sandwiches in front of George Grundy and Grundy picked one up, leaned over and dropped one sandwich in front of Doodlesticks, who squealed in delight and dove into it, with his little spin of a tail wiggling on his backside.

"Go easy, big guy. You are costin' me a fortune and you will be two hundred pounds in a week," Grundy said as he patted him on the back. Grundy then tugged at his waist, smiled, and dug into his sandwich.

Oliver Crump picked up his refreshed pint glass of brew and took a sip.

After he set it back down on the bar counter, Crump leaned over the bar, looked over toward Odell and Marlin, and said, "Say, Lyle, don't want to talk too much shop, but you were right about the hunting camp. The boys found pretty much what you predicted. A steel burn barrel with remnants of burned items inside. All burned beyond identification. No weapons. They are most likely in the lake. Not worth it to dive for them. Not now, at least, since Clark is history. There were three cars parked on the property. All Japanese compact sedans, same colors, same models, same makes and one with the remnants of a Go Navy sticker on the rear bumper. Clark took a rental car to Albany. Phony name, phony identification and credit cards under a dual identity for the cars and for the hotel room where he stayed. I think he was going to commit the next murder in the rental," Crump paused and his eyes went all over Marlin before he spoke once more, "well, let's just skip it. It is over and done with."

Grundy spoke up between chews, "Yeah. Good idea. Skip those awful details, Crump. We have eatin' and drinkin' to do."

Annie set the whiskey glasses in front of Odell and Marlin, and Odell grabbed the faceted whiskey glass and fingered it with the tips of his fingers. Odell spun it with his fingers and the whiskey licked at the edges of the glass and slowly settled back into the mass of liquid in gentle flows that left telltale whiskey runs along the inside edges of the glass. Other than Doodlesticks snorting at and gobbling down the grilled cheese sandwich, and Grundy chewing, the team grew silent, and they studied Lyle Odell as he pondered the aftermath of the case. His gray eyes showed that he was deep in thought. Odell ran his free hand through his hair and now that it was high and tight, it no longer stuck out in all directions when he did so.

He shook his head and lifted the glass up, but did not take a sip yet.

Instead, he held the glass in the air and said, "Yeah, it is tough stuff. I reviewed the records that the military sent over to me. Clark was a hero in combat. He served as a United States Navy corpsman assigned to United States Marine Corps platoons. He also performed combat photography. Photographed dead brothers in arms and other awful scenes from combat that bred his sickness. It is a shame because he saved lives. Served proudly. Won ribbons and awards and made rank. Petty Officer First Class Clark. It is so ironic that he saved lives and then took them, too. In Afghanistan, one day, a routine combat patrol went bad, with an outnumbered ambush by the enemy. His best bud was shot and killed and Clark tried, but he could not save him and a few others too. It was a bad scene, and Clark blamed the platoon sergeant for leading the platoon into the ambush. I guess he cracked and flipped his lid. He became a ticking time bomb of death. After discharge and failed therapy, he enacted revenge on all combat vets. He had hours and hours of therapy from the V-A and private therapists and doctors and consultants. His combat-related PTSD was severe, he had some schizophrenia, and after months of hospitalizations, medications, therapy, finally, a team of experts and doctors declared him cured. So much for that bullshit diagnosis. It seems as if Cap Moore's sterling military record and his return to Mohawk City set Clark off once again. Crazy stuff."

Odell took a sip of the Irish whiskey and then set the glass back on the bar counter.

"The military and horrible situations and circumstances created the monster. I wonder if it was really Clark's fault. Does he alone bear the burden of his guilt? I dunno? I guess it was, and I guess it wasn't."

George Grundy nodded and said, "I was in combat but never in Hellfire situations as what it seems that Clark went through. Some days sucked, but never faced an intense ambush or an outright assault of many enemy soldiers, just a few unorganized stragglers testing our perimeters. I do know that my mental health screening when I returned from my tours was total bullshit. It lasted all of about two minutes with what appeared to be a civilian screener asking pre-programmed questions from a sheet. I do not think she was a qualified therapist, a nurse or a doctor. Two minutes and they stamped my big ass clear to go. It seems as if it would be common sense to screen combat vets a little more and maybe even a follow up after discharge. At least, review military records to understand what the Hell the veteran experienced."

Odell stared at the wall of liquor bottles displayed in front of him, his eyes wandered across the lights and the colors of the bottles, and after a careful study, Odell said, "That is the problem with common sense. It has a deceiving label. In reality, it is not so common. It is actually very rare."

Sensing the mood change, Captain Moore lifted his glass and nodded to Marlin and Odell and then to the rest of the group to do the same.

Captain Moore said, "Anyway, regardless of the horrible circumstances, here is to the team. It is not always fun or pleasant, but someone has to do this job and we did it safely and I guess that is what counts. We are all alive and well. Here is to our health."

They all downed the drink, but the taste was somewhat bitter.

Captain Tucker leaned over the bar and into the conversation.

He asked George, "So, Grundy, after this case, are you finally going to retire?"

George did not hesitate in his answer.

"No way, Cap. Wife says we still have to pay off those stupid parent loans for college.

"Still? Geez, George."

"Yeah, gonna work 'till I'm dead, but I gotta keep goin' and follow alongside of Odell. After all, someday, I might learn sumthin' from him. Other than baseball statistics, names, and titles of classical music and composers and stuff like that. Say, Odell, how many walks did Derek Cramer have in his career?"

Odell listened carefully to Grundy's question. He tilted his head a little but did not immediately answer the question. Odell tapped Marlin's arm and nodded at the glass of whiskey. To coach her along, he lifted the glass a little, and Marlin did the same as they smiled at each other. Odell counted softly to a three count, and they lifted the glasses together and they downed the whiskey at the exact same time. Marlin leaned in and gave Odell a kiss on his cheek, and they set the glasses down on the bar while the onlookers clapped and cheered. After the spontaneous and rather joyous celebration of their display of unison drinking and a touch of their connection and a smattering of their love, the group patiently waited for the answer.

Nearby patrons waited.

Annie stopped serving, and she waited for the answer with her hand on a beer tap handle.

The food runner stopped in her tracks. Doodlesticks snorted and looked up at Odell. Was the answer evading the good detective? Did this random, surprise, and obscure question finally stump the great mind of Homicide Detective Lyle Odell? Patrons pulled out cellphones, dialed up the stats on the internet and once they had the answer, they looked up and over to Odell for his response. For a few seconds, the entire world stopped spinning. At least, the world inside of Gulliver's Bar and Grille on Fifth Street and Main Street in downtown Mohawk City, New

York.

Odell cleared his throat and broke the tension with his voice, "That would be one-thousand-eighty-two times. In the regular season, that is. Thirteen times in the World Series."

Odell finished speaking, and he then nodded and thumbed at the empty glasses to Annie to request refills.

"The numbers stuck in my head. For some reason. I am not sure why. Nevertheless, they did. Please, Annie. Refills of the Irish for Marlin and me. When you have a free moment or two. Thank you."

Everyone smiled and went back to their worlds. Odell did not let them down. He never did.

"Say . . . it is time for a smoke. Who wants to join us?" Odell said as the good detective went to tap his pockets and began his usual search routine, when he realized that he wore his casual attire today. His Mohawk City Police Department tee shirt had no pockets.

He sheepishly looked at Marlin, who smiled and said, "I gotcha, Odell. In my bag here. C'mon. George, can you watch, Doodlesticks? He does not sign autographs unless we get payment in advance. Might be a way to raise cash to pay your tab. You might consider it because I hate to tell you this but . . . Sarge . . . Doodlesticks is still hungry. He is kind of like a bottomless pit."

George frowned, and he slowly nodded while mumbling, "This is costin' me a damn fortune."

Marlin grabbed the cigarettes and lighter from her bag as Crump and Odell slid out of their barstools, and as Odell walked by his old drinking pal, Odell stopped in his tracks and said to Grundy, "Oh, George. Once Marlin turned him onto the scent and the proper commands, Doodlesticks would most likely easily smell the cash in your wallet except for the simple fact that you have no cash in there. You always feel the edges of your wallet to feel how much cash is in there. I happened to notice that when you did so before, you realized that you forgot to fill it this morning. You would have to use the credit card that Mrs. Grundy gave you for emergencies and she will chew your big ass out when the bill comes in the mail in twenty-eight days, because it is for emergencies only. You know . . . the red one that you keep next to the black one that you are supposed to use only for gas. Don't worry. I got the tab."

George Grundy's eyes widened. Even after all of these years together, Lyle Odell never ceased to amaze him with his incredible skills of detection and perception.

George nodded, smiled, and said, "Thanks, Odell. I owe you, buddy."

"George, you don't owe me jackshit. You don't owe me nuthin'," Odell said as he grabbed Marlin's hand and together, they walked out the side door of the bar and grille to enjoy the smoke.

Odell added as Marlin playfully patted Odell on his backside, "You are already paid in full, George. And then, some."

Detective Lyle Odell was good at his job.

Very, very good.

Exceptional.

CHAPTER ELEVEN

The following Monday morning. . . .

It was a beautiful day in Albany, New York. Blue skies and sunshine and puffy clouds with a strong foretelling of autumn in the air.

The crows arrived with one quick call on the crow call. Hastily and eagerly, they flew across the pond. They were patiently waiting for Odell and Marlin to arrive.

Apparently, in the secret world of crows, peanuts are a special snack.

This time, after Marlin scattered the peanuts on the asphalt path, under the guidance of the faithful leader of the murder, the crows had no qualms at all at swooping in and gobbling up the snacks and offerings while Marlin and Odell sat upon the bench and watched them enjoy the food. The trust they displayed was not only because the murder knew that Marlin and Odell eliminated the evil threat, they also could look into their hearts and see their souls. Crows have a certain uncanny way about them.

"When did you send the email?" Marlin asked.

"Last Monday," Odell quickly answered.

Marlin squinted against the early morning sunlight. She looked over at Odell and then tossed a peanut out upon the pathway where a crow gobbled it up into their beak and, with the prize in hand, flew up into the branches of the safe haven tree to enjoy it.

"Even before you solved the case?" Marlin asked.

"No, Marlin, *we* actually solved the case long before that. Yupper, I sent it on that Monday."

Marlin smiled at his inclusive use of the word, we. She loved this man more than words could ever describe or capture.

"Okay, so noted. Why did you send it?"

"Because it was the right thing to do for you in your life. It is your fate. It is what will make you happy and fulfilled in your life. Because you are going to solve many crimes and stop a lot of evil things from happening in this weary world. That is what we do. What we are supposed to do. When did they call you to schedule the interview?"

"Yesterday."

"Interesting. They should have called sooner. I could have married you by now. They took a helluva chance. When I wrote the letter and attached it to the email that I sent to the police chief there in Des Moines, I emphasized in my email introduction how he blew it the first time, when they ignored your application . . . he damn well better get his head on straight and not blow it this time."

Marlin's heart jumped at his words, but somehow, she found an answer and a question in the rubble of her torn soul.

"Even if I make it through the interview, and they proceed to hire me, and then I make it through the academy. . . I will never be the detective that you are, Odell."

Odell carefully listened to her words. He shifted his backside on the park bench. He motioned to Marlin for her to hand him some peanuts and Marlin reached into the bag and handed him a handful of the peanuts. Odell tossed them out to the crows. It seemed as if the entire murder of crows arrived to patiently waited for the snacks.

"That is the leader. There is the leader of the murder, Marlin. We owe the leader a lot. That crow is strong, intelligent, has faith, and is an outstanding leader. You can tell."

After the leader crow grabbed the snack, Odell turned, and he looked at Marlin and smiled. She loved when he smiled and how she wished that she could stay in his life and make sure that he smiled more often.

"That is an accurate statement that you just made, Marlin.

Very correct and accurate. You will never be the detective that I am. You will be better than I could ever be or could ever dream of being. You will be amazing. You will be the best there is. Because you are Detective Marlin Santini and . . . I am Detective Lyle Odell."

Marlin could not hide her tears at his words, nor at his love, nor at his faith in her, and she took her glasses off, set them on the bench, and wiped at her eyes to chase the tears away.

The tears danced away into the light of the day. More arrived on her cheeks.

Odell jumped in and saved her run of emotions with his logic, as he tended to do.

"You will be the oldest applicant in the academy. You are just over the age limit. It is fine. Cap Moore helped plow the road too. He is a cool cat. I am gonna like workin' for 'em. He is an honest, brave, and a powerful man. They will make a dispensation for you. You will make it. You are in fantastic condition. You can go all day and all night too," Odell winked at her with the duality in the meaning of his words.

Marlin's right knee bounced along with her words. It was a release of her nervousness.

"So, can you, Odell. So can you. I mean . . . if I get this job . . . I don't know. My mother and sister want to stay in Des Moines . . . they told me they don't want to come back to Albany. Knowing you, Odell, you already knew that fact. As well as the fact that my sister will finish school out there. At home. However, it is an easy flight. Only a few hours or so. Right? You could come out there. Or maybe I can bag all of this and Cap Moore can find a job for me here? Or I can open my business here. For real?"

Marlin was rambling in her thoughts and words and her soul and her heart were openly exposed as she did so.

Odell stopped her rambling. He gently put his hand on her knee and quieted both.

"Your flight out of Albany airport leaves in two hours. I will get you there in time. Easy flight? Maybe. Will I come out there? Probably not, because the best thing to do for us is for me to stay here and stay out of your life and out of the way. It is the best thing to do. Actually, the flight is four hours and eighteen minutes with the Chicago connection. Six hours and ten minutes if you connect through Atlanta. Tailwinds and headwinds not accounted for in those figures. Atlanta is the busiest passenger airport in the world. Great bars, though. Especially in the C terminal. I love the joint with the sailfish hanging over the door at the entrance. It is worth it."

Odell took a deep breath. He was suppressing his emotions, too.

"Cap Moore understands. Marlin, you need to go home. Iowa is your home. To be with your family. I am old. Very old and gettin' older and older and more worn out. I am severely flawed. You will do great things. Finish your education. You will be an outstanding patrol officer and receive a promotion to detective in a few years. Two years at the most. Find a wonderful man who is your own age. Marry him. An extremely lucky man he will be. Life will be grand. I am not your destiny. I need the whiskey to think. It is my crutch, and I am a slave to the magic in the bottle. I need it to dig in deep where the phantoms tread. Someday, I will find my way . . . but not now. Someday, I will say goodbye to the Irish and it will wave goodbye to me. I will thank it and it will thank me. But not now. There is still too much evil and too much to do. I don't want you to be changing my diaper and wiping up my drool and caring for a teetering old wreck of a man. You are too rare and precious for that. There are bad guys waiting in the future that Doodlesticks and you need to nail before they inflict more of their madness on the world. It would be selfish of me to allow them to escape your brilliant detection and justice."

Odell swallowed at his own words.

He earnestly believed them; however, they caused him great pain in delivering them. Odell dug deep into his words and pulled some poignant words out to minimize the impact of this incredibly painful situation. Yet, as Odell always did, he mastered the words as if he was a fine novelist, weaving the words into a tapestry of beauty and depth of color.

"Romance is for chumps." Odell used Marlin's own words against her, but because he loved her deeply, fully and wholly, he added, "Unless it is between Lyle Odell and Marlin Santini. Yet, we both have a higher cause and calling. We need to honor that mission. You need to fulfill your dreams."

Marlin was openly weeping now, and Odell leaned over and gently used his finger to wipe her tears away from her eyes.

Even in the protection of their beloved trees, the crows were full of empathy and, for the moment, remained silent.

They, too, wept at the situation.

"I love you, Odell," Marlin whispered as she gently circled his lips with her finger as a prelude for a kiss.

"As I do you, Marlin. That is why I wrote the email and sent it off to the Des Moines police chief and a few others that I thought would want to meet you. That is why I asked Cap Moore to help me and not offer you a job here. I wouldn't'a done it . . . if I didn't love you. You gave me respite from the madness, and peace in my soul for a time, and for that and so much more, I will be eternally grateful and will always love you."

Marlin sighed at his words, and she leaned into Odell and studied his gray eyes. Marlin fell into them once more.

They kissed long and deep. After the kiss, Marlin gently cupped Odell's head in her hands.

She smiled as she said, "When I return here after the interview to pick up Doodlesticks and my things . . . we can have pizza from Frank's West and Matty will deliver it. You will give him a nice tip. A generous tip. Way too much for a pizza delivery guy to make for dropping off one pizza. You roll that way, Odell. You understand everyone's struggles. Especially the common working people of this world. We will have ice-cold beer and Irish and you will tell me the name, the performer and the composer of the music on the radio. We will then go upstairs and we will make love all night and hold each other all night until the sunrise wakes us by dancing in our eyes through the shades in your room. Then it will be a wretched and painful last goodbye, but, in the end, it will be fine. All will be well. Because you are Lyle Odell and I am . . . Marlin Santini. Right?"

Odell kissed her hand and said, "Yes. Correct, Marlin. All will be well."

Marlin stood up. She gathered the pieces of her broken soul from the park bench, and picked up her faithful bag, and she stood up straight in the gleaming sunlight. Marlin looked around and took a deep breath. The sky was so blue and perfect. She looked to the murder of crows gathered in the tree next to the bench and the leader of the murder bobbed his head and danced on the branch to support her plight and of the mission and of their love.

After a long exhale of pain and emotions, Marlin said, "Then, Odell, I proudly say that I will love you forever. Please drive me to the airport."

Marlin Santini left a voicemail message on Lyle Odell's cellphone to tell him that she arrived safely in Des Moines. She was not concerned that he did not pick up the telephone call because she knew that the chances were very good that the battery was dead on his cellphone. Marlin knew that Odell would eventually make the connection.

In his chair in his humble home in Mohawk City, amid an empty bottle of Irish, the overflowing ashtray, and the pizza box at his feet from Frank's West, that Matty delivered a few hours earlier, Detective Lyle Odell opened his eyes when the classical music piece playing on his old radio ended.

In his deep haze, his mind filled with dreams and thoughts of Marlin Santini. She consumed him, enveloped him, and Lyle Odell knew that would always be the case.

Until the end of his days.

Odell wiped a single tear away from his left eye, and then he wiped a single tear away from his right eye.

In a low whisper Odell said, "Pietro Mascagni. Intermezzo. Cavelleria Rusticana. It sounds as if it is the Boston Orchestra or maybe the Evergreen. Damn, that is one of the most romantic and sad pieces ever composed. How ironic."

Odell kicked in the footrest on his easy chair. He kicked at the empty pizza box at his feet to push it away. Odell leaned forward, put his head in his hands, and wiped another tear away from his left eye. Then he wiped away the tear from his right eye. The tears remained stubborn. They kept coming.

Odell leaned over and he felt for the power switch and shut the old radio off. Then he shut off the light on the end table.

There in the darkness, he closed his eyes and gently and eventually drifted off to sleep.

THE END

EPILOGUE

The late September wind blew strong, with just a hint of crispness buried within it. Autumn had finally arrived in upstate New York after a long and unusually hot summer. Some days, the heat had been brutal. Terribly brutal.

Even on the warmest of days, cemeteries are cold places.

An Albany, New York city police car dragged up to a curb alongside a roadway within the Holy Angels Cemetery. In the passenger seat, Detective Lyle Odell scanned the graves for the location that his eyes sought to find.

"Sorry, Officer Winthrop. I am not exactly sure where the grave is located. I checked the map that the cemetery office gave to me and I think it is over here. I really appreciate your patience with me. Honestly, the excess consumption of Irish whiskey today has not helped me much. However, I had to feed the crows. I promised Marlin that I would. Okay, wait," Odell studied the map that he held in his lap, and then he pointed at a spot. "Please, stop here, Winthrop. Thank you."

The police cruiser slowed to a stop, and Officer Winthrop placed the gearshift lever into the parking gear and looked over at Detective Odell.

"You okay . . . Detective Odell? Do you want me to walk with you?"

Odell smiled and shook his head to show no. "I am a little tipsy, but no, I will be fine. Thank you for picking me up at the hotel, Winthrop. I was in no condition to drive, and I had to complete this mission today. In my meager defense . . . it is my day off today and I had to drive in from Mohawk City last night after an investigation suddenly came up. Damn killin' never stops in Sin City."

"No trouble. Detective Palmer told me that you are the man. I have heard about you. All police officers here and maybe, even everywhere, have. You are a legend. I wish I could be like you. Someday. Palmer told me it was okay to pick you up. My lips are sealed. Please be careful, sir. You are a little wobbly. I will wait here."

Odell nodded, flipped open the passenger door handle, and the door swung open.

Odell grabbed the single red rose from the seat, he scooted his legs out the door, stood up and before closing the door, he leaned in and said, "Thank you, and, Winthrop," Odell said while staring in at the young police officer.

"Yes, Detective Odell?"

"Please, no sir stuff. Dreadful memories. Just call me Odell or Lyle or Detective Odell. Anything but sir. And don't be like me, kid. I am not a legend. Far from it. Be anything in this world and in your life, but don't ever be like me."

Officer Winthrop shrugged his shoulders at Odell's words and his advice and said, "If you say so. Okay. Yes, Detective Odell. Gotcha."

Odell closed the door, and he slowly walked across the sprawling lawn marked by thousands of grave markers. His messy hair blew all around his head in the chilly wind, and he looked even messier than he usually did. He tied his necktie too short, and it was askew. His pants fell around his waist and his suit jacket had a coffee stain on the front of it. His shoes were dull in luster, one shoe had a lace that was loose, and it flapped along as Odell walked.

Odell wobbled while he walked, and he tapped his suit jacket and said, "Right side suit jacket pocket."

After fumbling with one hand while he balanced the peanuts in his other hand, he pulled out his pack of cigarettes, tapped one out, and stuck it in his mouth. As the cigarette dangled from his lower lips, Odell mumbled, "Just need to taste it."

His eyes scanned the grave markers until he found the one that he wanted, and when he approached it, his keen eyes scanned the grave marker while he mouthed the name inscribed on the elegant marker stone. A marker stone with an American flag perched on top of it. A flag that flapped all around in the strong late September wind.

"Thomas Wesley Rollins. World War Two. United States Army. Purple Heart and Bronze Star Recipient," Odell mumbled as he read the stone's inscription aloud.

Odell lowered his head and mumbled a prayer. Yes, indeed, Lyle Odell prayed.

Often.

He finished his prayer, tossed the peanuts onto the grave, and mumbled, "You are only guilty of being a courageous hero of honor. I am so sorry. I feel as if I know you so well, even if we never met. You suffered such pain, displayed such courage in combat, and survived only to die at the hands of one of our own. You fought for freedom. For all that, we all stand for each and every day. It is such a shame. Old soldiers are not supposed to die in such a horrible manner. He killed so many others . . . yet . . . my compassion compels me to visit here. To visit your grave. Not to minimize the others, but to honor them all. You were so kind. I feed the crows too. Marlin and Odell. We do. For your honor and for the honor of all the others. It is what we do. I have to tell you, Rollins, that I am miserably flawed, but the whiskey dulls the pain of this wretched and weary world. I will always do my best to stand for your honor and for justice and for what is right. Marlin will too. She will do wonderful things. I can tell. Despite the pain and the anguish, it was the correct decision to make."

Odell stood and saluted the grave. He wiped some tears from his eyes. He turned on his heels and as he did so, he tapped the right rear pocket of his pants and muttered, "Right rear pants pocket."

He reached into the pocket and pulled out a small flask. Odell stopped and lifted the flask toward Heaven. He unscrewed the cap and, with the dangling cigarette still holding onto his lower lip, Odell put the flask to his lips and took a swallow of the Irish.

"To you, Mr. Rollins. To you."

Odell then turned and plodded the rest of the way to the waiting police cruiser. The wind blew hard, and it suddenly blew cold. It is always so cold in cemeteries. No matter the season.

It is always so cold.

ACKNOWLEDGEMENT

Thank you to all the readers who wrote to me and told me how much they enjoyed the character of Detective Lyle Odell, his cases and adventures, and his associated cast of characters. Especially, thank you to the Sergeant George Grundy fans. Thank you to Harry M. Rogers Junior, Ms. Cali Rose, and my family and friends for the support. It is very much appreciated.

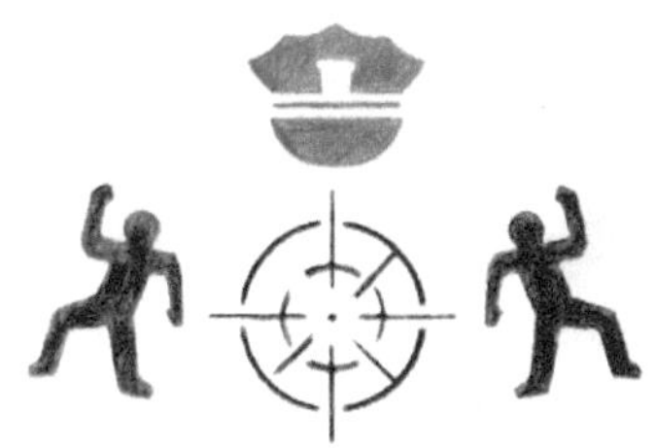

ABOUT THE AUTHOR

Paul John Hausleben

If you ask Paul John Hausleben, he will tell you that he is not an author, he is just a storyteller. His mission is to continue to write and tell stories to warm your heart, make you laugh, make you think, and sometimes make you cry, just a little. Most of all, he deals in memories, and helps you to remember the good times of your own life, and the special people who touched you along the way. He displays amazing versatility in his writing by covering a wide variety of genres. Paul was born and raised in Paterson, and then nearby Haledon, New Jersey, and began writing at an early age. He revisited a writing career later in his life, and he now is the author of a number of novels, compilations, short stories, music reviews, and audio and video works. Most of his work touches upon nostalgic remembrances of simpler times, and tells the stories of heartfelt, humorous, and special human relationships. Mr. Hausleben is the owner, and the driving creative force of God Bless the Keg Publishing LLC. Paul is a skilled and award-winning photographer, and his publishing company features much of his photographic work. Other than writing and photography, among many careers both paid and unpaid, he is a former semi-professional hockey goaltender, a music fan and music reviewer, and an avid ice hockey, football, soccer and overall sports fan, and a former military radio operator. Mr. Hausleben is an avid amateur radio operator. He holds an extra class amateur radio license with the call letters WA2ASQ. Paul is a Morse code and digital mode operator and he enjoys on-the-air radio contests and chasing long distance (DX) stations from all over the world while using very low power (QRP) transmissions to do so. Mr. Paul John Hausleben now resides in Somewhere, U.S.A., but his heart always remains along Belmont Avenue in good old Paterson, and Haledon, New Jersey.

THE CASES OF DETECTIVE LYLE ODELL

Homicide Detective Lyle Odell is disheveled, eccentric, and seemingly absent minded. His primary diet is pizza from a local pizza shop. He sucks down endless cups of black coffee, chain smokes cigarettes, has such a short-term memory for things that he has to remind his own mind where he places things, and to top it all off, he consumes gallons upon gallons of Irish whiskey. Detective Odell is haunted by his enemies and by the horror of homicide; but he is a super-genius. Beyond brilliant.

In the pages of Mr. Paul John Hausleben's novel, O'Malley, Homicide Detective Lyle Odell was a minor character, yet, the character resonated with readers. In O"Malley, the good detective helps the main character solve the mysteries of his past as well as the brutal homicide of a fellow police officer. The character proved to be so popular with readers that Paul John Hausleben decided to write ensuing novels detailing the cases and investigations of Homicide Detective Lyle Odell while elevating Odell to the starring role.

Here in this series of crime-drama, murder mystery novels, the reader is entertained by the methods used to solve intricate homicides as the eccentric, systematic, hard-drinking gumshoe detective continues to hunt for the clues that no one else can find and track down criminals as if he is a modern-day Sherlock Holmes.

Read along as the author weaves stories of murder mysteries

and crime-drama, and with Homicide Detective Lyle Odell, the author creates another amazing and unforgettable character to add to a line-up of unforgettable characters in his many pages of written lore.

Where Phantoms Tread: A Detective Lyle Odell Novel (The Cases Of Detective Lyle Odell Book 1)

Homicide Detective Lyle Odell is Mohawk City, New York's finest homicide detective. He also is the old city's only homicide detective. He chain-smokes cigarettes, and his diet consists of pizza, black coffee, and too much Irish whiskey. Odell is disheveled, eccentric, and absentminded. Often, he is teetering and tottering on his drunkenness while being haunted by his enemies and by the horror of homicide. Despite his flaws, Odell is a super-genius. Beyond brilliant. Odell is a modern-day Sherlock Holmes that does not miss a trick. His enemies dismiss him as a has-been—an alcoholic shadow of his former self. That is their second mistake. Their first mistake is committing what seems to be the perfect crime in Odell's city. A city where Odell treads along with the phantoms.

In gritty Mohawk City in upstate New York, there has been yet another death. A wealthy and beautiful young socialite from one of the richest families in Mohawk City turns up dead on a weekday night in a hotel room in the fanciest hotel in the old city. It seems as if she is the victim of her hard partying-lifestyle and her promiscuous and risky past and present. Outwardly, her sad passing is a cut and dry case of mixing drugs and alcohol . . . a terrible tragedy. Adding to the tragedy and the intrigue, the young woman works in Washington D.C. for the popular federal senator from New York. A senator who is a rising star in politics with his goals set upon the White House. Yet, is it a cut and dry? Or is there more to it? Homicide Detective Lyle Odell knows all too well the horrors of Mohawk City, and he knows how and why it earned the nickname of "Sin City." The phantoms of crime, evil, and death haunt him and even gallons of whiskey cannot end their constant invasion into his heart, soul, and mind. As the case unfolds, Odell digs in and finds there is nothing cut and dry about this case. At all. As the good detective unravels the mystery and the case deepens in evil and in tragedy, he dives in where phantoms tread to solve much more than just the young woman's tragic death.

Plucked out of the pages of the novel O'Malley by his creator, Homicide Detective Lyle Odell proved to be a hugely popular character with readers. In O'Malley, the good detective helps the principal character solve the mysteries of his past and the brutal homicide of a fellow police officer. The character proved to so popular with readers that Paul John Hausleben wrote a novel starring Homicide Detective Lyle Odell. Here in his first solo adventure, the eccentric, systematic, alcoholic gumshoe detective proves why his creator earns the title of "The Master Storyteller" as the author weaves a masterpiece of murder mystery and crime-drama and creates another amazing character to add to a line-up of unforgettable characters in his many pages of written lore. Grab your copy today!

OTHER WORK BY MR. PAUL JOHN HAUSLEBEN

The Time Bomb in The Cupboard and Other Adventures of Harry and Paul

The Night Always Comes, Another story from the Adventures of Harry and Paul

Reunion, A sequel to the Night Always Comes and Another story from the Adventures of Harry and Paul

The Miracle Tree, Another story from the Adventures of Harry and Paul

The Chronicles of Henson

Heaven's Gain, The Final Adventure of Harry and Paul

Geyer Street Gardens, Beneath the Mask of a Hockey Goaltender, Another story from the Adventures of Harry and Paul

Where the River Bends and Curls

Tales of the Quiet Stranger in the Black Hat

Crows on a High Wire

Flying

Christmas Cocktails

Flashes, Spark, and Shorts: Flash One

And a few others too!

CONTACT INFORMATION

You may write to the author at ctte27@gmail.com
Published by God Bless the Keg Publishing LLC

Henrico, Virginia, U.S.A.

You may write to the publisher at
godblessthekegpublishing@gmail.com

Find us on Facebook

"Life's simple pleasures are so often the best ones!"

Follow Paul John Hausleben on Facebook and enjoy samples of his photography, receive updates on new releases, and enjoy his general meanderings. Book reviews are important to authors and publishers! Please consider leaving a book review for this publication on your favorite book website, blog, or publication. Thank you.

www.ingramcontent.com/pod-product-compliance
Lightning Source LLC
LaVergne TN
LVHW041925090826
845145LV00015B/690

* 9 7 8 1 7 3 3 0 9 2 7 7 7 *